SISTER OF THE BRIDE

SISTER OF THE BRIDE

LAUREN MORRILL

YELLOW
HOUSE
MEDIA

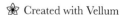

Fuck it, this one's for me

Chapter 1

Polly's flight is due to land in an hour, and I still have seven lasagnas to make.

"Time?" I call, and Fernando shouts back, "One thirty."

At the prep table in the back of the kitchen, I'm

surrounded by cauldrons of Bolognese and béchamel, stacks of noodles Nonna made fresh this morning, and enough cheese to build a scale model of Noah's ark. For the last eight years, this has been my Thursday task: layering pasta and sauces and cheese into enormous cast-iron trays that keep my arms in the kind of shape that usually requires a very malevolent person trainer. I can do it in my sleep. I often *do* do it in my sleep, if you count the nightmares I have where I forget to make the lasagnas and have to try to bang them all out in the fifteen minutes before the restaurant opens.

When I was a kid, this was Dad's job, but I could usually be found perched on a stool nearby, talking through my school day or the latest Red Sox scores and occasionally pitching in.

"Noodles, Bolognese, béchamel, cheese…noodles, Bolognese, béchamel, cheese." I mutter it to myself over and over like an incantation. Between layers I wipe my hands on my apron. I pause only to brush stray hair from my eyes with the back of my hand or to call for a time check; Fernando's always ready with a response.

There are already thirteen finished lasagnas on racks in the walk-in cooler. These seven will make an even twenty, each ready to be cut into a dozen pieces that are individually baked until their edges are nice and crispy, then served atop a pool of Nonna's marinara, made from the same recipe her father brought over from Sicily almost a hundred years ago. Two hundred and forty portions to last the restaurant through the weekend. Our regulars know they have to get in early, because once the Thursday lasagnas run out, they're out of luck until the next weekend. For almost a hundred years it has been this way, and it's one of the things I made sure not to change when Dad died. I had to make some alterations to cut costs, of course—running a restaurant is expensive, and the books were starting to creak by the time I took over—but the lasagnas? Those stayed.

"One carbonara, one risotto, and one spaghetti, hold the marinara, hold the meatballs," Evie calls as the door from the dining room swings closed behind her.

A groan rises from the kitchen, and Evie throws her hands up, her order book flapping. "I know, I thought we'd made some progress last time, but the Buttered Noodle King of Back Bay has returned with a vengeance."

Fernando stills his chef's knife, which has been making rapid work of a pound of garlic for tonight's dinner service, and tilts his head back as if to plead with god.

"That kid is going to be the death of me," he says.

For the decade and a half that he's worked at Marino's— first as a busser, then in the kitchen as a prep cook, then a sous chef, then eventually the head chef—Fernando has been known for two things: his killer tomato risotto, and his relentlessly positive attitude. But one redheaded five-year-old might be the thing that finally breaks him.

"You chill out," I say, pointing a silicone spatula at him. "I got this."

I take a moment to try and pull back the curls that have escaped my messy bun, once again cursing the stylist who convinced me that a "lob" was a good idea for someone who has to keep her hair up at work. I'm dangerously close to requiring a hairnet, and while I'm not particularly vain, I draw the line at lunch lady chic. I finally give up on the rogue strands, tucking them behind my ears with a sigh, and head for the swinging door that separates the kitchen from the dining room.

"Don't you have to go soon?" Fernando asks.

I pull my phone out of my back pocket and swipe at the screen. The app shows Polly's little animated airplane still hovering over the Atlantic, but it's running on time for a 2:35 p.m. landing. Forty-five minutes to do some quick child psychology and assemble six and a half more lasagnas, and then—if I'm very lucky—a few minutes to spare to swipe on some lip gloss and make an attempt to tame my hair.

Easy-peasy.

"I've always got time for the Buttered Noodle King," I say with a wink. Fernando gives me a two-fingered salute, and I head off into battle.

The lunch rush has ended, leaving just a few customers lingering in the dining room. At table six, there's a couple who told Evie that they were on a first date. And it's going pretty well if those moony looks and her foot stroking up his calf are any indication. There are two tables of tourists, identifiable by their sweaty T-shirts and backpacks, and in the back banquette, my tiny target.

"McKeevers!" I cry as I approach the table, arms wide. I push away a little tickle at the back of my brain that makes me feel as if I'm stepping directly into Dad's shoes, but unlike the size-twelve clogs he wore in the kitchen, these fit me just fine.

The family that awaits me has been coming to Marino's since before it was even a family of two. Ian and Lindy McKeever had their first date at Marino's when they were undergrads at Emerson. Ian proposed over Mom's tiramisu, and three years later, when Lindy McKeever was eight days overdue with little Jamie, she waddled into the dining room to see if our famous eggplant parmigiana could get the show started. (Her water broke on the T ride home, but I think that was probably more because of the eight-days-overdue thing than the eggplant parm.)

"Jamie, my man, how's it going?" I kneel down to his eye level. He's hard at work on the maze printed on the back of the paper kids' menu. Focused, despite the fact that he's completed the thing at least two dozen times before.

"Good," he replies with the kind of shrug that will be rude when he's fifteen but is adorable at five.

"Whatcha having for lunch today?"

"Spaghetti."

"With sauce and meatballs? Yum, that's my favorite meal."

Jamie shakes his head, his flaming curls bouncing as he tightens his grip on the red crayon. "Just noodles."

I glance up to see Lindy McKeever mouth the word *help*, and I silently reply, "On it." I turn my full attention back to Jamie, beaming down on him like a happy ray of sunshine. I nod as if to say, *Yeah, that sounds good too, impressive palate, kid.* "Hey, what's your favorite food?"

"Chicken nuggets," Jamie replies without missing a beat. I already know this, of course, because more than once the McKeevers have brought Jamie in with a greasy McDonald's bag and guilty faces. I've told them time and time again that it's *fine*, but it drives them out of their hipster foodie minds. So when they asked me a couple of months ago to help them attempt to steer Jamie toward a wider palate (one not made up entirely of ground-up chicken bits), I was more than happy to try.

"Oh, nuggets are pretty great too. I've been thinking maybe we should add them to the menu," I lie, hoping my Italian ancestors aren't rolling over in their graves. "What's your favorite sauce to dip them in?"

"I like sweet-and-sour, but honey mustard is okay too. And ketchup if there's no good sauce."

"Oh, excellent. You know, I could bring out a little cup of red sauce, and maybe you could dip your noodles. You know, like you dip chicken nuggets."

Jamie scrunches up his face, ready to protest, but then a realization seems to wash over him—he's been given permission to pick up his noodles *with his fingers* and dip them into sauce. Which is likely to be messy. And if I know anything about Jamie McKeever after several years of hands-and-knees level cleanup beneath his seat, it's that he loves a good mess. He's as serious as he is slovenly, and I love him for that.

Jamie's parents glance over at him, their eyebrows up at their hairlines, the nervous expressions of anxious parents waiting to see if their little lordling is going to protest. His crayon hovers just short of the center of the maze as his wheels turn.

"Yeah, okay," Jamie finally says. And then he returns to the maze, narrowly avoiding a dead end to bring the alligator to the swamp.

It takes everything in me to avoid fist-pumping, because Jamie will know immediately if we're trying to put something over on him. (Ask me about the great eggplant fries fiasco of last spring, #neverforget.)

"Excellent. I'll tell Fernando to add a side of sauce to your noodles. And if you run out, Evie'll bring you another, okay?"

"Thanks, Miss Marino!" Jamie says, flipping the page over to tackle the word search.

I smile and ruffle his hair, even though I've told him a million times that he can call me Pippin. He seems to like that my last name is the same as the name of the restaurant he's eating in, like maybe that makes me famous or something. And in some Boston restaurant circles, it kind of does. Marino's has been open in this very Beacon Hill location since 1931, when my great grandfather won the entire building in a very questionable game of poker and decided to feed the hoity-toity denizens of Boston's most venerable neighborhood the food of his homeland. Marino's has been a mainstay ever since, an institution. Ben Affleck ate here once. And more than a few Kennedys, plus half the Whalbergs.

It's our regulars who are like family, though. This restaurant has been my home (literally, since I live upstairs with Mom and Nonna) all my life, but I try not to forget that strangers see it as a kind of home too. The McKeevers are just a few of many.

As I head back to the kitchen, I run my fingers over the red paint splatter on the mahogany molding like a ritual. It's an accident from when Polly and I were nine and Dad let us "help" him repaint the dining room in exchange for being allowed to get our ears pierced. A minor paint fight ensued, and Dad said he liked that the splatter always reminded him of his girls.

Another thing about Marino's that I'll never change.

"Plate of noodles, put the marinara in a little salad dressing cup on the side," I call to Fernando as I hustle back to my lasagnas. "I've talked him into dipping noodles like chicken nuggets."

"Whatever works." Fernando shrugs, tossing a handful of pasta into a boiling pot of salty water. "I'm making it my life's mission to get that kid eating osso buco before middle school, you hear me?"

"Dream big, Chef."

I resume ladling Bolognese into a pan, working in satisfied silence as the plate goes out to Jamie. Minutes later, Evie pops her head back in with a double thumbs-up. My diabolical plan has worked. Success! At least for today.

Midway through my sixteenth lasagna, the door to the alley clangs open, and tall, rangy guy with floppy curls practically trips into the kitchen. "Excuse me, can someone please tell me where the Freedom Trail is?"

For a split second, I stare open-mouthed at the square jaw and easy grin of the man standing in front of me, his hands shoved into the pockets of his well-fitted jeans, a soft, faded Citgo logo stretched across his sculpted chest. But then that image dissolves, and all I can see is my best friend in the whole world since we were five.

"Holy shit, Toby!" I drop my ladle into the Bolognese, narrowly avoiding the splatter, and race across the kitchen, practically leaping onto him. He lets out a little *oof* as I collide with his chest, his arms wrapping around my waist as he pulls me in for an epic hug. "What the hell are you doing here? I didn't know you were visiting!"

"I'm not," he says, pulling back with a wicked grin. A lock of his curls flops over his forehead, and he reaches up to tuck it away like a reflex. As always, it springs right back. "I live here now."

I blink at him in shock. "Wait, *what?*"

"Pippin, inside voice," he says with a wink.

"I'll talk in any voice I please, are you *serious?*"

His grin widens, my best friend entirely too pleased with himself. "I absolutely am. You're looking at the newest member of the emergency medicine residency program at Mass General. I start tomorrow!"

"Oh my god! I'm so happy!" I fling myself back into Toby's arms, squeezing him with all the joy that comes from knowing my best friend has finally, *finally* come home. Eight years ago, I bid Toby a tearful goodbye as he boarded a flight to California for undergrad at USC. Four years later, he was on to medical school at Stanford. It's been eight years of sporadic visits, threaded together with FaceTime calls and text messages and a steady stream of the worst Dad jokes of all time. "But what happened to the PhD program? Medical research or something?"

Toby shrugs. "I changed my mind. And someone dropped out of the program here, so my advisor at the med school made a call. I wanted to surprise you. Surprised?"

"Absolutely! I had no clue. First because you've had your nine-step plan or whatever for as long as I've known you, and second because you forced that god-awful dad joke on me this morning. I was sure that thing had to be coming all the way from Palo Alto."

He ignores the comment about the nine-step plan, which is definitely a first. "No, that one came to you live from the Silver Line. I just got in this morning."

"You little shit!"

"It was worth it to see that look on your face," he says. He squishes my cheeks between his large, warm hands. "It's really hard to put one over on the great Pippin Marino."

I stick my tongue out at him, and when he laughs, I turn my head and lick his hand.

"Pippin, you're still here! You're going to be late!" Mom bursts into the kitchen and yanks an apron off the rack by the wall. She has it tied on in two seconds and is midway through pulling her silver-streaked hair back beneath an orange floral bandana by the time she reaches the prep table.

"She doesn't land for another half hour," I say, because I've had this day planned down to the minute for weeks. Not that it matters, because I'm already being shoved toward the door before I can even open the schedule in my notes app.

"Delta says she's arriving early," Fernando says, holding up his phone on the other side of the kitchen. "Oh, and welcome back, Toby."

"Good to see you, man," Toby says with a little salute.

"Yes, good to see you as always, dear," Mom says before turning her attention back to me. "You gotta go."

"She landed!" Evie calls, poking her head into the pass-through. Because apparently the whole restaurant is tracking my sister's trek across the Atlantic. Not surprising, since London, where Polly has spent six months doing research for her dissertation, is the farthest any of us Marinos have strayed from the nest in almost a hundred years. Even when Polly left for grad school, it was just to New Haven, a quick scoot down I-95. To say that I felt like a piece of me disappeared into the ether when she left is a massive understatement. Six months without a late night at J.P. Licks, trading stories over frappes with my womb-mate, has been the absolute worst.

And then my traitorous phone vibrates a full thirty seconds

later to let me know that yes, my twin sister is indeed on American soil.

"You're late," Toby whispers, his eyes wide and teasing.

"I'm not late, she's early," I grumble. I take off my apron and hang it on my hook by the door, doing my best to brush the flour off my jeans. So much for time to swipe on lip gloss. I'm not even going to be able to change clothes.

"You've got a little right here," Toby says, rubbing the tip of his nose.

I reach for a shiny new saucepan and peer at my reflection in the bottom to check for any other stray food particles. I pull my hair out of its stubby ponytail and try to shake my curls into what might charitably be described as "Doc Brown from *Back to the Future* gets a perm."

"Before you go, is Everett coming for dinner tonight?" Mom calls. She's already halfway through a lasagna and doesn't even raise her eyes from her work. Her tone tells me she already knows the answer—she just wants to make me say it.

"Who's Everett?" Toby asks, and I just wave him off.

"No. We're not…" I trail off, trying to figure out a way to say it without, you know, *saying* it. But I come up empty, and I don't have time to get creative. "We broke up."

A series of groans rises from the kitchen, including from Evie, who's on her break by the sink slurping leftover gazpacho, and Emile, the dishwasher, who's rinsing out his water bottle between loads.

"What did *this* guy do?" Fernando asks, crossing his tattooed arms over his chest. "Wait, let me guess. He breathed too loud."

"My money's on him saying 'that's hilarious' instead of actually laughing," Evie tries. I shoot her a dirty look because *hello*, girl code or something?

"If you must know, he ordered for me at dinner last

Friday," I say. And I'm gratified when Fernando lets out a low whistle. He knows this reason isn't frivolous. That's a major foodie faux pas. But Mom just sighs.

"Pippin, why must you be so picky?"

"I didn't realize having standards was a problem."

Still never looking up as she smoothes out a layer of pasta sheets, Mom shakes her head. "I just want you to be happy."

"Being with a man who doesn't presume he can make decisions for me when we've been dating all of five minutes *will* make me happy."

"Or one who doesn't chew with his mouth open like Julian, or pronounces Subaru as 'Soo-boo-roo' like Ben, or owns too many pairs of khaki pants like that guy, what was his name?" Fernando asks.

"His name was Holston, and the problem with him was primarily that his name was Holston," I say. The khaki pants didn't help, though. People were always asking him for help every time we shopped at Target, and he had the gall to be annoyed despite the fact that in the three months we dated, the man wouldn't put the damn red polo shirt away. That alone probably meant he was a serial killer.

"I don't blame you on that one," Evie chimes in. "I'm sorry, but *yes, Holston, don't stop, Holston, just like that, Holston* isn't exactly the stuff of fantasies."

Toby attempts to cover his laugh with a hiccup, which I follow up with an elbow to his midsection.

This is another reason why I need Polly back. *She* never razzes me about my breakups. Of which, okay, there have been many, but come on. I have so little free time; why waste it when the signs are all there that a relationship isn't going anywhere? That's just good time management. Why spend your evenings with someone who annoys you—or worse, orders for you at a restaurant and picks the *chicken*? I'd rather curl up in my jammies and watch old episodes of *Grey's Anatomy* with Nonna.

Honestly, I have never spent a minute with a guy that was all that much better than being on my own. I'm an excellent cook, and I own a really good vibrator. Dudes had better be coming correct if they want to beat that, and in my experience they're just all kinds of wrong.

And now that Polly *and* Toby are back, what the hell do I need a relationship for? All that getting to know someone, rehashing your flaws, telling your stories, training them how to find your clit? No thank you. I'm much better off on my own.

"You want to help me out here?" I ask Toby, gesturing to the peanut gallery, who are attempting to roast me. "You owe me after forcing 'impasta' into my life."

"I would, but I got off a red-eye this morning, and the man next to me snored like a longshoreman for the entirety of the flight. I haven't slept in something like thirty-six hours, and at this point I barely know my own name. You're on your own, kid."

"Traitor," I say, poking a finger into his chest.

"Tired," he says, grabbing it in his fist. He turns back to the back door and holds it open for me. I duck under his arm and out into the alley. "Tell Polly I said welcome back."

"Will do," I say, grateful to have an excuse to walk away from everyone's favorite topic—why Pippin runs through guys like a movie theater rotating through new releases. As if being twenty-six, busy as hell running a family business, and picky is enough to qualify me for spinsterhood. It's a conversation that always makes me want to walk into the Atlantic.

And besides, Polly has landed.

Chapter 2

TOBY

If April showers bring May flowers, what do
May flowers bring?

Pilgrims

PIPPIN

You're better than this Toby

TOBY

Oh I'm definitely not

I've always loved Boston in the summertime. It's as beautiful as the winter is bleak, our reward for enduring months of cold and damp and snow that sometimes stretches all the way into April (and more than once into May). Spring is a day that you might blink and miss, but summer? Summer is a *season*, and today is the kind of late-June day that makes you wonder why anyone would live anywhere else. The sun is warm. The breeze off the water feels like nature's air conditioning. And sure, the sidewalks are crowded with tourists pointing their iPhones at everything instead of watching where they're going, stumbling around looking for Cheers and lining up for photos on Acorn Street. But when the sun is shining and I'm not sweating, I can overlook it all.

Hell, I can overlook anything today, because not only is Polly finally coming home, Toby is back.

As we walk side-by-side down the cobblestones of Charles Street, I give my best friend a little hip check. He looks over and gives me his megawatt smile, the one I know he pulls out only for his absolute greatest triumphs (and absolute worst Dad jokes).

"It's good, right?" he asks, throwing an arm over my shoulder.

"The best," I say, so happy I can barely stand to look at him. "So did Jen come with you? Or are you guys doing the long-distance thing?"

Toby's toe catches the corner of a wonky brick in the sidewalk, and he pitches forward a step. When he rights himself, he shoves his hands into his pockets.

"No," he says, then clears his throat. "Actually, we broke up."

Now it's my turn to stumble. Toby and Jen have been dating since the beginning of med school, when they met at some weird future doctor costume party that involved dressing as an injury. She's beautiful and smart and nice, like the grown woman equivalent of a golden retriever.

"Seriously? When?" I ask.

"Uh, I don't know. A few weeks ago?"

I pause on the sidewalk, reaching up to grab his arm and pulling him to a stop. I don't know Jen or the inner workings of their relationship very well, because Toby has rarely talked about it with me. I've met her only a handful of times on quick visits to Boston, and while I cannot fathom being in a relationship with the same person for that long, ending one seems kind of intense.

"Are you okay?" I ask.

"I'm fine. I'm just tired. Seriously, that flight was like being strapped in next to a Weedwacker." The corners of his lips lift, and he shrugs. "Look, the breakup sucked, but it's absolutely over. I just want to move on."

I watch as Toby does what he does best: wills away whatever dark clouds are hovering around him. His furrowed brow relaxes, and his lips quirk up into a smile. He bounces up and down on the balls of his feet, always a bundle of energy, and I can't help but throw my arms around him again. I knew I missed him something fierce when he was gone, but I'd had no idea how wide that void felt until he showed back up.

"Okay, then, moving on," I assure him. "You sure you don't want to come with me to the airport to pick up Polly? You could surprise her too."

"Nah, I really need to crash. My parents are expecting me to go to dinner with them at the club tonight, and if I fall asleep in a twenty-five-dollar martini while they grill me about my life choices, they won't let me live in the basement apartment. You going that way?" Toby points in the direction of the Charles Street T stop, but I shake my head and nod in the other direction.

"I think I'm gonna walk over to Park." I'm in the mood for a nice walk, and it'll be just as fast as walking to Charles and waiting for the train. Besides, it'll give me a few extra blocks with Toby as he heads back to his parents' town house on Louisburg Square.

"Well, I start my residency tomorrow, but the first week is just a lot of orientation and social stuff. I want to get in as much Pippin time as possible before the hospital swallows me whole," Toby says as we dodge a group of Gen Xers looking for the Real World Boston house.

God, I missed him. It's been so long since we've actually lived in the same place. When he left for college, I didn't realize how final it would feel. Toby, always the go-getter, the achiever, the golden boy, spent all his summers in college doing internships and study abroad trips and acts of do-goodery that earned him top honors and entrance to one of the best medical schools in the country. Once there, he continued to spend his summers working his tall, skinny ass off to be at the top of his class. I wasn't a bit surprised when he called to tell me that he'd been accepted to a prestigious PhD program doing neuroscience research at Stanford, the first step on his way to following in his mother's footsteps and becoming some fancy-pants award-winning medical researcher.

That's how the dad jokes started. Toby, always overwhelmed with classes and studying and projects and internships, could barely find time to talk. When we realized we'd accidentally gone several months without speaking, he started firing off the most groan-worthy dad jokes in an attempt to make peace. And they stuck. They've become our love language, even though I mostly love to hate them. At least I've still had a bit of him in my days, even if the eye rolls nearly gave me migraines.

"Hey, now that you're back, does this mean the dad jokes are over?"

Toby turns and gives me the kind of puppy eyes usually reserved for animal shelter ads. "I thought you loved me just as I am."

"I do, but maybe we can just, you know, turn down the volume on that part of you?"

He flutters those infuriatingly long eyelashes at me, and I groan.

"Fine. But no more than one a day. Please."

Toby pumps a fist, narrowly missing taking the hat off a man in a fanny pack photographing a Dunkin' Donuts.

"Oh my god, you're really back!" I cry, the realization hitting me once again. "What should we do first?"

"Christopher Lloyd film festival, *obviously*."

"Did we settle on Lloyd? I thought we were leaning toward Mike Myers." For years, whenever we can manage to cram in a free night to veg, we pick an actor and watch a selection of their classic films. Last time Toby visited at Christmas we did Julia Roberts, and let me tell you, *Mystic Pizza* still slaps.

"Yeah, but then I looked up Mike Myers's filmography on IMDB, and I realized that a lot of his classic roles have not, shall we say, aged well? I think I'd rather just leave them in the past and watch *So I Married an Axe Murderer* for fun."

"True. I'd like to pretend *The Love Guru* never happened."

"I'm thinking Mr. Myers might too. So Lloyd, then? The only question is, do we watch all three *Back to the Future*s? Or do we pick one?"

"First of all, I submit that it's *Backs to the Future*, like attorneys general or courts martial," I say. "And if we're going to pick only one, two is obviously the correct choice."

"Fair. I'll text you tomorrow when I've slept enough to operate my fingers." Toby yawns and is about to peel off at Mt. Vernon Street, but before he can cross, I spot a flash of red between groups of tourists. A pair of khaki pants steps around an Asian family, and the next thing I know, I'm leaping behind Toby to avoid being spotted by Holston, the ex-boyfriend with the unfuckable name.

"Oh my god, Toby, please hide me," I whisper, even though there's no chance of Holston overhearing me on a bustling city street. Thankfully, my best friend tops six feet by several inches and makes an excellent hiding spot.

Toby looks around, and I point at the offending polo shirt waiting for the walk sign on the opposite corner of Charles and Mt. Vernon. "That's Holston, and I can't see him because the *last* time I saw him was on his birthday when I told him I didn't want to date him anymore."

Toby groans. "Pippin, you broke up with the man on his *birthday?*"

"I didn't *know* it was his birthday. But thank god I ended things when I did, because he was about to take me to what turned out to be his surprise birthday party, where I would've met his entire fucking family, and it's a lot harder to cut and run once you've met someone's mother."

Toby yawns again, his shoulders slumping. I duck down lower.

"Pippin, he didn't take the walk sign," he says over his shoulder, where I'm cowering like, well, a coward. Desperation is creeping into his voice. "He's looking at his phone. And I'm so tired. I'm fading fast. Please don't make me stand here much longer."

"What am I supposed to do?"

"I don't know, walk past him like a grown-ass woman who accepts the consequences of her actions?"

"I'd rather step in front of an oncoming Uber."

Toby groans again. "What did you do while I was in California?"

"I missed you. And also I had a lot of awkward conversations. I really need to stop dating guys in my neighborhood."

Toby sighs, a full-body experience that I swear lowers his height by a full three inches. Then he turns around, wraps his arm around me like he's trying to hide me from paparazzi, and leads me to a green wooden door.

I look up to see the sign for Harrison's Hardware (est. 1948) and gasp. "I can't go in there! I have to go meet Polly, and if I go in there, I'll be late for sure!"

"It's this or you face *Holston*," Toby says, and even though he's exhausted and a little exasperated, he can't mange to say the name with a straight face.

"Fine. But I'll make you pay for this. We're watching *Who Framed Roger Rabbit* even though Judge Doom gives you nightmares."

Toby rolls his eyes and opens the door, the little bell strung up over the frame announcing my arrival. I give him a glare, and he gives me a shove, then turns and heads for his parents' apartment and, I assume, the first flat surface upon which he can pass out.

The bell on the door does its job, and Mr. Harrison's head pops up from behind the tall counter. I remember standing at the base of that counter staring what seemed like a very long way up while Dad talked Celtics and Bruins with Mr. Harrison. He would give Polly and me caramel apple pops that he kept in a plastic bin behind the register, and we'd spend forever trying to lure out whatever incarnation of shop cat was currently lurking among the shelves. The space smells exactly the same as it did then, like pencil shavings and grease, and for a moment I can almost hear Dad calling us back to the front of the store to go meet Mom for lunch.

"Pippin! Good to see you! Did your nonna lose her keys again?" Mr. Harrison asks.

"Nope. I just popped in *really quick*," I say, in what I already know will be a fruitless effort to dissuade him from a full-blown conversation. Mr. Harrison has always been a talker, but it got more pronounced a few years ago when his wife died. I usually spend a few minutes chatting with him while picking up steel wool for the saucepans or a handful of screws to fix a wobbly prep table, but I don't have that kind of time today. Polly landed fifteen minutes ago, and if I want to be there to help her get her bags when she emerges from customs, I need to *go*.

I glance over my shoulder and watch Holston's head bob past the front window of the shop. Crisis averted. Well, one of them, anyway.

"Anything I can help you find?" Mr. Harrison asks.

My eyes dart around the nearby shelves, trying to find something that won't spark a conversation and preferably costs less than ten dollars. I land on the display of candy to the left of the register—boxes of dusty Paydays, Chunkys, Skor bars, and other things kids think they want because they're candy but actually don't because they're disappointing (woof, what a metaphor for adulthood, huh?).

"Looking for a snack? Because my distributor just sent me a box of hot nuts."

"Excuse me?" I blink at Mr. Harrison, who, by the way, is *very* appropriately named. The man is covered in tufts of snow-white hair, and it's so thick it looks like he's wearing a mohair sweater beneath his flannel shirt. When Polly and I were little, we used to torture each other by whispering, "Do you think you can braid Mr. Harrison's chest hair?" just before the other was about to fall asleep, leading to squeals and mental images that would keep the victim up for an extra twenty minutes at least. So hearing this seventy-five-year-old Sasquatch say the words *hot nuts* to me is, well, jarring.

"I said *hot nuts*," Mr. Harrison repeats, his voice clanging through the store. He reaches for a red bag hanging from a rack and gazes down at the image emblazoned on the packaging. "They're quite tasty, though they do leave a bit of an after-taste on your tongue. I think the spicy coating gives an odd mouthfeel."

An unholy combination of snort-laugh and gag gets trapped in my throat, and I have to clamp my hand over my mouth and convert it all into a cough. God, what I wouldn't give for Polly to be here right now, hearing this right along with me.

Mr. Harrison glances up, and I quickly drop my hand and plaster on a smile.

"I'll be honest, I was skeptical, but the hot nuts aren't bad.

Though I haven't sold as many as I'd hoped. Maybe because people don't like their nuts spicy," he says. "You game?"

At this point, I can barely contain my guffaws, and I'm wondering if I can surreptitiously start recording on my phone so I can play this conversation for Polly as soon as I find her at the airport. Speaking of, this stop was definitely *not* on the minute-by-minute schedule. I need to get out of here ASAP if I'm going to meet Polly in enough time to yell "hot nuts" in a pitch-perfect imitation of Mr. Harrison's gravelly voice directly into Polly's face enough times to make her pee her pants.

"I'll take them," I say. If nothing else, they'll make an excellent visual aid for when I relay this story to Polly.

"Well, good," he says as he punches buttons on his cash register. "Can't imagine why these things aren't moving."

"It's a mystery," I reply, waving off the receipt and grabbing my purchase before he can launch into an explanation of the pros and cons of bagging the hot nuts. Oh god, the unintentional innuendos. "Thanks, Mr. Harrison!"

"Tell Polly to come by and say hello," he says, and before I can bolt, he slides two caramel apple pops across the counter. "Good seeing you, Pippin."

I smile, suddenly wishing I could hop up on the stool by the counter and chat about the Stanley Cup finals. I make a mental note to come back by on a day when I'm not on such a tight schedule. Dad would want me to.

"Bye, Mr. Harrison," I say before stepping through the door, the ding of the old brass bell announcing my departure.

Chapter 3

Polly and I are identical twins.

Allegedly.

But as Polly exits customs pulling a pale pink suitcase, a vintage leather tote over her shoulder, it's hard to see. Polly's sun-streaked brown hair falls in beachy waves around her shoulders, while mine (markedly less sun-streaked and curled from the steam of boiling vats of pasta) still has a kink in it from the hair elastic I used to keep it out of the lasagna. If you put us next to each other and asked a hundred people which one of us just got off a transatlantic flight, ninety-nine would pick me, and one would be lying. And I wouldn't blame them! The international traveler is wearing an airy maxi dress with delicate straps and a pattern that looks like the waves off the Amalfi Coast. I'm wearing an old tomato-stained Universal Hub shirt and jeans with flour on the butt.

At the sight of Polly, I rise up on my toes and hold up the sign I made last night. PIZZA, it reads in bright red Sharpie with a cheesy little illustration at the bottom. I can tell the moment Polly spots it, because she tips her head back in a deep and familiar laugh before digging into her tote bag for a wrinkled, folded piece of paper. She stops on the linoleum and grins, holding it high above her head. It reads, in Polly's trademark artfully messy scrawl, PEPPERONI, invoking our dad's favorite twin nicknames. A business bro in a rumpled suit who is too busy staring at his phone to notice Polly's Norma Rae moment stops just short of smashing into her back. He starts to flash her the stink eye, but after one look at her sparkling blue eyes and bright smile, it seems like he's suddenly about to ask for her number instead. But Polly isn't paying attention to him at all.

"Pepperoni!" she cries as she launches herself through the crowd, the sign crinkling against my back as she envelops me in a hug so forceful that I stumble back four steps.

"Good to see you too, Pizza." I breathe in the familiar scent of green tea and citrus. Polly calls it her signature scent. I remember the summer sophomore year when she discovered it at the Nordstrom perfume counter and worked double shifts at the restaurant to afford it. She's worn it ever since. Because Polly is the kind of person who *has* a signature scent and looks flawless after stepping off a transatlantic flight, and somehow you still don't want to push her down the nearest flight of stairs.

"You're lucky I love you, because it should be a crime to

look that good after seven hours on an airplane," I say, pulling back to give Polly a good once-over. "Seriously, did British Airways have some kind of organic spa on board? And was it staffed by acolytes of Gwyneth Paltrow?"

"This look is brought to you by an upgrade to first class and no seat mate," Polly replies. She strikes an Instagram influencer pose, arms over her head, one hip popped out, her smile pointed up toward the fluorescent lights as if they're a sunbeam. Then she crosses her eyes and sticks out her tongue. "It's amazing what ample leg room and complimentary champagne will do for you when sky-bound."

"Lucky bitch," I say before pulling her into another hug. As a person who's usually not much of a hugger, my touch-meter is off the charts today. But to get to hug my two very favorite people in the world upon their return to me? Worth it.

Polly takes a deep breath, inhaling the ambient smells of Dunkin' Donuts and Sbarro. "I missed this place," she says, and I know she doesn't mean Logan Airport.

"This place missed you," I reply, smiling. I take her suitcase and pull it around next to my thigh. "Now, let's go get the rest of your luggage. Mom's making tuna noodle, and you know if it sits too long it turns the consistency of kindergarten paste."

"*Yesssss*, my favorite."

"We *know*. You can be sure that Nonna missed you since she's agreed to eat it without complaint."

Polly's love of our mother's Midwestern casseroles has long been a subject of great consternation in the family. Well, amongst everyone except Mom, who is just happy to have someone to share her love of the "cream of" creations from her Minnesota childhood. She has a collection written on notecards in a little metal box in our tiny apartment kitchen. It was the same rotation for a while, but then the Pioneer Woman burst onto the scene, and we had to start limiting her to one casserole a month.

"Hush, you," Polly says. She hikes her leather tote higher onto her freckled shoulder. "Let's go to baggage claim."

"Okay, and on the way I can tell you all about Mr. Harrison's hot nuts."

<hr>

I suggest an Uber, but Polly is adamant that she wants to take the T—something about it being vital to her reentry into the United States.

"I've been listening to delicate British voices implore me to mind the gap for months. I'm ready for garbled Southie accents to bark at me about Green Line delays," she explains.

So we board the Silver Line to South Station, gratefully letting the bus driver heave Polly's suitcases onto the luggage rack.

"Did your stuff multiply?" I ask, eyeing the two extra-large suitcases along with the rolling carry-on and her tote.

"I bought an extra suitcase to bring stuff home. It was cheaper than shipping!"

We make our way to the open seat in the middle that straddles the two segments of the bus. As kids, we loved to ride in this spot when we headed to Logan to pick up Nonna's cousins visiting from Sicily. Nonna always had to leave us alone there, because the way the floor twisted and the seats bounced made her carsick. But we loved it. And still do, apparently.

I eye the two enormous suitcases and wonder where Polly's going to put all that stuff. Our attic room has always been a cozy little nook with barely enough space for our twin beds, desks, and dressers, and as we've grown over the years, it's only become more dorm-like. I've mostly had it to myself over the last eight years, since I lived at home while going to UMass Boston, working at the restaurant between classes. Polly spent her four years at Harvard living on campus, then headed off to a cramped studio in New Haven for grad school. This will be the first time we've been back together in the attic since we were eighteen, and I'd be lying if I said I wasn't excited. Polly will be spending the summer revising her dissertation and preparing to defend it while she job-searches. Until she knows what college will be lucky enough to have her as its newest art history professor, we'll be roomies again. I will happily overlook her clothes hoarding and the fact that she talks in her sleep. I'm just so damn happy to have my sister back.

"Okay, so I've got a whole list of ideas to facilitate your, what did you call it, *reentry* into Boston life." The bus shudders to a start, and I pull out my phone, where I've been making a list basically since the moment Polly took off six months ago. "The MFA has a new Basquiat exhibition that we should for sure check out, and the Brattle is showing *Empire Records* next week. Oh, and Mr. Tanner said he'd be happy to spot us some Sox tickets this summer, we just need to pick a date." I make a note to follow up with one of our favorite regulars, who happens to work in the Red Sox front office. "There's also the summer concert series on the Esplanade, so we should go through and see what looks good, and I want to plan a trip out to Mendon to hit the drive-in. Pizza, beer, and a double feature of some Marvel something. Sounds good, right? *Very* American."

"Easy, trigger." Polly reaches over and covers the screen of my iPhone, lowering it gently to my lap like a hostage negotiator. "Put the calendar down slowly so no one gets hurt."

"Ha-ha. What's the problem? Don't worry, I'm not expecting to monopolize *all* your time. I know you've got your dissertation, Madame Genius."

"It's mostly written," Polly says. She bites her lip, a telltale sign that she's holding something back. She glances at her own phone for, like, the eleventy billionth time since we sat down.

But before I can ask what's on her mind, the bus shudders to a stop at South Station and passengers jump up as if there's a prize for getting off with all your luggage first. Joke's on them —it's just extra time spent inhaling hot bus fumes in the tunnel.

We wrestle Polly's bags off the rack, down the steps, and onto the platform, me pulling the largest suitcase and Polly dragging the other two. And with the crowds streaming towards the various train lines, there's no chance to question her about summer plans, because we're swallowed up in a sea of commuters and tourists, couples consulting maps and parents wrangling tantrumming toddlers. We reach the Red Line platform just as a train whooshes into the station, and it's not until we're cramming into the car that we can finally talk again.

"I missed this," Polly says, though I notice she doesn't inhale quite as deeply as she did at the airport. Which is wise, because the man dressed as Ben Franklin sitting next to us smells like he hasn't had a shower since 1776.

"I'm sorry, you missed rickety cars that smell like an unholy mix of Dunk's and BO?"

"Believe it or not, yes?" Polly leans against the pole and braces herself as the train departs the station. "I mean, I loved London. It was an incredible experience, and I'm so lucky that I got to travel around Europe a bunch too. Tuscany, Mykonos, Barcelona, Brussels…oh my god, I ate so much food and saw so much art, it's a wonder my stomach didn't explode and my eyeballs didn't fall out of my head."

"Where'd you get the nose ring?" I ask, poking my finger at the thin silver ring, shiny and new.

"We did a weekend in Capri, and I decided to go for it," Polly says, catching her reflection in the darkened glass of the subway car. Her cheeks flush with a rosy glow as she tilts her chin.

"Ah, so that explains the tan," I say. I run my fingers across a constellation of freckles on Polly's shoulder. "I thought you seemed a little too sun-kissed for someone who just spent six months in a country famous for its rain."

Polly blushes from her cheeks to her chest. There's definitely more of a story here than a few European side trips.

Polly's always been the more adventurous of the two of us. She was first up the tree, off the top of the monkey bars, and under the biggest waves. As a person who likes to make sure something is safe before I do it, it was unbelievably helpful to be born with my very own crash test dummy of a sister. When Polly pumped her legs on the swings until the chains felt loose, then jumped off and broke her arm? I knew not to do that. But when she popped up on her second try surfing on the Cape, I decided maybe I could give it a whirl too. (I wiped out three times and lost my bathing suit top before I decided surfing wasn't for me.) I wasn't at all surprised when Polly announced that she was moving to a new country where she knew nobody. And from the tan and the smile and the general sunshine oozing off of her, maybe it's something I might want to do too.

If I can find a reason to leave the restaurant for six months.

"It's just nice to be home, you know?" Polly says. "Familiar."

"Love that dirty water," I reply like a reflex.

"*Boston, you're my home,*" Polly sings, her voice lilting along to the melody of the Standells song Dad used to sing while stirring giant pots of Bolognese. It's the kind of memory that jumps up and catches me by the throat every once in a while, a hard shake that reminds me Dad is actually gone. And as good as it feels to have Polly back, it also serves as a reminder that things can never be like they once were, like they were the last time Polly lived at home and Dad would clomp up the attic stairs to wake us up for school singing "That's Amore."

The day Dad died marked a clear before and after, a fracture point when something in our family felt like it broke apart. I feel like I've been holding the pieces together with my bare hands ever since.

And my hands are getting awfully tired.

Chapter 4

Why did Billy get fired from the banana factory?

Because he distracted everyone with his terrible jokes and someone lost an arm in the packing machine?

That's grim, Pip...

He kept throwing away the bent ones

I like mine better

The Marino's building hasn't changed much in the almost one hundred years it's been in my family. And while HGTV has tried to convince everyone that happiness is a new coat of paint or a sledgehammer to a wall, the continuity suits me just fine. There's no shiplap to be found here. No stainless steel appliances except for the ones in the commercial kitchen of the restaurant. I like that the steps are covered in scuff marks from generations of Marinos. I like that just inside the front door there are pencil lines marking the heights of not just Polly and me, but Dad too, and even Nonna as far back as the 1940s. I don't care that the furnace can't keep up in January and the window air conditioners can't keep up in July. I love that the dining room table came over from Sicily with Great-Grandpa and Great-Grandma Marino, a wedding present from her parents, and bears all the dents and scratches and stains of a hundred years of family dinners.

And while I know it's probably a little pathetic to be twenty-six years old and still sleeping in your childhood twin bed, sharing an apartment with your mother, your grandmother living a floor below, I don't care. Because I love the voices that greet me when I walk in the door.

Mom gives me a quick peck on the cheek before lunging to pull Polly into one of her famous of hugs.

"Get over here, you!" Mom says. For a tiny person, she hugs like a longshoreman, and Polly lets out a little grunt as Mom squeezes her. "Six months is too long to go without seeing one of my babies."

"I wish you could have come to visit," Polly says, her face still buried in Mom's hair.

"Yes, well, you know how things go with the restaurant. It's so hard to get away." Mom sighs, her shoulders dropping several inches. She pulls back and gives Polly a sad smile that makes my heart constrict. Mom had planned to go visit in the spring, but Fernando broke his arm in a weekend pickup soccer game, and everyone had to pitch in for the five weeks he had a cast. I hated that she had to cancel her trip; lord knows she deserved it. I've been working so hard at the restaurant these last few years so Mom could work *less*, but so far it seems like we've all just been grinding harder than ever. Hell, *I* would have liked to go visit Polly, but that conversation never even started.

Mom was always happy to be a restaurant wife when Dad was alive, pitching in on busy weekends, pouring wine and running plates along with her pastry work. But it was never her plan to run a restaurant. Mom left Minnesota to be a Wellesley girl, studying studio art and education. She met Dad in the beer line at a Red Sox game, where he was double-fisting sweating cups of Sam Adams. She said it was love at first sight. He said he was the luckiest bastard in New England. They married right after she graduated, and she took a job teaching high school art just across the river in Cambridge. Mom left that job when Polly and I were born and taught community art classes part time while we were growing up. She was planning to go back to work full time when we left for college, but when Dad died of a heart attack that fall, everyone's plans changed.

Mom used to have an easel set up in the corner of the living room and was always working on a painting. When she finished a few, she'd sign up for a booth at a craft fair and sell them off, then use the money to take us down to the Cape on the ferry for a day to eat lobster rolls and splash around at the public beach. But that easel has been empty ever since she and I had to take over the restaurant.

"Cuore mio!" Nonna screeches as she comes rushing in from the kitchen, a stained apron tied around her waist. Mom may be making dinner, but Nonna is in charge of dessert, and my stomach grumbles as I inhale the smell of fresh cannoli shells radiating off her in waves. Nonna grabs Polly and pulls her in like an aggressive dance partner. Never mind that Polly is a good head taller than our grandmother, who is small and round and warm in all the ways that make you feel loved with every hug. We always used to wonder how our father, all six feet three of him, could have come from such a tiny woman. But of course those were his father's genes—the man who got

Nonna pregnant when she was nineteen and spent exactly four seconds considering fatherhood before lighting out for Southern California in a shiny new VW Bug, never to be heard from again. Whenever he's mentioned, Nonna mutters all the Italian swear words she knows under her breath.

"Nonna! I missed you!" Polly says, and Nonna immediately grabs her by the shoulders, pushing her back to make a long, narrow-eyed assessment.

"You look…" Her eyes roam up and down Polly's figure before landing on her freckled face, and she breaks into a wide grin. "You look *happy*, my darling."

If Polly's grin were an electric current, she could power all of Fenway for a full nine innings.

"I *am* happy," she replies, the words warming the entire room.

"I'm so glad, cuore mio," Nonna replies. "Now, I have to go fry the last of the shells before the oil gets too hot, so settle yourself, because dinner, *such as it is*, will be done soon."

"Hush, you," Mom says, playfully snapping a dish towel at Nonna, who is giving Mom what can only be described as the most loving of stink eyes. "You ate seconds of last week's casserole."

"A broken clock is right twice a day," Nonna says, flapping her hands in Mom's direction. Nonna loves to tease Mom about her casseroles, but on more than one occasion I've caught her reheating leftovers in the middle of the night and eating them surreptitiously over the sink.

"Fifteen minutes, okay, girls?" Mom says. And then she lifts a hand to her chest, her eyes getting watery. "Oh, I've missed that. *Girls*. It's so good to have you back, Polly."

And then Mom scurries off to the kitchen before the sentimental tears begin flowing in earnest.

"Should we drag the bags upstairs?" I ask. The pile of suitcases is taking up basically the entire entryway. If a fire were to break out, we'd definitely have to go out a window, but the thought of dragging them up two more flights to the attic makes me want to take a ten-year nap.

"Nah, leave 'em. We'll let dinner fortify us for the climb." Polly drops her tote bag on the floor by the largest suitcase and wanders into the living room, gazing around like Tom Hanks after he finally got rescued from that island. Not a single thing has changed since she left six months ago. The house still smells like olive oil and the sharp tang of tomatoes. The back wall of the living room, all bookshelves, is still full to bursting with novels and art books and cookbooks, not to mention over-stuffed photo albums and scrapbooks—though there may be one or two new murder mysteries, courtesy of Nonna. And perched along the edge of every shelf are framed photos, starting with one of Great-Grandpa and Great-Grandma Marino's wedding in 1926, a stiff black-and-white portrait of two Italian teenagers looking more than a little terrified. Which was warranted, since they were about to board a ship to America, where they knew not one word of the language. There's a photo of Nonna holding Dad as a baby in 1961 and a photo of him and Mom shoving cake into each other's faces at their very eighties-errific wedding. But most of the photos are of Polly and me, first as chubby babies, then as awkward kids, tweens, and teens.

Polly picks up a gold frame. Inside is Dad in a brown suit, flanked by my sister and me in our caps and gowns at high school graduation. Dad has a beefy arm thrown around each of us, his grin a mile wide beneath his mustache. Dad always had a bushy, dark Tom Selleck–style mustache, even though those definitely weren't fashionable in the mid-nineties, not even ironically. But Dad leaned hard into his burly-Italian-dude persona despite being an absolute cinnamon roll of a human being. He sang Rat Pack songs to wake us up, tripled the garlic in every recipe, and doled out bone-crushing bear hugs like they were free money.

"I can't believe it's been eight years," Polly says, clutching the frame. Her eyes glisten, and I wonder if she's having the same sense memory as me of Dad's heavy arms pulling us close, the smell of cigars and Dial soap wafting off him.

"Sometimes it feels like it's only been eight minutes," I reply.

"I know, right? Like, I walked into the house and half expected him to body check me to take my suitcases," Polly says, and because she's always been a crier just like Mom, her eyes well up. "There's just so much he's missed. So much more he's *going* to miss."

My chest constricts, and I have to take a practiced deep breath to keep from following that feeling down the twisty slide into full-on tears. I've gotten pretty good at keeping the tears at bay, letting them out only every once in while when my heart feels too full of them and I need to press the release valve on my sorrow.

But now is not one of those times. Polly is back, and this is a *celebratory* dinner.

I quickly descend into fix-it mode, making it my job to keep Polly from dissolving into sobs. Or at least to try and turn them into happy tears. It's one thing I've gotten very good at over the years. One of the many, I guess.

"If he were here, he'd be shouting out the windows about how his Ivy League little girl is back in town," I say, taking the frame and gently setting it back on the bookshelf. "He always loved that you were such a giant nerd."

Polly looks at me sidelong, a single tear dripping down her cheek, but she smiles and swipes at it with the back of her hand.

"You think he wouldn't be thrilled to see you boss babe-ing it at the restaurant?"

I roll my eyes. "Mom's the boss."

"Marino's couldn't run without you." Polly flops onto the couch, her golden highlights spilling over her shoulders. "Mom told me how close we came to closing back then. If it weren't for you, Marino's would be some insufferable tapas bar and Mom and Nonna would be living in the 'burbs."

And where would I be living? But I don't say it out loud. I can't, not even to myself, because I know it's the wondering that can get you. My job is here. My home is *here.* And Polly's right—Marino's *was* close to closing, and I did make enough changes and work enough extra shifts to save it. But I still can't afford to take my eyes off the ball. The restaurant is the only thing we have left of Dad. Losing it is not an option, even though keeping it running hasn't been easy.

Because while the family business keeps us going, it isn't making any of us rich. Which is sort of what you have to be in Boston, unless you want to live with three roommates eight T stops from here. At least my current roommates are known quantities. They love early bedtimes, hate parties, and Nonna keeps the wine rack well stocked with delicious spicy reds. Sure, Mom loves to blast yacht rock, and I can't exactly bring a guy home to my attic twin bed, but at least I can count on Nonna for impromptu *Grey's Anatomy* binges.

Still, I can't help but wonder sometimes what comes next. It's not like running Marino's was my childhood dream. But what else can I do? Mom needs me, and while Polly has wanted to burrow into ancient paintings since the first time she stepped into the Museum of Fine Arts on an elementary school field trip, I've never really had anything like that. If someone had asked my parents when I was little what I'd grow up to be, they probably would have said bossy. So I guess running Marino's is in my blood one way or another. I just kept waiting for my dream to jump up and wave itself in front of my face, like, *Hey, Pippin, I'm the thing you're supposed to be doing with the rest of your life!* But honestly, at this point, even if it did, I'd probably be too busy planning the weekly specials or sourcing semolina to notice.

"È ora di mangiare!" Nonna calls from the dining room, cutting off Polly's tears and my quarter-life crisis. "Mangia, mangia!"

"Coming!" I reply. I take Polly by the hand and pull her through the living room. We all take our seats as Mom sets the casserole dish down on a trivet in the middle of the table and Nonna fills the wine glasses. Once our chairs are scooted in, Nonna silently crosses herself, and then we all dive into the steaming food.

"I'll have you know that I talked your mother out of putting *cottage cheese* in this," Nonna says. The corners of her mouth turn down in a sharp frown, but I notice the bite on her fork is pretty hearty for someone who often pretends to spit in the dirt when Mom serves tuna noodle casserole.

"I bet it would give it a nice richness," Polly says, and it reminds me that we've been missing the diplomatic member of our family these last six months. I've had to broker peace during several dinner table spats, and while I'm good at a lot of things, diplomacy is not my forte. "It would be like the ricotta in a lasagna."

"My father better be deaf in his grave, I swear," Nonna mutters. Mom rolls her eyes and shoves the casserole dish down the table toward her, and Nonna takes seconds without making eye contact. At this point, it's Nonna and Mom who are like an old married couple, taking care of each other with a side of loving teasing.

I let everyone get a few more forkfuls down before pulling out my phone. "Okay, so *now* can we talk summer plans? Because Evie told me about this beach rental on the Cape that her roommate's parents own, and I think we can get it for super cheap. I mean, cheap for the Cape," I say. I click over to my calendar. "But we need to get on it quick, because they can't hold it for long."

"Um, well…" Polly says, chewing in a way that can only be described as circumspect. She swallows hard but doesn't say anything else, her eyes still on her plate. Something is *up*, and I'm done wondering.

I put my fork down with a hard clink and lean forward on my elbows. "Okay, what's the deal? Suddenly you're iffy about a week on the Cape? What do you have against sun, surf, and lobster rolls?"

Polly sighs, and for a brief moment I wonder if she got a quickie lobotomy on a weekend trip to Prague or something. I know she's not the biggest Sox fan in the world, but Mr. Tanner's seats are in a corporate box where there's an unlimited supply of ball park food. Polly has never in her life turned down a chicken finger buffet with a full array of sauces.

"Actually, before we make plans for the summer, there's something I need to tell you all," Polly says.

"Oh god, please tell me you're not going back to Europe." That's been my greatest fear since Polly left. Because come on, it's *Europe*. Of course my sister, who is basically 50 percent school nerd, 50 percent wanderlust, would want to go back. But losing her for six months was hard enough. The idea of her permanently relocating three thousand miles away makes me feel like a piece of my heart has broken off and is floating around in my body, searching for an escape route.

Polly shakes her head, dropping her eyes to her lap. She seems to be twisting something in her hand as she grapples with what looks to be a major announcement.

"No, no, nothing like that. I'm definitely here to stay," she says, a little flush starting to creep up her neck. Then she sits up a little taller and spends entirely too long straightening her fork on her plate.

"Well, what is it?" Nonna finally squawks, making Polly jump a little.

"I met someone," Polly says finally, only it comes out really fast and all one word, like *imetsomeone*. Everyone leans in slightly, trying to untangle the meaning. "Her name is Mackenzie—"

"The investment banker?" I ask, because I remember something about a girl Polly met in London from one of our family text threads. Frankly they can be hard to follow, because Nonna has discovered gif reactions and has been using Cristina Yang to reply to basically *everything*.

"She's not an investment banker, she was freelancing with an investment bank," Polly says.

"I don't understand how those are different things," I reply.

"Is Mackenzie the one from the thing with the laundromat?" Nonna cuts in.

"What's the thing with the laundromat?" Mom asks.

"You know, the time Polly mixed up the detergent amounts because she didn't convert to metric—"

"And the suds! Oh, I remember that story," Mom says, laughing. "Wait, is she the one in the photo of you eating haggis in Edinburgh?"

"It was Glasgow," Polly says. She sucks in a breath, her eyes firmly planted on her plate, which I suddenly notice she's barely touched despite her love of Mom's casseroles and their six-month absence from her life. "But yes. That's her. We've been dating. And we sort of...well, we fell in love, and she's beautiful and brilliant—she has an MBA from Harvard and is, like, this financial computing wunderkind, and—"

Polly nervously rambles on about Mackenzie's resume and vital statistics, but I stop listening after *wunderkind* because I'm busy watching my sister slip something onto her finger that was definitely *not* there when we all sat down to this meal. But that sparkly something is big enough to drown out the sound of

Polly's voice and make the entire room disappear except for the light glinting off that…that *rock*.

"Are you fucking *engaged?*" The words come flying out of my mouth at a volume I usually reserve for scaring pigeons away from Nonna's terrace tomato plants. It's so loud that Mom's fork clatters to the floor and Nonna gasps, clutching her hands to her heart.

And then everyone's eyes swing to Polly and her left hand and the *ring*, which she is now gazing down at like it's a golden retriever puppy.

"Yes," she says finally. And when she looks up, her cheeks are flushed, her eyes are shining, and she looks for all the world like she's just won an Oscar *and* a Pulitzer. She laughs, this sort of hysterical, joy-filled noise that only makes the shock smack me harder in the back of the head. "It happened really fast, obviously, but when you know, you know. You know?"

No, I definitely do *not* know.

"You're getting married?" Mom whispers, and I wait for the meltdown. Because one of the Marino women has just announced her plan to marry someone none of us has met. Hell, *Polly* just met her six months ago. How can this be real? Polly was never one to play wedding growing up. She wasn't obsessed with being a bride. She was more likely to hang her finger paintings on the wall and lead everyone around, pretending to be a curator.

Polly as a *bride?* She just turned twenty-six! On the ladder that leads to Mount Bad Decision, this is one of the top rungs for sure—just above asking your stylist to help you bring back mall bangs, but below eating raw oysters at a discount buffet in Las Vegas. What could possibly have possessed her?

"Are you pregnant?" I bark out. The words, I swear—they just come tumbling out of my mouth independent of my brain, and Polly sort of half yelps in indignation.

"Pippin! Jesus," she says by way of an answer, and I'm glad

she doesn't actually dignify that with a response. Instead she turns to Mom and Nonna, who appear to be a much more receptive audience. "Don't worry, you're going to meet her in about"—she glances down at her phone—"twenty minutes. Because I invited her over for dessert and coffee."

A layer of silence hangs over the table like a wet flannel blanket. I glance from Nonna to Mom and back again. They're both staring at Polly with their mouths open. I imagine they're starting to formulate all the same arguments I am: *You're getting married to a person you've known for five minutes whom none of us has ever met? Are you out of your mind?*

But instead Mom pushes her chair back and stands, leaning over to throw her arms around Polly, muttering, "My baby" into Polly's hair. Nonna throws up her arms and exclaims, "More like dessert and *champagne*! Splendido, cuore mio!"

Which leaves me, sitting across from my sister with the list of summer plans I had for us. Plans for *us*, and now there's someone else. Once again, Polly is skipping ahead, but this time I can't even trail behind, because I don't even recognize the path.

Chapter 5

I don't trust those trees. They seem kind of shady.

I see we're vastly expanding the definition of "joke"

I had twenty minutes to imagine what this financial wunderkind who's swept my sister off her feet might be like, and in none of those minutes did I imagine *this*.

Sure, Mackenzie Bryan is beautiful, with dark tan skin and chocolate-brown eyes, her shiny black hair pulled back in a sleek low bun. But she looks like she just finished giving a boardroom presentation in her navy pantsuit. Underneath is a sleeveless white linen blouse that's so crisp it looks like she pulled it out of the dry cleaner's bag just before knocking on the door. I can't remember the last time I wore white, much less anything that needed to be ironed. I spend way too much time around tomato sauce and olive oil for something like that to be in my closet. My free-spirit sister is still in her flowy dress, and sitting side by side, Polly and Mackenzie look like two beautiful dolls from very different play sets.

Mackenzie's only fault seems to be that she's wracked with nerves. She's sitting ramrod straight on the couch, her shoulders trying to migrate up to the gold hoops in her ears, and thus far most of her answers have been of the one-word variety. It feels more like a very terse interrogation than a joyful family meeting.

And honestly? Good. She *should* be nervous meeting her future in-laws (a word that turns my mouth sour) for the first time. We're Polly's family, and we're *close*. Our opinions matter, and I like to think that if Mackenzie walks out of this room having disappointed us, this whole ridiculous engagement thing will be over before it even begins.

We're all gathered in the living room, with Polly and Mackenzie both perched on the edge of the couch, their knees brushing together. Polly has Mackenzie's hand clasped in hers, their fingers threaded together, and I can't stop watching as Mackenzie's thumb traces a soft circle on the inside of my sister's wrist. It's the only part of her that appears the slightest bit relaxed. It's the only indication that they've even met before.

Polly, meanwhile, looks absolutely radiant, and when she spots me staring at Mackenzie's thumb, she clears her throat and gives me a patented twin look that I read immediately as *Don't be weird, Pippin.*

I'm trying, I reply with my eyes. *This is a massive shock, and I'm still catching up to the fact that you're marrying an absolute stranger, much less the supermodel businessbot sitting across from me.* I don't know if Polly gets all of that, though. I'm not sure I have the facial dexterity to convey the entire message accurately.

It's so bananas to me to watch my sister sit next to someone she's calling her fiancée. We're not at this stage in our lives yet, are we? This feels like playing dress-up, like a very in-depth game of pretend. Polly's always been a romantic, but marriage? Seriously? This can't be real.

"I've heard so much about you," Mackenzie says. She seems to be directing it nonspecifically at the lot of us.

Like what? I want to say, but that seems rude, so instead I go with, "That makes one of us." Which I guess sounds *more* rude? I'm doing that thing where I let my mouth run without engaging the filter first. I try to follow it with a laugh, like, *Hey, it was just a joke!* But it clearly doesn't translate, because Polly mutters a low scolding, "*Pippin.*"

Mackenzie's shoulders rise another half an inch, and a little muscle jumps in her jaw. I try to tamp down my satisfaction that she seems intimidated. Again, she should be.

"Of course, I know this all must be a tremendous shock," Mackenzie says.

Tremendous? I nod, but both Nonna and Mom are shaking their heads as if they get news like this every day.

Mackenzie barrels on as if she prepared this speech before she walked through the door. Like maybe there's a PowerPoint presentation to go along with it or notecards in the pocket of her blazer. Are we about to get a TED Talk on why Mackenzie needs to make my sister a child bride? "I mean, it's the twenty-first century. Who meets, falls in love, and gets engaged in six months?" she says.

"Exactly!" I cry with what, okay, I can admit is probably a *smidge* too much volume. Especially considering the look Polly is shooting me. Our twin-speak is definitely rusty, but I'm pretty sure this one means, *I'll drown you in the Charles River if you don't start acting right.*

"It did happen fast, but Polly is so easy to love," Mackenzie says, and if it's possible, Polly seems to glow even brighter. (Not like Mackenzie has actually articulated anything specific about my sister that she loves.) Mackenzie seems to feed off the energy of her fiancée's grin, because she visibly relaxes into the couch. "And when you meet the person you want to spend the rest of your life with, you want to start right away."

"*When Harry Met Sally!*" Mom exclaims. And that's the moment I know there will be no skepticism from our mother. Because there she goes, tearing up. The Marino women *love* a good rom-com.

"Excuse me?" Mackenzie shifts in her seat, adjusting her black-framed glasses and cocking her head slightly. She looks like she could pull out a file folder at any moment and start trying to sell us 401(k)s.

"The movie. It's a line from the movie," I say. I wait for this to jog Mackenzie's memory, but it appears to be lingering at the starting line.

"I've never seen it," Mackenzie says. "I'm more of a documentary person."

What?! I glance over at Polly to see if this information is new to her. It must be, because we've watched the Nora Ephron collection so many times we wore out Mom's old DVDs. How could Polly marry someone who hasn't seen *When Harry Met Sally* and—what's worse—doesn't seem to *want* to?

"That's actually how we met!" Polly jumps in, because I'm just sitting here blinking in confusion. Even Mom seems a bit befuddled. "We were the only two people at a matinee of *Too Big to Fail*. Five minutes into the movie, I picked up my popcorn and sat down next to her and said, 'Might as well watch together!'" They're now gazing into each other's eyes, transported back to this magical moment when it all began over talking heads discussing the largest financial collapse since the Depression.

"*Too Big to Fail?*" I ask Polly. "I'm sorry, but *why?*"

"I was homesick and wanted to hear some American accents. It was playing at the little theater near my flat." Polly shrugs and turns back to Mackenzie. "Who knew I'd meet the love of my life hunting for some hard *r*'s?"

"Certainly not me," I say, letting the filter drop again. This time it's Nonna who clears her throat and shoots me the narrow-eyed look she used to give us when we got chatty in church. Shit, if I'm losing Nonna, I have no hope of talking sense into Polly. So I decide to try and throw a conversational bone to smooth things over. "Polly says you work for an investment bank?"

Mackenzie nods, and I realize I've never met anyone to whom I could apply the word *prim* until now. "I do cybersecurity assessments for international financial firms," she replies.

"That sounds like a good job," I say. "Do you live in London full-time?"

I notice Polly stiffen slightly and file that away for a later conversation. Before Mackenzie can reply, Polly squeezes her hand and jumps in. "Mackenzie is usually based in Boston, but she spent the last eight months in the London office. It was fate," she says in the gooey, in-love voice I remember from when she dated Lorelei Davis senior year. They broke up when Lorelei told Polly that majoring in art history was "a one-way ticket to living in a cardboard box." Lorelei *also* got an MBA.

It seems my sister has a type.

"I'm a consultant, so I just finished up a contract with a London firm. But yes, I'm based here," Mackenzie says. "I keep an office in Kendall Square."

"So Mackenzie, who are your people?" Nonna cuts in. Mom sighs and Polly gasps.

"Nonna, that's—" I start to gently admonish her, but Nonna blows me off with a wave of her arthritic hand.

"Please, Pippin," she says before turning back to Mackenzie. "They're Red Sox fans, yes?"

Mackenzie laughs, which a) I didn't know she could do and b) is good, because it looks like Polly is still recovering from her heart attack over our little old Italian grandmother's method of proving respectability.

"My dad's actually more of a Celtics guy, but he would definitely never root against the Red Sox," she says. "He's lived in Boston most of his life."

"Celtics are fine," Nonna says with a firm, approving nod. "I'm not trying to say I couldn't learn to love you if you came from Yankees fans, but it would certainly take effort." Then she mimes spitting in the dirt. My grandmother, ladies and gentleman. A real dame.

"Forgive my grandmother—she takes her baseball very seriously," Polly says.

"What's the point of watching the game if you don't?" Nonna replies.

"Nonna, it's called a pastime, not a blood sport," Mom says, but Nonna brushes her off with a wave and a *pshaw*.

"Speaking of my parents, they are very much looking forward to meeting all of you and wanted me to extend an invitation for dinner next Saturday," Mackenzie says. I suppress an eye roll at *extend an invitation*, because who the hell talks like that? Mackenzie sounds like the voice that lives inside your home security system, not a person who should be marrying my sister. Polly must be *really* high on romance, because it's obscuring the fact that she and this woman have nothing in common.

"Oh, well, that's not going to work," I say, the words just exploding out once again, blowing right past the suggestion of a filter.

"Pippin!" Polly shoots me the classic twin-speak look for *what the hell is wrong with you?*

"What? Saturday night in the restaurant business? You know how it goes," I say, even though at the moment I'm starting to wonder if Polly still remembers. Turns out a lot can happen when you leave the country for six months.

Maybe your entire childhood just plumb falls out of your memory.

"Fernando can handle it," Mom says, shooting me the look that is clearly the one Polly's descended from. "And Evie can handle front of house."

She mutters, "Honestly, Pippin," under her breath the same way she did when I was little and used to ask loud questions in the middle of mass.

"Sunday brunch, then," Mackenzie says, and now I have nothing to say, because I eliminated Sunday brunch at Marino's three years ago when I realized it was losing us money because no one goes to an Italian restaurant for waffles and eggs.

Mackenzie's thoughtful accommodation seals the deal for Mom, who turns to her, smiling warmly, and says, "We'd love to. Please tell your parents we look forward to getting to know them."

Mom and Nonna walk Polly and Mackenzie to the door. Polly wants to give Mackenzie a Beacon Hill tour and then go for drinks, and I have to bite my tongue to keep from reminding her that she saw Mackenzie a week ago but hasn't seen her family in six months, and also Mackenzie has lived in Boston her entire life, so why does she need a damn tour? But the filter is powered back up, thank god.

My mind is whirring. Surely this can't last. Can it? No, truly, it can't. They're just engaged. It isn't like they're already married. It takes, like, a solid year to plan a wedding, and surely the relationship will reach its inevitable conclusion before then. There's no *way* my art history–loving, romantic comedy–watching, free-spirit sister is going to spend the rest of her life with an uptight computer nerd who works in international finance and looks like she was born in a three-piece suit.

If this were a Nora Ephron movie, I'd already be hatching

a plan to break them up. But this isn't a movie, and I don't think I have to do a damn thing here. Mackenzie and Polly were meant to date, maybe fall in love for a bit, but they definitely won't end up together.

I give it three months tops. My only job is to be there to hug my sister and feed her Oreo frappes when it all goes to shit.

"I guess we'll see you next Sunday for brunch, then," I say as Mackenzie and Polly head for the door, hand in hand. I feel much calmer now that I've figured this shit out. I don't have to work as hard not to be a total idiot asshole when I open my mouth. I just have to wait this out, and then things will go back to normal. Hopefully soon, so we can still get down to the Cape and hit a Red Sox game. "It was nice to meet you."

Polly turns and gives me a smile, then mouths a silent "Thank you." I almost feel bad that in my head, I'm already stocking up on Kleenex and planning a Nora Ephron film festival to comfort Polly when this whole thing ends.

Chapter 6

PIPPIN

PIPPIN

What is the worst thing someone could bring home from study abroad?

TOBY

I don't know this one!

PIPPIN

It's not a joke, you ding-dong! This is a best friend SOS! My sister brought home a fiancée!

Toby is already on our bench, the one beneath the willow tree at the edge of the swan boat pond in the Public Garden. It's the bench we used to meet up on after school, him coming from his fancy private school in Cambridge and me from public school in the South End. We took Halloween photos on that bench, and prom photos, and surly teen selfies where we stuck out our tongues and flipped off the camera. It's the bench where he told me he was going away to USC. The bench where he held me after my dad died while I cried for so long I thought I'd never stop.

It's almost nine, and the sun is long gone, the garden nearly empty save for a few people passing through after a late night at the office and a few couples enjoying the quiet oasis in the middle of the city. Toby's got his head back, his eyes closed, his face bathed in the golden light of the streetlamps. His long legs are splayed out in front of him, and for the first time I look at my friend and realize that he really is all grown up. Gone are all traces of the coltish, gawky boy I grew up with. If I weren't so excited to have him back, I might be a little sad. I know it's been eight years, but I sort of didn't realize that was actual time passing, you know?

"Nice pj's," I say as I slide in next to him and pluck at the soft flannel printed with the Dunkin' Donuts logo.

"Pips, bring it in." Toby lets out a yawn that sounds like a migrating goose, then throws his arm around me, tugging me into his warm shoulder. I rest my head and sigh.

"I'm guessing you haven't gotten much sleep since I last saw you?" I ask.

"I got a solid hour of a power nap, then three hours of a five-course meal, each course accompanied by my parents grilling me about my future. I was a good thirty minutes into my much-needed evening slumber when you issued your SOS."

"Sorry about that. But what's going on with your parents? You'd think they'd be pleased to have a doctor in the family."

Toby shrugs, sending my head bobbing up and down.

"My parents are not big on change. They're a bit like you that way," he says, poking me in the ribs. I swat his hand away in protest. "Speaking of, I hear congratulations are in order?"

I don't even have to say anything. I sit up, and the glare on my face apparently speaks volumes, because Toby raises his hands in surrender. "Okay, we hate this. Got it," he says.

"It's not that I hate it, exactly, it's just...I don't understand it."

"What's to understand?"

I sit up, pulling my legs up onto the bench and turning to face him. "Why is she getting *married*? Is there some kind of Victorian-era marriage contract she's fulfilling? Is Mackenzie a scammer? Is Polly under the thrall of a witch's curse?"

"Maybe they're just in love," Toby says.

"That's fine! Be in love all day and all night. I just don't get why she's getting married. That seems...extreme. I mean, you were with Jen for *four years*, and you guys didn't get married."

Toby shifts beside me but doesn't say anything, so I guess we're still not talking about *that*.

"What can I do for you, Pip? How can I help?"

God, I've missed my best friend.

"Honestly, just you being here is good. I've really missed being able to put out the Bat-Signal. I don't think I have any other friends who I could drag out of bed in the middle of the night to listen to me whine on the shores of an artificial pond."

"It was an actual bullet point on my pros and cons list when I was deciding whether to come back," he says. He leans forward and rests his elbows on his knees, his gaze on the grass below. "I'm sorry if I ever made you feel like you couldn't call when I was in California. Even when I was all the way across the country, you were still one of the most important people in the world to me. I would have dropped everything."

He didn't *make* me feel that way, but I definitely did. I mean, not only could I never manage to remember the time difference, but Toby was living this whole other life. He was doing big, important things. And he had Jen. It was pretty clear their relationship was serious, and I didn't want to be the weird friend who seemed like she was peeing in a circle around him to claim him. So I didn't call every time I felt like I was having a come apart, or every time I needed to talk something out, or every time I decided to finally press the release valve on my feelings and let the tears flow.

But that was *my* choice. It was never him.

I reach out and lay my hand on his thigh, giving it a squeeze. Damn, his quads are stacked—when did that happen?

"You've always been there for me, Toby. Even when you were on the other side of the country. No apologies necessary."

A cheer rises up out of the dark, and a gaggle of kids dressed as pirates comes marauding through the garden, swords raised. I spot a stuffed parrot flopping on the shoulder of one, and another has a girl in pantaloons thrown over his shoulder. She's pounding theatrically on his back and yelling something about treasure.

"Emerson kids," I mutter as the theater students from the liberal arts college that borders the Common and Garden parade by.

"I never realized how weird this neighborhood was until I left it," Toby says with a low chuckle. Then he yawns again.

I'm just about to release him from his best friend duties and send him back to bed when he sits up, his gaze searching for the moon in the sky.

"Do you think you'll ever get married?" he asks.

I recoil, blinking at him. "What?"

Toby looks down and meets my eyes, his head cocked slightly. "Not soon, I just mean *ever*. Do you see that for yourself, when you look into your future?"

"I don't really look into my future very much," I say. I turn my focus to the spot on the bench where the green paint is chipping. I flick at it with my fingernail. "There's too much going on in the present."

Toby shakes his head. "You're very pragmatic, Pippin. I think that's why you're having a hard time with Polly's engagement. She's always been the whimsical one, and you've always been the practical one. But love isn't practical."

I wonder if he's talking about Jen now, and the end of their relationship. Something happened that resulted in their breakup and him on the other side of the country, in him scrapping his entire life plan and winding up by my side. But if he doesn't want to talk about it, I won't force him. He'll tell me when he's ready.

"Maybe it should be," I say instead. I huff and cross my arms over my chest, hunching down on the bench. Toby may be grown up, but I have gone full-on sullen teen.

"Everyone gets to have their own outlook, I guess," Toby says. "Just promise me you won't unload this on Polly. Your only job right now is to be supportive. When you need to let it out, you come to me, okay?"

"I know, jeez. I'm not a monster."

"I'm not saying you're a monster, Pip. I *am* saying that you can be a little...*vocal* about your opinions."

I shoot him a look. "Are you saying I can't keep my mouth shut?"

"I'm saying your greatest weakness is that whatever you're thinking is written all over your face. You can never play cards or watch bad improv, nor can you *ever* be in the audience for any kind of slam poetry event."

"Maybe it's just that you know me too well to let me get anything past you," I say.

Toby drops his chin with a laugh. "Yeah, that's definitely it, Pip."

Chapter 7

TOBY

I don't trust stairs. They're always up to something.

PIPPIN

How long are you going to do this?

TOBY

For as long as we're friends. So ... forever?

Later that night, the bedroom door creaks open, and Polly creeps in, her sandals in her hand.

"Hey," I say from my bed, where I'm tucked up with my iPad watching an old episode of *Grey's Anatomy*. I pause the show, freezing a particularly gruesome heart surgery on the screen.

At the sound of my voice, Polly yelps, her hand flying to her chest, her shoes smacking her square in the face.

"I appreciate the attempt at stealth, Pizza, but it's not even eleven." I tuck the iPad under my pillow. Despite my reassuring chat with Toby, I'm still full of adrenaline from dinner earlier. I was hoping an episode of doctor drama would lull me to sleep, but it hasn't yet worked. "What kind of late-stage spinster do you think I am?"

She grimaces. "Sorry. I wasn't sure if you had to work in the morning."

I stifle a sigh and flip on the lamp for her. Polly does have one thing right: my entire life revolves around whether or not I have to be at the restaurant. That's usually the difference between one episode of *Grey's* and a solid binge of four. And since I have to be at the restaurant more often than not, Polly was probably right to assume I was tucked in for an early night. Not that I haven't been trying to pull back.

Sort of.

A little bit.

"Evie's opening up, and Fernando's got a new kid doing prep," I say. I pull out my phone and add an item to my to-do list: check in with my head chef to be sure the new kid—Jacob? Joseph?—is working out. "I won't go in until after lunch."

Polly nods, slipping out of her dress and digging through her suitcase, which has exploded on the floor next to her bed, stray shoes and tank tops starting to creep over and disappearing under my bed. She emerges with a fistful of silk that is apparently meant to be pajamas. "I can help out while I'm here," she says as she pads into the tiny bathroom Dad built into the corner of the attic when we were in third grade. "I still remember how to make the lasagna."

I laugh quietly to myself, because even when Polly used to help out full-time during summers, her lasagnas always came out lumpy with questionable layers and pockets of too much sauce or not enough cheese. I can only imagine that now, after so many years out of practice, they'd best be described as "abstract."

Even in the dim light, Polly can read the skepticism all over my face. "What? You don't have to do everything yourself, Pippin."

Don't I? The retort is on the tip of my tongue, but I swallow it. "I know. That's why Fernando's got the new kid," I reply. *Josh*—I'm pretty sure his name is Josh. "I almost never work lunch anymore." I don't mention that it's because I had to lay off our bookkeeper and now I spend lunch filing and categorizing expenses myself.

"That's good to hear." Polly pops her head out of the bathroom, her face covered in some kind of tangerine-colored oil that she massages into her cheeks. I swear, if art history wasn't her passion, Polly could have become a chemist with all the concoctions she puts on her face. "You spend too much time in the kitchen. Mom told me about Everett."

"How do you even know Everett existed?" I realized pretty quickly that he wasn't a keeper, so I didn't waste my time bringing him up in any of our texts or calls while Polly was in London. We only had sex once, and he didn't ask me one single time what I liked or if it was good. I faked it, and it wasn't even a strong performance, but he wasn't paying a bit of attention. "He was barely around to begin with."

Polly emerges from the bathroom, her skin dewy and pink, and climbs into bed before tossing me a heaping helping of side-eye. "My point exactly. You need to spend less time in the restaurant and more time on *extracurriculars*." She waggles her eyebrows.

"I get laid plenty," I reply, tossing a pillow that Nonna embroidered at my sister's head. Even though I'm out of practice, I score a direct hit.

"Okay, but are you actually finding anything in all that sex? Or is it just an endless string of first through third dates and some uninspired banging and then you serve them their walking papers?"

Ugh, I hate how close she's stumbled to the truth.

"First of all, they're not all boyfriend material, but some of them put the *extra* in *extracurricular*, as you say. And second of all, excuse me, but when did you go all family values on me? You took enough gender studies classes to know not to shame me for dating." Polly rolls her eyes, but I shoot her a look, and suddenly, despite Toby's warning, I can't hold back. "Seriously, Polly. Why do you have to get *married?* This isn't 1950. Move in together! Get to know each other! What's the rush?"

"I *knew* you couldn't hold back!" Polly says, her voice equal parts triumph and frustration. She wings the embroidered pillow back my way, but it flies over my head and thuds against the window. She flops over on her side to face me, a pillow tucked under her head, and even though this is nothing like the conversations we used to have when we were kids, whispering over the dim yellow lamp on the bedside table between us, I can't help but be transported right back to those times. And I can't help but wonder how much longer I'll have Polly across from me now that she plans to run off and get married.

Polly lets out a frustrated sigh. "We *do* know each other, Pippin. And when you know, you know. Why would I put off happiness?"

I have the sudden urge to reach over and switch off that dim lamp, because it's providing entirely too much light right now. I can see the look on Polly's face, and I know exactly what's hiding behind those words, the thing she's not saying. Because every day since Dad died, Polly has pursued her dreams as if the punishment for missing an opportunity is death itself. And I can see her eyes welling and feel the itch at the back of my throat, so I flip off the lamp and change the subject.

"Hey, so I forgot to tell you…Toby's back," I say.

I can practically hear her mouth drop open in the dark. "Like, *back* back?"

"Yeah. Apparently he decided he didn't want to do the

medical research thing and left Stanford to do his residency in the ER at Mass General."

"Oh wow. So he's really back. Right-around-the-corner back."

"Yup, he's living in the basement apartment of his parents' town house," I say. "And he broke up with Jen, apparently."

I hear Polly's sharp intake of breath. "*Wow.* So he blew up his whole life, huh? How is he?"

I roll over and stare at the ceiling, which is spider-webbed with delicate cracks in the plaster. "Good. He said he didn't want to talk about the breakup, but he didn't seem, well... broken up over it. He seems really happy, actually."

"How's he look?" she asks after a beat of silence.

"What do you mean? He looks like Toby," I say, thinking about his ferocious yawn and those ridiculous pajama pants. "A very tired version of Toby, but still Toby."

"*Pippin.*"

"What?"

"I don't even like men, and even I can admit that grown-up Toby looks like the kind of guy who could really blow your back out."

"Ew, stop," I groan. Polly has always liked to taunt Toby and me, even when we were kids and *Pippin and Toby sittin' in a tree* wasn't ironic. But Toby's my best friend, and okay, yeah, he came back from medical school significantly less gangly, but he's still...Toby. I could never go there. I never *want* to go there, no matter how tall and muscular he gets. I don't do relationships or romance, and I'm not about to blow up our friendship because Toby is cute now.

"Are you honestly telling me that even now that you're both all grown up and he wears scrubs that look straight out of an on-call room scene in *Grey's*, you haven't thought about it?"

My face contorts into an expression I usually reserve for when someone tries to feed me mushrooms or any vegetable that's been converted into a foam. "I can honestly say *no*, I have never looked at Toby like that."

"Looked at him like what? With your eyes?" I feel Polly staring at me, and when I look over at her bed, she's giving me a look that is the human embodiment of the heart-eyes emoji, hands charmingly under her chin.

I roll over, stretch to retrieve the pillow from beneath the window, and chuck it back at her, wiping that look right off her face. "Stop it," I say, "or I'm going to start asking you about all the times you pictured Cynthia Mills naked." Cynthia was Polly's best friend all through high school until Cynthia went off to college, joined the campus evangelicals, and decided she needed to pray Polly's gay away through a series of increasingly hysterical emails. But before she became a homophobic loon, she was gorgeous.

Polly lets out a theatrical gag and mimes tossing the entirety of her dinner onto the carpet between our beds. "Message received," she says, reaching for the lamp to switch off the light.

But as I lie back on my pillow, I let Polly's words roll around in my head for a moment. Has Toby gotten hot? Objectively, yes. When he threw his arm around my shoulders tonight, I felt the presence of firm biceps and the corded muscle of his shoulder. His hair seems to be less teen frizzy and more grown-man floppy, and he's got this one dimple—just one, on the left side—that used to look rascally but now has a bit of a model bent to it. Those are just facts. But that doesn't mean I'm *attracted* to him. I never have been.

We've been best friends since we were five years old. Mom brought Polly and me to splash around at the Frog Pond because it was too hot to do anything else. Toby was there with his nanny, who was perched on a bench, deeply engrossed in some paperback thriller. That meant she didn't notice when Colton Baker, a real asshole even at five years old, tried to pants Toby right there in the middle of the Frog Pond in front of god and the Massachusetts State House.

Toby, who I would later learn has never been one for confrontation, just stood there, mouth agape, with his lily-white butt crack hanging out of his Ralph Lauren swim trunks. And because I have from *birth* been a person who thrives on confrontation, I marched my chubby little legs over to Colton, put my hands squarely on his chest, and shoved him straight down on the ground. Then I reached behind Toby, yanked up his swim trunks, took his hand, and marched us both off to beg Mom to buy us popsicles from the ice cream truck parked at the edge of the Common.

We've been best friends ever since, through middle school awkwardness and high school wildness, through three thousand miles and eight years of distance. Toby was there for me when my dad died, even though it was only a week into freshman year and his parents didn't want him flying back across the country. He missed a week of classes to hold me while I sobbed and tried to understand what my life was going to be. He even filled in at the restaurant that first summer before he started doing internships and couldn't get home as much.

Toby and I have twenty years of history that means almost as much to me as my family and the restaurant. Toby's my person, my constant. You don't fuck around with that, literally or figuratively. But as I drift off to sleep, my mind (that dirty asshole) suddenly takes me directly to a *Grey's Anatomy* on-call room. Only it's not McDreamy or McSteamy inside; it's McToby in scrubs, his hair flopping over one eye as he grins down at me, that one rascally dimple catching the moonlight. His biceps bulge as he holds himself above me, his hands bracketing my face, lowering himself slowly, so slowly, and—

Ugh!

I have to flip over and stare out the window directly into the streetlight to burn the image away.

Chapter 8

Why don't eggs tell jokes?

They'd crack each other up!

Come on, that one was good!

PIPPIN

I really thought that you being back would put an end to this

We're an hour from closing, and thank god, because this has been an absolutely brutal Saturday. Turns out the new kid—whose name is Justin, which I will for sure remember now because I had to shout it so many times tonight—fucked up the prep and left us scrambling an hour before the bulk of our reservations showed up. And I don't know if it was the heat or that the Sox lost earlier in the day, but people were *spicy* tonight.

Which is why I'm standing out in the alley, trying to catch a moment of quiet, even if that means taking in a big gulp of hot dumpster air. Evie has joined me, and we lean against the warm brick of the back of the building, staring out into the darkness like GIs after an air raid.

"I got yelled at because I brought a woman a Cabernet Sauvignon that was red," Evie says with a thousand yard stare directly at the wall of the building across from us. "She swore to me that Cabernet Sauvignon was supposed to be *white.* What do you even do with that?"

"Exactly what you did: bring her a glass of white wine and smile like she's a culinary genius, thus saving your tip," I reply.

"I just want to make sure you know that a little part of my soul died when I did that," she says, closing her eyes and rubbing at her temples. Evie started working at Marino's five years and about thirty tattoos ago. She moved to Boston to go to Berklee and become a songwriter but dropped out after her first semester. She's been trying to figure out what she wants to be when she grows up ever since.

"No more than when I had to ask Fernando to please go easy on the garlic on a customer's *garlic bread*," I reply. "Like, maybe just take your sensitive white-lady palate to the Olive Garden."

We return to silence, both of us trying to battle headaches the size of Fenway. Only Toby's approaching footsteps interrupt us.

"What, are we having a meditation moment?" Toby asks as he ambles up in light blue scrub pants and an unzipped hoodie, a Dunkin' Donuts T-shirt visible underneath. It's been almost two weeks since Toby returned and Polly got engaged. He's started his residency now, and it's still weird to see him in scrubs that aren't a Halloween costume.

"You're awfully chipper for someone who worked a seven-to-seven shift and just got off"—I glance at my watch—"a whole two hours late."

He shrugs. "I promised this kid I'd go to CT with him, but they were backed up, so I had to hang around," he says. "But otherwise it was a good night. The kid's CT was clear, I did, like, forty million stitches, nobody was seriously injured or ill, and nobody yarfed on me. Best kind of shift you can ask for on a peds ER rotation."

"Don't you need to go home and fall face-first into bed?" I ask. "Or have you come here to torture me with more 'jokes'?"

"I hear the air quotes, and I will not respond to them," he says, grinning. "Nonna said she left me a box of cannoli in the walk-in. I'm going to eat four of them, *then* fall face-first into my bed."

"What did you do to earn cannoli?" I ask.

"I looked at her ingrown toenail and assured her it wasn't infected," he says, his grin expanding like a kid who just aced his AP exam.

I grimace. "Ew. Enjoy, because you *definitely* earned that." I nod toward the door. "You go on in and grab them. I'm not going back in until I have to."

"Rough night, eh?"

"You have no idea," I groan.

"Good to see you, Evie," Toby says, tipping an imaginary hat as he ducks in the door.

I lean my head back against the wall, close my eyes, and try not to think about my grandmother's ingrown toenail.

"Hey, so what's Toby's deal?" Evie asks.

I crack one eye open and squint over at her. "What do you mean?"

"Is he single? Because *I'm* single, and he's cute."

I open my mouth to say yes, he's available, but before I can do that, I hear myself saying, "He just got out of a long-term relationship, and I think it was pretty rough? I don't think he's dating right now." Which…is not even remotely true. I mean, he *did* just break up with Jen. But he doesn't seem too messed up about it. He still hasn't talked to me about it at all, actually.

I only met her a few times when she accompanied him back home for holidays. She seemed nice, but I'll be honest, I was always surprised it lasted as long as it did. She was just... quiet. She always acted like she needed permission to be anywhere or do anything or join a conversation. Since he hasn't said a word about the breakup, I've kind of been assuming that Toby finally noticed Jen has the personality of a nervous kindergarten teacher and dispatched with her. Honestly, why everyone doesn't listen to my romantic advice from the get-go is beyond me. I have *very* good instincts.

But yeah, Toby would probably be fine with going on a date right now, but for some reason I feel weird about offering him up to Evie. I mean, we work together. I'm actually kind of her boss. That would be weird, right? If she dated my best friend? Surely there's some kind of blurred line there, something employment ethics-y that we should steer clear of.

Evie shrugs. "Too bad. He's *hot*. Like, George Clooney in season one of *ER* hot, with the floppy hair and the muscles under the scrubs. I'd let him inspect my tonsils any day of the week."

"I hope that's a euphemism for making out and not some weird strep test fetish," I reply.

"You guys have never..." Evie waggles her eyebrows in the universal sign for *get down and dirty*.

"No! No," I say, sticking out my tongue to keep from repeating it six or seven more times. "I've known Toby way too long. We're just friends."

"Are you sure? Because he looks like Shawn Mendes's dirty older brother."

I grimace, but my mind also snags on the description. Because...okay, maybe a little bit? He *is* very tall, well over six feet, and he's got those wily curls that sort of flop over his eyes and ears of their own volition. He's got warm brown eyes and a wide smile, and yeah, I can see it. But dirty? What does she mean by dirty? *That* I don't get. To me, Toby will always be this gangly little cinnamon roll who I've known since I was five. Has Toby gotten hot? Objectively, yes. Is Evie right that he looks like season-one Clooney in his scrubs? Sure, okay, I see it. Have I had a handful of inappropriate dreams since he moved back to Boston? I admit nothing. And besides, *inappropriate* is the operative word. It's not like I ever have those thoughts when I'm awake and in charge of where the good ship *Mental Image* steers. I'm no more responsible for that than when I dream that my limbs are spaghetti and Ben Affleck is trying to dip me in marinara.

So I have a hot best friend. So what! That doesn't change the reality here, which is that Toby and I are just friends. Always have been, always will be, and neither of us wants to change that.

And *dirty*? Toby, my Labrador retriever of a best friend, is definitely *not* dirty.

The door to the kitchen pops open and Trevor, another server, sticks his head out. "Table four asked about dessert menus," he says to Evie.

"Shit. There goes my tip," Evie says. Because everyone knows that if your table flags down a server who's not you, it's because they think you're not paying attention.

"Comp them some affogati," I say before she disappears through the door. "That should redeem you."

"Thank you!" she calls, and before the door clangs shut, Toby emerges through it with a white bakery box tied up in red ribbon. Nonna loves a nice presentation, but Toby immediately grabs one of the tails and yanks, leaning against the wall next to me to crack open the box. He pulls out a perfectly piped cannoli with mini chocolate chips on the ends and a snowy dusting of powdered sugar on top and consumes half of it in one bite. He tilts his head back, and a moan escapes his throat as he chews, this rough, deep sound that makes me forget for a second that it's coming from Toby. It also reminds me that it's been a few weeks since I got laid, and clearly that's making my imagination do weird, wild things. Maybe I should give Everett another shot? I could provide him with a map to my clitoris, which is about a quarter of an inch north of where he thought it was.

I glance over as Toby chews, trying not to notice the way his Adam's apple works as he swallows. I let my eyes wander along his rounded biceps and corded forearms, and right as they reach his waist, he reaches up in this ridiculous catlike stretch that exposes a couple of inches of his stomach beneath his scrub top and *oh my god*, when did Toby start hitting the gym? Those are real-life abs, the kind you can't get accidentally, especially not with the way Toby eats. (I wouldn't be shocked if he ate all the cannoli *and* the box.) He *worked* for those. I have to force my eyes away to keep from following the trail of chestnut hair that disappears beneath the low-slung waistband of his scrubs, and holy shit, why am I having hot and horny thoughts about *Toby*?

I blame Evie. Seriously, Shawn Mendes's dirty older brother? And Polly too. She's the one who planted the seeds of that pesky on-call room dream I've had twice now. I don't have feelings for Toby; everyone *around me* has feelings for Toby, apparently, and they need to stop splashing that shit all over me.

I drag my eyes back up to his face and see that he's clearly caught me staring. I open my mouth to explain, but he just offers me the box. "You want one?" he asks, because of course he thinks I'm lusting after the cannoli.

Which is good, because for a moment there I was *definitely* lusting after Toby, and that *cannot* happen.

Chapter 9

TOBY

What kind of car does an egg drive?

A yolkswagen!

PIPPIN

You know how I feel about puns

"Okay, so what do these people do, exactly?" I ask as I crowd onto the wide granite stoop of the Bryan family home with Mom, Nonna, and Polly. It's time to meet the in-laws, and I'm suddenly wicked nervous. I didn't realize the Bryans were rich.

Like, *stupid* rich.

I mean, the expansive stone mansion, with its leaded windows and gas lamps flanking a front door big enough to drive a Mini Cooper through, sits on a sloping green lawn the size of an NFL regulation football field. And when you live in a city like Boston, large-yard rich is a whole different kind of rich.

"Mackenzie's dad is an attorney," Polly replies, reaching for the doorbell.

"For the mob?" I ask, turning to take in the full scope of the emerald-green grass, which looks like it's been cut with a ruler and scissors.

Polly takes a deep breath and blows it out like she's steeling herself to leap off a cliff. "No, he's a partner at a big-deal corporate law firm, and her mom is a psychologist who's written a bunch of bestselling books."

Something pings in the back of my brain, and when the pieces snap together, my jaw drops open. "Wait, is Mackenzie's mom *Dr. Nora?*"

"Yes," Polly replies, as if it's meaningless, like I just asked if Mackenzie's mom is a Sagittarius.

"Oh, I love her!" Mom says.

"Who's Dr. Nora?" Nonna asks.

"She's a self-help guru! She has, like, seven million Instagram followers and a bunch of books. She's friends with Oprah, and I heard she helped Serena Williams before her last French Open, which she *won*," I explain. I'm a little surprised Nonna hasn't heard of her, but Nonna also can't figure out how to set an alarm on her phone, so the podcast app is probably a little beyond her.

"Should I have worn a nicer dress?" Mom asks, looking down at the floral number she selected. It was one of *seven* different dresses she tried on this morning—well, four dresses and three pants/blouse options, because apparently we need to act like we're *all* marrying into the Bryan family, not just Polly.

"Please be cool," Polly says through gritted teeth, her words running together in a last-ditch plea as the front door swings open.

I expect to see a housekeeper, or maybe a butler in a pinstriped waistcoat and tails like the guy on the Monopoly box. I expect to see white walls and minimalist furniture that no one actually sits on. Based on the lawn alone, I expect an *Architectural Digest* spread or at least something worthy of the pages of *Vogue*. But those expectations are blown to bits as soon as Mackenzie's parents open the door and a festival of color appears behind them.

"Welcome!" Dr. Nora Martinez-Bryan says. Just like in her Instagram posts, she's wearing a flowy, classy linen ensemble in vibrant colors, her hair cut in a shiny black bob. She just *looks* like someone who has the answers to all life's questions and will gladly allow you to sit at her knee while she shares them with you over a steaming cup of tea.

"We're so glad to meet you, Marinos!" A dark-skinned bald man with a salt-and-pepper beard, who I assume is Mackenzie's father, welcomes us in with great big bear hugs. "I'm Frantz, and this is my wife, Nora."

"It's so wonderful to meet you," Mom says, stepping through the door and smoothing out the imaginary wrinkles in her dress. "Your home is just lovely."

And truly, it is. The walls are painted rich jewel tones and are covered with framed photos, art, and hanging sculptures. The sweeping mahogany staircase is carpeted in a plush wine-colored runner that bears signs of years of feet hustling up and down. The living room to the right is filled with mismatched, well-loved furniture that begs you to flop down on it.

And there are books everywhere.

Everywhere—bursting from bookshelves, piled in teetering stacks on tables, discarded on the expensive-looking Persian rugs. Nora even has one tucked under her arm, which she was apparently reading just before answering the door. She quickly places it on the nearby entryway table, dog-earing the page first, before pulling Polly into a hug.

"So good to see you, mi querida," Nora says before stepping back and welcoming the rest of us into her home. "We got a chance to visit the girls this summer in London. It was a real treat, and we fell in love with Polly just as fast as Mackenzie did! My daughter, by the way, will be down in just a moment. Please excuse her—she's negotiating a deal, and we are still working very hard on establishing a proper work-life balance."

"Oh, she's just young and hungry," Frantz says with a chuckle, and while I figure in this she must take after her father, I'm still hard-pressed to see how uptight, type-A, prim Mackenzie could have come from either of these people. Everything about them is joy personified. Mackenzie seems like she'd have to have joy shocked out of her with a cattle prod. "Please come in."

We all shuffle after Frantz and Nora into the living room, where we settle into seats that are as comfortable and welcoming as I suspected. Frantz ambles over to the bookcase in the corner, and that's when I realize the house isn't full of *only* books. There are also records. Lots and lots of records. Frantz flips through a shelf and pulls one out, sliding the vinyl out of the sleeve.

"I hope you don't mind—I always love to set a mood," he says with a mischievous grin, then drops the needle on Prince's *Purple Rain.*

"Dad is deep in a Prince phase at the moment," Mackenzie says as she marches down the stairs—truly, the woman *marches* as if she's never been relaxed for a moment in her life. "I hope you're all ready to party like it's 1999."

"Prince is not a phase, my darling," Frantz replies. "Prince is a lifestyle."

"My husband has been collecting vinyl since before the CD boom," Nora explains. "It's his passion."

"I was doing it before it was cool," he says.

"My dad, the original hipster," Mackenzie quips. She walks over and takes a seat next to Polly, slipping her hand into hers and doing that thumb thing again. This time it bothers me a little less, or maybe that's just because of the insanely cozy

71

wingback chair I'm sitting in. I'm about to ask Dr. Nora if she ever needs a house sitter, because I'll do it for free.

"We all must have vices, and vinyl is mine," Frantz says, dropping into another wingback chair with a shrug.

"Me, I like baseball and medical dramas," Nonna says.

"Books, obviously," Dr. Nora says, gesturing around at her library. "Also gardening."

"Yes, I was just noticing your yard," Mom says, moving to the window to peer out. "It's just lovely."

"It's my pride and joy," Nora replies, sharing a Cheshire grin with Polly that clearly has some kind of inside joke buried within it. "Would you like a tour?"

I have never wanted anything less, since it would require me getting out of this chair, but everyone else seems jazzed to go look at plants, and so off we troop into the morning heat. All but Mackenzie, who stops short at the sound of her ringing phone and quickly peels off to answer it. Polly doesn't seem to mind that her fiancée is spending the first meeting of their families on the phone, but it bugs me. I have to work to arrange my expression into something other than a scowl, Toby's warning about how loud my face speaks ringing in my ears.

I don't know a thing about gardening, but I have to admit that the yard is impressive. I half listen as Dr. Nora talks about gingkoes and fig trees, peonies and daffodils and roses. Plants are nice and all, but the thought of having to keep something other than myself alive makes me want to take a ten-year nap. Who has time for all that watering and pruning? I got a basil plant for my windowsill once. It was dead within a week, and I remembered why they sell fresh herbs at the grocery store.

I hear the sound of bubbling water, then come upon a pond the size of a sedan in the middle of the sloping yard, surrounded by natural-looking stones. A tangle of brightly colored fish the size of small cats comes rushing toward the sound of feet, flashes of orange, yellow, black, and silver swimming back and forth, rushing for the rocks.

"They're like dogs," Frantz says as I step closer to the edge. The fish scramble as close to me as they can get, and I get the sense that if they could grow legs, they'd climb out of the pond and beg right at my toes. "They get excited at the first sign that someone has food. Want to feed them?"

He picks up a bucket of pellets and hands it to me. "Just a scoop. Toss it out in the middle so they don't try to beach themselves. They're as dumb as they are pretty, unfortunately."

I follow his directions, pleased that feeding the koi has gotten me out of the garden tour. Too much discussion about the growing conditions of annuals and perennials makes my brain ooze out my ears, and this gathering has only just begun. I can't pass out from boredom too early. I don't think that's the impression Polly is hoping to make: *This is my narcoleptic sister, Pippin, who can't be arsed to keep her eyes open while you talk.* I'd be picking my belongings up out of the middle of the street later for sure.

I toss the first cup into the water, and the fish pounce on the food, swallowing up pellets with their wide, gaping mouths.

"You guys seem like you're starving," I say as I dip the little cup into the bucket and toss another helping to my new fish friends. They swarm the pellets again. Watching them splash about, the sound of the burbling water filling up the space around me, I can almost forget why I'm here. "More?"

"Don't let them fool ya—they're not hungry. Carp will just eat and eat and eat until they explode," Frantz calls as he trails off after his wife and my family.

A loud splash sends my gaze straight back to the pond. I'm hit with panic at the idea that I've just exploded some bougie fish. I brace for the sight of floating fish guts, but it turns out it's just the yellow one lunging for a pellet wedged between two stones. Thank god, because I don't know how I'd explain an exploded fish.

Mackenzie's home life is absolutely nothing like mine and Polly's. I know opposites attract and all that, and certainly ending up with someone who is just like you would be a major snooze, but there's something to be said for…understanding the other person? How could Mackenzie possibly understand Polly when she grew up on an estate and my sister grew up sharing a 180-square-foot bedroom with sloping ceilings? As much as I already love Frantz and Dr. Nora and their cozy mansion, I'm still not confident this relationship will go the distance. But I remind myself that all I have to do is wait for the inevitable.

Unfortunately, patience is not a virtue I possess.

I hear rustling from the far side of the pond, which features a retaining wall and a drop-off below into the lower part of the yard. I spot Mackenzie's sleek bun bobbing back and forth as she paces the grass below.

Suddenly her voice cuts through the serenity of the bubbling pond. "That's not at all what we discussed," she says, her tone full of nails. If I weren't so dead set on being unimpressed by Mackenzie, I'd be giving her a *you go girl* right about now, because those are some major #girlboss vibes. "I agreed to an NDA, and you agreed to make my contract reflect that. Where's the money?"

I freeze. Sure, I don't have a fancy-pants Ivy League MBA, but I know what an NDA is. And I've seen enough movies that when someone whisper-yells, "Where's the money?" into a cell phone, I can conjure up some very specific scenarios. I don't *think* Mackenzie would engage in corporate espionage, but then again, I don't know her very well. And even if she *is* on the up-and-up, this kind of ruthless business nonsense is not going to mesh well with Polly's free-spirited artistic side. I owe it to my sister to at least listen in…right? Maybe look and see if

Mackenzie is using a burner phone? Anything that might prove my future sister-in-law is about to commit some serious white-collar crimes?

I don't bother to interrogate the impulse, just sort of semi-squat and creep along the rocks that surround the pond. I can only make out some of what Mackenzie is saying because she keeps pacing and half the time she's too far away. But if I can just get a little bit closer, maybe I can—

And then my foot lands on a slick little stone that wobbles. Just a bit, side to side, but it's enough. I reach up, scrambling for something to grab—a branch, a passing stranger, the hand of God himself—but there's nothing. My fists close around handfuls of air as one foot shoots forward and the other flies back. I try to use my core to catch myself, but unfortunately I haven't had a whole lot of time for core workouts lately, and I only manage to pivot so that when I finally do hit the water, it's in a full belly flop.

As murky pond water begins seeping into my underpants and the frilly tail of a fish that costs more than the shoes I'm wearing swats me in the face, I realize I need to get my shit together or my family is going to disown me.

If only I'd had that realization *before* I nearly drowned in Dr. Nora's koi pond.

Chapter 10

How does a taco say grace?

Lettuce pray!

I like how you use the exclamation point, as if that makes it funnier

"Pippin, we've got a seat for you right here," Nora says, patting an empty spot at the dining room table to her left, and I wonder if it's intentional—maybe Dr. Nora is going to take this opportunity to offer me some self-help tips. Maybe she wants to revolutionize my life.

Maybe I should let her.

I smile and drop down into the empty chair, my hair dripping onto the shoulders of a T-shirt Mackenzie found in her old dresser. It reads, THERE'S A FINE LINE BETWEEN NUMERATOR AND DENOMINATOR; ONLY A FRACTION WOULD UNDERSTAND. It pairs perfectly with the red-and-green flannel pajama pants she's loaned me, which have yetis doing what looks like the Macarena on the butt. In this whole house, are these the only clothes Mackenzie left behind when she grew up and moved out? Is she fucking with me? Because if so…honestly, bravo. It's the most personality I've seen out of my financial documentary–loving future sister-in-law. It makes me like her just a little bit.

But when I glance across the table, Mackenzie gives no indication that the loaner clothes are part of an elaborate revenge prank. Instead, she's busy making sure her champagne flute is perfectly aligned with her knife, which is resting with military precision beside an elegant china dinner plate. Ah, yes, there's the Mackenzie I barely know and have lukewarm feelings for.

Not that I'm in a place to complain. I'm the one who was trying to eavesdrop on her when I took a header into the koi pond. I'm the one who let one too many Jason Bourne movies (all of which I fell asleep during) go to my head.

And from the venomous looks Polly keeps flashing my way, it's clear I'm the one who has acted like a full-on idiot and embarrassed my sister on a scale heretofore never imagined. I'm sure that as far as Polly is concerned, I have earned the hand-me-down Mathlete T-shirt and holiday pajama pants. As far as Polly is concerned, this is a light punishment. If it were up to her, she likely would have handed me a sixth-grade ballet recital costume and wished me the best. Frankly I'm lucky she hasn't called an Uber and sent me home in my wet clothes. The fact that I'm still welcome at the table at all is a supreme act of charity on my sister's part, and as I sit here trying to ignore the sneaking feeling that there's algae in my ear, I vow to be on my very best behavior for the rest of this experience.

At the head of the table, Frantz reaches for a bottle of champagne to the right of his plate and raises it. "I thought we might start with a toast?" His wide, jubilant grin is enough to distract me from my aquatic faux pas, and I grab my glass with my very best smile on my face. Frantz pops the cork expertly, and when everyone's glass is full, he stands.

"Polly, we were so lucky to get to spend some time with you this summer when Nora and I visited, and we knew right away that you and Mackenzie made quite the pair. We could not be happier to welcome you and the rest of your family. So a toast to family, both old and growing. Marinos, we are so glad to have you at our table today, and Polly, we are so blessed to be able to welcome you into our family, today and every day." At this, his voice catches, and he raises his glass high. I glance around the table and see that both my mother and Polly are caught up in the emotion of the moment, and Nonna reaches for her napkin to dab at her eyes. "Felicidades!"

A chorus of *felicidades* and *cheers* rises from around the table, and I focus on the bubbles bursting on my tongue instead of the pit in my stomach. I can't believe I just met Mackenzie and now my sister is being welcomed into somebody else's family by somebody else's father. How did this all happen so fast? And is there a way to slow it down?

"Please, everyone, dig in," Nora says from her seat opposite Frantz. There are so many hulking dishes of eggs, chorizo, croissants, crispy home fries, and fresh fruit—enough food to feed ten armies and still wrap up the leftovers—that I am surprised the table isn't groaning under the weight. "I may have gone a bit overboard, but between my Mexican heritage and Frantz's Haitian heritage, we're both from cultures that feel an unending sense of shame if someone leaves the table hungry."

"Well, then that makes three because I've never met an Italian who didn't want to send you home groaning with a covered dish in your arms," Mom says. "And if you add in my Midwestern roots, I'm pretty sure no one in this family will ever have a grumbling stomach."

"Cheers to that," Frantz says, raising his glass while simultaneously balancing a croissant on a pile of eggs. "Speaking of the big merge, we though this might be a good time to talk about wedding plans, since we're all sitting around the same table—so much simpler than email. It'll be here before you know it!"

"Oh, I didn't realize you'd set a date," I say, and since these are the some of the first words I've spoken since my swan dive into the koi pond, they come out sounding slightly froggy. Which is how I feel, honestly, at the idea of my sister "merging" with anyone.

"Well, we haven't nailed anything down, but there are a few things we have to work around," Polly says. She pushes a strawberry around her plate. Mackenzie reaches over and rubs her back, and it's at that moment that I realize Polly looks nervous. Nearly as nervous as she looked the other night when she made her big announcement about this blessed union. Now I'm nervous too, because what other bombs could there possibly be?

Nora nods at Polly. "Mackenzie's abuela is flying in from Mexico City and staying for a month in October. She's not well, and the trip is long, so it seemed like it might be smart to try to plan the wedding for when she's already here."

"We want to make sure the people who are most important to us can be there, so October fourteenth seems like a good date," Polly says.

I'm doing math, but Mom is faster. "But that's just five months away," she says.

My mental calculator may be slower, but it turns out it's also a bit more accurate. "That's four months. *Four.* How are you going to plan a wedding in the busiest month in New England in just four months? Is there even a venue available in the entire city?" I realize the Bryans are stupid rich, which means their money probably opens a lot of doors. But an

October wedding in Boston is a hot ticket, and unless another engaged couple breaks up between now then, they'll be out of luck.

"Well, we were thinking we could have it here." Polly reaches over and grabs Mackenzie's hand, and her fiancée smiles back at her.

"My parents have hosted a number of events here, so we know it can be done beautifully," Mackenzie adds.

"Oh yes, there's plenty of open space for tables and a dance floor, and we've had a tent back there more than once," Nora says, and it hits me that this whole discussion has already happened. Somehow my sister got engaged and started planning an actual wedding without filling me in *at all*.

And that? Well, it hurts.

But this is not the place for that kind of reaction—you have exactly no high ground when you're wearing novelty pajamas pants at a dining table—so I tune back in to what Nora's saying. "Remember that fundraiser we did for the children's adaptive ballet program? That was in October, and the trees were absolutely on fire. I swear we doubled our goal thanks to Mother Nature alone!"

Having been fairly up close and personal with the back garden, I can attest to its beauty. Though we'd have to be careful with drunken guests around the koi pond. But still… even with a venue, planning an entire wedding in four months? My sister, married and gone in *four months*? And that's almost as long as Polly and Mackenzie have known each other.

"Aren't you trying to finish your dissertation? And defend it? And search for jobs? Come on, Polly, this seems…not possible." I don't want to be a downer, and I know I'm on thin ice with my sister, but still. This is a little bit ridiculous, and if I don't say something now, it's all going to get too far down the road. Turning the car around will be costly and painful. I'm doing my sister a favor by speaking up. "Surely you can't think planning a wedding on your own in a time crunch while doing everything else you have to do is a good idea."

"You're right. I can't do it on my own," Polly says, and I let out a breath. I took a big risk opening my mouth at this table, and it feels good to be acknowledged. "We're definitely going to need some major help."

And that tone of voice…*oh shit*, I know it well. It's the one Polly used in fifth grade when she decided we should be Sonny and Cher for Halloween and she wanted me to wear the mustache. There are some very embarrassing photos that prove just how well that tone of voice works on me.

"I was hoping you might want to help," she continues. "I mean, you're very organized and have a good eye. Plus you have so many connections in the hospitality industry."

I have to hand it to her—Polly is *good*. She gives me a look that's swimming in guilt, because she knows that sitting here in front of all these people, still clad in the humiliation of my last mistake (seriously, I'm pretty sure there's a lily pad tangled in my hair), she knows I have to say yes. And even if the stakes weren't so high, Polly's my twin sister. She's my other half. *Of course* I'm going to help her plan the wedding, even if I think it's absolutely ridiculous to do it in four months, much less to a woman you've known for barely six.

With the soft strains of "I Got You Babe" tinkling through my brain, I smile. "Of course I'll help," I say, and even though my heart's not in it yet, the grin that spreads across Polly's face brings me a few steps closer to that finish line. That smile—full of joy and hope and anticipation—lets me know that it's time to shut my mouth for real.

Filter: *activated*—permanently.

This wedding is happening, and now that I'm on board— or at least standing on the jetway, ticket in hand—I'm going to make sure it's the best damn wedding you could possibly plan in four months.

Chapter 11

TOBY

Why didn't the skeleton climb the mountain?

PIPPIN

Shouldn't you be busy saving lives?

TOBY

It didn't have the guts!

PIPPIN

I weep for your patients

TOBY

I'm still on peds rotation. I've finally found my audience!

It's a quiet Monday morning in the Boston Public Garden, but my mind is loud. I've come here to find a bench where I can sit and start chipping away at the Marino-Bryan wedding plans. I figured the rustling leaves, rippling water, and passing duck tours would provide me with the perfect amount of white noise to help me concentrate, but instead all I can do is panic. Panic that my sister is actually doing this, and panic that I won't be able to pull it off. Which is an odd, warring mixture of emotions, to be sure.

I pull out my phone and click on the app I downloaded as soon as I got home from the Bryan family brunch. I-To-Do is the highest-rated wedding planning app on the internet, which is why I chose it even though it set me back a whopping $19.99. I'm going to need all the help I can get if I'm going to put together the perfect wedding for my sister and my sister's deeply uptight fiancée in just four months.

The app loads, and I type in the date Polly mentioned: October fourteenth. I half expect the app to laugh at me. Instead I get a pop-up box that informs me that I'll be working through the "accelerated" checklist. I sigh. As much as I'm dreading this wedding, I do love a good checklist, accelerated or otherwise. And when the checklist appears, I feel a surge of serotonin when I see that the first item—*select a date*—is already checked. I fall in love with the app immediately for serving me up that reward.

I scan the list of tasks ahead of me, scrolling and scrolling and—my god—*still* scrolling, my jaw dropping at the lengthy list. It seriously never ends. Good lord, how are we going to do all this? Flowers, officiant, music, dresses and shoes, vows, a cake, special utensils to ceremonially cut the cake, invitations, place cards and menus, a photographer and videographer and something called a soundscape? Guest travel plans and hotel room blocks and calligraphy and monogrammed robes and... custom dress hangers??

I take a hard right turn from hoping this wedding doesn't happen to wondering if I can convince Polly and Mackenzie to pop down to Boston City Hall this weekend and tie this thing up for fifty dollars. (Yes, as soon as I saw a check box for custom ring bearer attire for dogs, I clicked out of the app and googled elopements.) I can see now why wedding planners make so much money. This is going to be another part-time job. At least.

Of course, Polly asked me to *help*, not run the whole show. But I can already feel high school group project Pippin rearing her ugly head. I've always been the queen of *just let me do it, okay?* And I have a feeling that I'm going to have to work very hard to remind myself that this is *Polly's* wedding and that I'm not a paid professional wedding planner and that maybe, just maybe, I should relinquish some control.

I add that to the checklist in the app.

Within minutes, my planning brain takes over and starts to break down the to-do list into smaller bites, eliminating things we don't need—transportation between venues, for instance, since both the wedding and the reception will be at the Bryan family home. There are no dogs, so custom dog attire will not be needed, and Frantz begged to curate a playlist instead of hiring a DJ, so that's done.

I'm deep in thought about the actual necessity of a wedding website when a flash of light blue catches my eye. I only have a moment to wonder what it is before a whole person hops over the bench from the back and thuds down beside me. I bite back a scream as I realize it isn't some random park psycho but my wide-smiling, floppy-haired best friend in light blue scrubs and a pair of hideously neon sneakers.

"Toby, Jesus Christ, are you trying to give me a full fucking heart attack?" I huff the words out, my heart pounding in my throat. It feels like maybe it's not hyperbole. Am I going to have to test Toby's medical skills right now?

"Sorry." He cracks open a plastic clamshell containing a salad and starts eating it like he's worried a pigeon is about to swoop in and steal it. "You look stressed."

"Maybe it's because a full-grown man snuck up on me in a public park."

"Nah, it's something else." He reaches up and points at the spot between my brows, his finger stopping just shy of brushing my skin. I feel an electric current zip up through my chest and zap me right where he didn't *quite* touch me, and *damn* everyone for putting ideas in my head. We've had a perfectly good twenty-one years where I didn't have one single dirty thought about Toby Sullivan, and now that's two in a week (to say nothing of the dreams). The only explanation is…well, it's like that salad Toby's eating. When you see enough people eating salads or scroll past tons of pictures of artfully arranged salads on Instagram, suddenly you start to think you want a salad. But you don't actually *want* the salad. Nobody *wants* a salad. You've just had the salad idea shoved into your head until your lizard brain picks it up and won't let it go.

Toby is a salad.

And I have never in my life *wanted* a salad.

I want a nice juicy steak.

Toby is nothing like the guys I usually date, who are broody and dark and mumble a lot. I like bad boys, okay? And yes, the bad boys often turn out to be bad in other ways, but that's okay, because unlike Polly, I'm not trying to marry anyone right now. I'm just looking for a good time.

I swat his finger away and growl a little, but he just laughs, shoveling another forkful of his lunch into his mouth.

"Since when do you eat salad?" I ask, hoping a change of subject will redirect whatever misfiring hormones were in charge of that feeling a moment ago.

"Since I realized that Slim Jims and Mountain Dew would not get me through medical school in one piece," he says, then quickly pivots right back. "You're all crinkled up. It looks like you're studying for AP chemistry again."

85

"For the record, I was right. I have never used any of that knowledge ever again."

"There were times in med school when I wished I could say the same thing," Toby replies. He taps my phone, which has gone to sleep in my lap. "Stop changing the subject. What has you all frowny-faced?"

"You know how Polly's engaged?" Toby nods. "Well, turns out she's getting married."

"I'm confused. Isn't that how it usually works?"

"In four months. Four months! And because she's also writing a dissertation and job searching, *I* will be planning this blessed event, which, in case this hasn't penetrated, takes place in *four months.*"

Toby sits back and lets out a long, low whistle. "That's definitely going to be intense. But, I mean, you love this stuff, so..." Toby stabs at a cherry tomato and cuts me a sidelong glance.

"What are you talking about?"

"Come on, Pippin. Checklists? Calendars? Budgets? Bossing people around and making things bend to your will? That's your love language."

"My love language is acts of service and you know it."

"Same thing! You love Polly, and doing this for her is how you're going to show her your love. I don't think the planning is the problem. Or even the four months part," he says, and then he pokes me in the shoulder with his fork, leaving a little tine prints of dressing on my sleeve. "You're skeptical."

"I *am* skeptical!" I cry, happy that I can finally talk to someone about this. Polly's certainly off limits, and Nonna and Mom just give me the evil eye every time I try to real talk with them about my reservations over Polly's impending (*very* impending) nuptials. Apparently everyone is fully on board the wedding train while I'm still dangling off the caboose. "They've known each other for *six months* and they're getting *married*. And I just don't understand why. What's the rush?"

Toby turns his gaze to a little girl tossing popcorn at some ducks in the pond while her mother clutches the back of her dress to keep her from going in after them. "To quote the late, great Nora Ephron by way of Harry Burns, 'When you realize you want to spend the rest of your life with someone, you want the rest of your life to start as soon as possible.'"

"At least you've seen the movie," I mutter. "How dare you use Ephron against me!"

"You're the one who made me watch *When Harry Met Sally* eleventy billion times."

I open my wedding planning app and add a check box for "Make Mackenzie watch *WHMS*," because if I'm going to learn to love my future sister-in-law, that's definitely a requirement.

"Do you need help?" Toby asks.

"From you? You want to help me plan a wedding? Just how comprehensive was medical school?"

"Hey, I got dragged to every appointment when each of my four sisters got married, so I know some things. Turner's wedding was just last year, so it's fresh. Plus, I did a psych rotation—surely that could be helpful."

As much as I would love to have Toby along for this ride, I shake my head. "Toby, you barely have enough time to feed yourself. You've been a resident for all of two weeks, and I've already seen you nod off into a bread basket. In what universe do you have time to help plan a wedding?"

He shrugs. "The beginning is called boot camp, but it'll calm down. It's not really like it is on television. You watch way too many medical shows, by the way."

"There's no such thing."

I wake my phone up, and the endless to-do list taunts me. It would be nice to do this with him. I may be the captain in a group project situation, but Toby is an invaluable cheerleader. And if I'm going to make it through this experience with my good humor intact, I probably need him.

"Okay, you can help," I say. "But you have to promise to tell me if you need sleep or just want to sit on your couch and veg instead of, I don't know, sourcing peonies or whatever."

Toby raises three fingers and solemnly nods. "Scout's honor."

"That doesn't mean much, since I know your fear of snakes kept you from earning basically any of the outdoor merit badges, but luckily I believe you anyway."

"Good. Because I'm always here for you, Pippin. For peonies or cake tastings or auditioning wedding bands or *cake tastings*. Did I mention cake tastings? I'm definitely here for cake tastings."

I arch an eyebrow at him. "Yes, I believe you mentioned that."

"I can also look up *tons* of wedding-related jokes."

"Thank you, I appreciate that. Not the jokes part, but the sentiment." I reach up and flick the end of his stethoscope, which is hanging around his neck. "Aren't they missing you at the hospital?"

"I've got just enough time to ask you if you want to be my plus-one to this fancy hospital gala. I won tickets by knowing all symptoms of rabies!"

I grimace. "You want me to go to a rabies banquet?"

"No, I just knew the answer to the question. The banquet is for...an anniversary of something? Or a dedication of a new wing? I don't really know. All I care about is that it's at the Fairmont Copley Plaza, there's an open bar, there's going to be a five-course meal that's supposed to be out of this world, and it's a whole night when no bodily fluids will be launched at me."

"You know I work weekend nights," I tell him, turning my attention back to my app.

He reaches over and swipes my phone from my grasp, forcing me to look at his big, stupid, puppy-dog grin. "That's the best part! It's on a Tuesday! Come on, come eat fancy food with me, it'll be fun. I don't have anyone else to go with. Everyone I'm friends with at work is on shift that night."

I think about the other night, when Evie asked me if Toby was available and I said no. I was talking completely out of my ass for reasons that pass all understanding, and now I feel guilty about it. Toby is single! I don't know what happened with him and Jen, but that was a very long relationship that's over now, and he deserves to take a real, actual date to fancy shit like this. And I am a terrible friend for standing in the way of that. Luckily, I can try to rectify it right now.

"Hey, you know Evie, the server with the blond pixie cut and all the tattoos?"

Toby blinks at me. "Yeah, what about her?"

"Well, she was asking if you were single the other night. She's interested in you. Maybe you should take her."

Toby pauses, his puppy-dog grin flickering just a smidge, like a light bulb that hasn't quite burned out. But it quickly reignites. "Nah, this isn't really a first date kind of thing. This will be way more fun with a friend."

A friend. Okay, well, if this is just a friends thing, then maybe I should do it. It does sound fun to get gussied up on a Tuesday and eat a five-star meal at one of the fanciest hotels in the entire city. Plus I might be able to get some ideas for the wedding in all that finery.

"Okay," I say. "Sign me up. But think about Evie. She's really cool. I think you guys would get along."

"Yeah, sure. Will do." Toby passes my phone back to me, then stands and stretches, his scrub top rising to reveal that damned sliver of toned stomach. I force my eyes up to his face so I don't feel like an absolute pervert. "Okay, once more unto the breach. Later, Pip!"

And then he turns and jogs out of the garden, heading toward Charles and the hospital, leaving me on the bench with my wedding planning app and a strange, low-simmering concoction of weird feelings sloshing around inside of me.

Chapter 12

TOBY

I have a joke about chemistry, but I don't think it will get a reaction.

PIPPIN

I don't get it.

TOBY

... sorry, I forgot science-based jokes are not your thing

PIPPIN

None of these jokes are my thing!

It's been a week since I downloaded I-To-Do, and I am finally —*finally*—getting to check off another box. Just not the box I was hoping.

"According to my checklist, we need to start with setting a budget," I explain, instinctively pulling out my phone and opening the app. I moved it to my home screen last night for easy access. As it loads, the screen promises me once again that

I'm on my way to planning a successful wedding. More than once I've wanted to email the developers of I-To-Do and ask them what the definition of a successful wedding actually *is*. Clearly one where the couple ends up, you know, *married* at the end, but besides that, I suspect it also includes things like "none of the guests vomited from food poisoning," and "everyone left with a tasteful mason jar full of artisanal gumballs." I need a scale somewhere between those two things so I know what I'm aiming for. Where on the scale from vomit to artisanal gumballs do we need to be?

"Well, obviously we're not going to go crazy," Mom says as we make our way down Newbury Street.

"And finding the dresses will establish the vibe of the wedding, which will help us budget for everything else," Polly adds.

"Plus dress shopping is the fun part. Start with the fun part, I say," Nonna adds.

It's a warm early-July morning, and the shops on Newbury Street are just starting to come alive. The four of us come to a stop in front of a gilded door with a classy, discreet sign on the front reading VOW'D.

"Okay, but none of you actually said *numbers*," I say, though I know this conversation, which I've been trying to have for *days*, will be fruitless. Nobody wants to start with an Excel spreadsheet when wedding dress shopping is an option. I can already tell I'm going to be the Debbie Downer of this whole experience, and I try to suck it up and make peace with it. Someone's got to be the heavy, crunching numbers and making calls. Someone's got to tend to the checklist. And that someone is *me*. "Plus, we need to figure out who's even paying, because you're both brides, which means the yoke of the patriarchy won't be foisting every single dollar of this shindig onto our shoulders. So three cheers for gay pride and all that."

Polly rolls her eyes and reaches for my phone, prying it

from my clutches and shoving it so deep into my back pocket that I stumble backward two full steps.

"Very romantic, Pip," she says. "The community appreciates your full-throated support."

"You better not have accidentally checked any boxes," I say, retrieving my phone and examining the screen. I-To-Do is sacrosanct. One small mistake, one accidentally checked box, and we could wind up with a wedding with no music—or worse, no booze.

"We're each going to buy our own dress, and we're going to split everything else evenly," Polly says.

"Excellent." I'm already adjusting the balance sheet in my head. I googled how much the average wedding costs, and in Massachusetts it's forty thousand dollars. *Forty thousand dollars.* That's practically a down payment on a condo. It's definitely a very nice car. We're saving money by not paying for a venue, but still, I'm happy to cut the budget in half. It's not like Polly, the perpetual college student, is flush with cash, and while Mom has savings, we're not forty-thousand-dollar wedding people. We're not even twenty-thousand-dollar wedding people, which is why I've been googling budget wedding ideas for the last week. Polly knows all this—I *know* she does—and yet here we are on Newbury Street, looking at dresses without first firming up a budget with her fiancée. Something is off. But at least now I have a ballpark, if "half of a number we don't know" counts as a ballpark. I make a mental note to adjust the actual Excel spreadsheet when I get home and smile to myself. Pivot tables are my love language.

"Stop doing math in your head. I don't want to see you doing mental calculations while I'm trying on dresses," Polly says.

"Fine, as long as you promise that after you choose a dress and establish said vibe, we'll sit down and talk numbers?" Polly rolls her eyes, but I level her with a twin look. "Hey, you asked me to help plan this thing. You knew what you were getting into."

"Yes, and we love you for it," Mom says.

Mom and Polly exchange a loaded glance, but before I can decipher it, the bell on the door of the bridal shop tinkles and we're being ushered into what looks like an Icelandic bag of cotton balls. Austere, sleek, and modern, save for racks bursting with ruffles and lace.

A woman of indeterminate age in an immaculately tailored black pantsuit is waiting for us at a table near the door. Her ice-blond hair is pulled back in a ponytail so tight it functions as an amateur face-lift. She's also wearing bright red lipstick the color of a child's popsicle, which feels like a bold move in a room full of thousands of dollars worth of white fabric. It's kind of a gangster move, honestly, and it makes me respect her instantly. I love a confident, professional woman with a hint of badass.

The woman passes us all delicate flutes of champagne and introduces herself as Birgit in an accent whose provenance I can't quite pinpoint: maybe equal parts Russian and one of those countries in the middle of the North Atlantic that's covered in ice. She nods with an approving smile as we introduce ourselves, like we've passed her first test simply by saying our names out loud without falling down.

"So vaht az-te-tique are you aiming for?" Birgit asks.

"Excuse me?" I say, causing Polly to elbow me directly in the ribs.

"*Az-te-tique*," Birgit says again, moving her red lips with an exaggeration that tells me she thinks she's speaking to a toddler. And when you combine her accent with my extremely limited knowledge of weddings, maybe that's what I am.

"Aesthetic," Mom whispers.

Oh. But still, *what?* White Wedding? Bridal? All I can think of is music videos with weddings in them, but something tells me shouting "November Rain" will not go over well with this woman. Honestly, is that the best first question? But Polly, who has the ring on her finger and a whole lot of hours of art history under her belt, doesn't hesitate.

"I'm thinking autumnal boho with touches of structure," Polly says, immediately in her element. "Soft fabrics that have a bit of heft to them, potentially velvet? With maybe rust or brass in the accents. Both color and texture, I mean. A nice blend of natural and industrial. But *not* modern farmhouse. This is Boston, not Waco. It's a backyard wedding, but no barns. No mason jars."

Birgit nods as if Polly has just laid out a detailed training plan for the next Red Sox championship season. I have no idea what she's talking about, and I'm starting to realize that it's going to take more than a few hours of Google searches and a twenty-dollar app to truly understand weddings.

Birgit leads us through the shop to a sleek white couch that's shockingly comfortable, though I'm almost too afraid to sit on it. I work with marinara sauce for a living. White furniture has never, ever been my friend. Toby's mother still has not forgotten the time I sat on a white linen ottoman in their library right after a dinner shift.

In the end, I wind up with half a butt cheek on the edge of the couch, my phone perched on my knees as Polly is whisked away behind a set of heavy drapes.

"I want her to do something sheer and lacy, like April's dress when she was supposed to marry that EMT but actually ran off with Jackson," Nonna whispers.

"Why are you whispering?" I ask.

"Because this place feels like church," Nonna replies.

"Amen," Mom says. "I think she would look great in something like Cristina's season-one dress, when she was supposed to marry Burke but he left her at the altar? But maybe with sleeves. Strapless is so overdone."

"I'm down for the dress from Cristina's second wedding. That red one was fire, and that wedding actually happened," I say. This family watches entirely too much *Grey's Anatomy*. "But mostly I just hope she picks something today, because we have fifteen weeks and seventy-three more boxes on my checklist to get through."

"Don't be such a downer, Pippin," Mom says. "It's not all about checklists and numbers."

"Says the person not in charge of pulling off a wedding in less than four months."

"But you're *not* in charge of pulling off a wedding in less than four months, you're *helping* to pull off a—" But Mom halts mid-sentence, her hand flying up to her mouth as her eyes settle on Polly, who is emerging in the first dress. Nonna gasps upon catching sight of her, and even I feel myself turning into a bit of a puddle.

The dress is an airy thing with light layers of gauzy fabric, nipped in at the waist, with some kind of crystal embroidery that makes it look a bit like a map of constellations. It drapes gently over Polly's shoulders and looks like it would flutter lightly in even the softest breeze. Nonna begins clucking about how Polly is glowing while Mom begins openly weeping.

Polly turns to me.

"Pip? What do you think?"

I cock my head, taking in the full picture, trying to look past the fact that it's my sister dressed as a *bride*, which still feels like an idea for an elaborate costume party, and actually evaluate the fashion. But it takes a moment, because *oh my god, Polly is actually going to be a bride.* My sister, my most trusted companion, is about to take someone else's hand and walk off into the rest of her life.

I take a deep breath and release it slowly before answering. I need to focus on whether or not she should be wearing *this dress* when she walks off into the rest of her life. "It's a really nice dress, and you look gorgeous in it. But I'm not sure it's the one."

I brace myself for the meltdown or the scolding from Mom about being a bridal grinch. But I know I'm right about the dress. If you didn't know Polly, you'd describe her style as girly and bohemian, but I know that what she actually loves is excellent craftsmanship attached to all that detail, which this dress doesn't have.

Everything's been slightly off-kilter ever since Polly announced her engagement. It's like the string that connects us as twins has started to fray. It's weird not being able to trust the twin thing we've shared our whole lives, and it's making me realize that string has been more of a lifeline for me. Just *knowing* another person and having them just *know* you is important. Powerful. But now Polly is in a wedding dress and we're in deep, uncharted waters.

But to my great surprise and delight, Polly nods. Quick and businesslike, crossing the dress off her own mental checklist.

"Agreed," she says. "Next?"

I'm right. The string is secure.

Polly proceeds to try on an endless parade of dresses in various shades of white and cream and champagne. There's even a pale pink one in the mix that Birgit calls "blush." There are ball gowns and mermaid dresses and delicate sheaths. Strapless ones and ones with straps and sleeves. I quickly establish a system, because otherwise I know we'll spend hours fawning over the dresses and leave blinded by white fabric with no final choice. And I wasn't kidding—we don't have time for an eternal dress hunt. This needs to happen *today*. So each time Polly comes out, I ask if she likes the dress she's in more or less than the previous dress. If the answer is less, the dress goes back on the rack. If it's more, then the previous dress heads back to the rack and this dress gets to wait in the dressing room for the next bracket. This leaves only one gown in the dressing room at any given time, and it means we're only ever comparing a dress to one other, not every other option. It's honestly genius and maybe is the way we should be electing the president. I should write a letter to my senator. Or maybe just send the suggestion to I-To-Do.

It's all going swimmingly, clipping along now that most of the tears from the first gowns have dried, and I can feel us coming close to a decision. A delicately beaded sleeveless dress with a deep V and pockets has remained in contention for the last six rounds. I think Polly is about ready to call it, but then Birgit emerges from the dressing room. Her face shows all the seriousness of someone about to engage the nuclear launch codes, and her hands are clasped behind her back.

"Polly vould like me to tell you zat zees eez zee dress, and she vants you all to be ready so no one makes face and ruin it for her," Birgit intones in her cold, imperious accent.

Nonna turns to Mom and me, waving her finger in the air, and says, "Arrange your faces, ladies."

Birgit pulls backs the curtain, and Polly emerges, gently holding up the front hem of a dress, and I can tell immediately that my sister is right. This is the one. And I didn't need a warning to prepare me. I couldn't control my smile if you paid me.

The dress fits her like it was sewn directly onto her body. The lace bodice is fitted down to the thin satin sash, and then the skirt flows gently to her feet. It has sleeves that stop just above Polly's elbows, an unusual length that looks delicate without being matronly. When Polly turns, I see a perfect line of silk buttons that begins at the nape of her neck and trails all the way down to the floor, ending just before the short but tasteful train that pools behind her.

I have spent days watching Mom and Nonna tear up every time the wedding is mentioned, but I've never felt that impulse myself. To me, the wedding is just stress. Or worse, dread.

Sometimes thinking about it still evokes shock. But now, seeing my twin sister in the dress that is absolutely meant to be her wedding gown, I get it.

"I'm thinking that instead of a veil, I can do flowers in my hair," Polly says, and that image sends Mom into gasping sobs as Nonna dabs at her eyes with an embroidered handkerchief.

"Greenery and fall leaves could also be nice," Birgit supplies, and Polly's eyes light up. Everyone is halfway down the aisle in this thing, but glancing at the app perched on my knees, I'm reminded of one very important question.

"How much?" I ask, and four heads turn directly to me with a look like I've just farted in church.

Birgit sniffs before answering, a sort of verbal punctuation that frankly I don't appreciate. "Vell, ve'll have to put rush on it if you vant in time, plus alterations on accelerated schedule. Zat vould put you just over eight."

"*Thousand?*" I bark.

Birgit nods, the corners of her mouth turning down, like my outburst has offended the dresses. "Yes. I write up invoice so you see zee breakdown and exact price," she adds, though I suspect this offer is merely a way to get out of the room so we can all have the meltdown we need to have right now.

"Quick, take a picture," I say to my Mom, who is fiddling nervously with her phone like it's a worry stone. "We can show the photo to a seamstress and have a dress just like it made."

"And you think that would be cheaper? Pippin, a dress like this takes a craftsman," Polly says.

"She's right. That kind of work costs money. Frankly that price is outstanding for all that lace," Nonna says.

"Okay, then, I guess we need to keep looking. Because eight thousand dollars for a dress you're going to wear *once* for like four hours is an *outrageous* amount of money."

But nobody moves. In fact, they all avert their eyes like I've farted *in the bridal salon*. Nobody seems to think this is a wild amount of money except me.

"You can't be serious. Where do you even plan to get eight thousand dollars? What is the vibe of this wedding, the Rockefellers? The Hiltons? The *Kardashians*?"

"I'm using my trust," Polly says, her voice high and full of air.

I gasp, unable to arrange my face into anything other than total shock. And I thought an eight-thousand-dollar wedding dress was a surprise. "You're using Dad's money?"

Our father had life insurance when he died, and Mom set aside some for each of us for school. But Polly, being the smarty-pants wunderkind she is, didn't use hers. She went to Harvard for undergrad on a full scholarship and grad school at Yale fully funded. I know she's dipped into the trust here and there for auxiliary school things, but she has always had a job to help pay her way, so she hasn't needed it much.

"But that money is for big things! Like a house. Or a car!" I try again, but Polly remains placid.

"I have a car, and Mackenzie already owns a condo," she says, watching the way the dress moves in the mirror. Her voice is calm and quiet. "And I want to spend the money on this."

"But why? It's *one day*."

And then Polly's eyes are off the dress and pointed directly at me, a fire igniting in them.

"Because Dad won't be there!" she cries, and it echoes off the mirrors. The seismic effect of the quiver in her voice causes my throat to constrict. "He won't walk me down the aisle. We won't have a father-daughter dance, and he won't make stupid dad jokes in a toast." Polly takes a deep breath, looking down at the dress before leveling her gaze back at me. "This way he'll be there. And I'll always have these memories, and they'll always be connected to him." She blinks once, releasing the tears that were welling up in her eyes. They stream down her cheeks, and I can barely hold back my own tears. I sneak a glance at Mom and see her leaning into Nonna, who is passing her a handkerchief.

"But Dad always told us to keep an emergency fund, and if you spend the money on this, you won't have one," I say, the words coming out in a whisper.

We've always lived lean, never taking big vacations or making huge purchases, so we could have a family emergency fund. That was why Mom was able to set aside most of the life insurance money. We experienced the worst emergency possible, and we were able to fall apart safely because of it. It's why I still haven't touched my own trust. I lived at home while I went to UMass Boston on scholarship and got my business degree, taking classes through the summer. I barely spend any money and am saving even more now by continuing to live at home while I run the restaurant. If the unimaginable happens again, I'll be prepared, and the thought of Polly being caught unawares because she bought a fucking *dress* makes my breath feel trapped in my lungs. I have to convince her that this is a bad idea.

"Girls, there's something I need to tell you," Mom says.

Nonna sits straight up. "Now, Penny?"

Mom nods. She moves to the edge of the couch, like she needs her feet planted firmly on the floor for whatever she has to say. "I was going to take you to lunch after this and tell you, but I think what I have to say answers a lot of the questions you have right now." She pauses and takes a deep breath through her nose, letting it out through her mouth. I recognize it as one of the calming techniques my mother picked up after Dad died. "Nonna and I have decided it's time to sell the building and retire."

The room is absolutely silent save for the growing ringing in my ears.

"I'm sorry, when you say sell the building, you mean sell

our *home*? And close Marino's?" I feel like I'm trying to speak Italian, a language that, despite my grandmother's valiant attempts, I've never mastered.

"Well, I hope Marino's can stay open. I've been talking to a restaurant management company that's interested in acquiring it. They'd buy the building as an investment and continue to run the restaurant under their umbrella."

Marino's under someone else's *umbrella*? It doesn't even make *sense*. It's been a family business for damn near a hundred years! And she's already talking to someone about this? Without consulting me?

"You've got to be kidding me," I say, because I can form no other words.

"I've talked to a real estate agent who thinks we can get close to ten million for the building. That's more than enough to take care of Nonna and me *and* the both of you."

I don't know what's more shocking—that mom just said ten *million* or that my entire life as I know it is about to disappear.

"But…why? Marino's is…it's *ours*. It's our *home*. Literally! I live there!"

"I know that. But running a restaurant was your father's passion, not mine. I've done it for eight years because I loved him and I owed it to all of us. But it's a hard, exhausting life, and it's never going to get easier. Selling the building is the only way I can ever retire. It's the only way Nonna can ever retire."

"And in very fine fashion," Nonna says as I gape at her. This is her beloved father's restaurant. She's lived in her apartment literally her entire life. How can she possibly want this? "Hey, don't look at me like that. This was my idea. I'm old, and the stairs and the people…and with that kind of money, we can buy a cottage on Nantucket and I can live the rest of my life on the beach instead of kneading pasta dough until I die."

I don't want to be selfish, but also… "What about me?

Mom, *I* manage Marino's. That's my job. It's my whole life! What am I supposed to do?"

"Whatever you want!" she says, with the nerve to sound almost exasperated. "Pippin, I know Marino's is your home and you'll always love it. But it was never your dream either. And if I don't sell it, you'll stay there forever, trapped. You're never going to leave the nest unless I push you out."

"So you're *selling* the nest."

"I am." She's resolute, that much is clear. This is not the opening of a discussion. This is an announcement. A press conference with no questions.

I look over at Polly, still standing there in eight thousand dollars worth of lace, looking stunning but very quiet.

"Polly?" I ask. I hope that on this, at least, we can still be a team.

"I really don't know what to say," Polly replies.

"Thank you!" Finally somebody is going to talk some sense.

"I'm really happy for you, Mom."

My jaw drops. Sure, Polly hasn't lived there in years, but how can she be fine with seeing our entire home, all that's left of our father, sold to strangers?

"Pip, life is short. We know that. We learned it in the hardest way possible. The only thing you can do is live it the best you can. And for Mom and Nonna, this sounds like the best way to live."

In my heart, I know my sister is right, but frankly I don't appreciate Polly using my heart against me. And excuse me for not being completely zen about the total annihilation of my life as I know it. Polly has her PhD and a plan. She's going to defend her dissertation, then find a job as a professor of art history. She'll move in with Mackenzie and live happily ever after. But what do I have? No home. No job. And certainly no happily ever after, unless you count the fact that I'm not saddled to any of the chucklebutts I've dated in the past. That makes me pretty happy, I guess.

"This is absolute bullshit. You're just throwing away one hundred years of family history for the beach," I say, pointing at Mom. "What would Dad say if he were here?"

Before she can answer, I whirl on Polly. "And shame on you for using Dad to justify this insane expense. That's not who you are. Seriously, eight *thousand* dollars, Polly?"

And before I can thoroughly lose it, I turn and bolt for the door just as I feel the scratch in my throat that tells me tears are en route. Because goddammit, I'm not about to cry inside this giant box of tampons that is a bridal boutique.

Newbury Street is now crowded with tourists and shoppers carrying bags from Burberry and Louis Vuitton. I turn to head home when I hear the tinkle of the bell inside Vow'd.

"Pippin Jane Marino, *stop right now.*"

I freeze in my tracks, a reflex after twenty-six years of my mother whipping out my full name only when I'm in the deepest trouble. I turn to see her staring me down on the side-walk. If looks could kill, I'd be in sixteen pieces, encased in concrete, and sinking to the bottom of the harbor in Southie.

"I'm sorry, Mom, I just—"

She softens immediately and holds up a hand to silence me. "Honey, it's okay. I know this is shocking, and I probably could have handled it a lot better. I know it means big changes in your life. Much more for you than for Polly. But honey, that's part of the reason why I'm doing this. I know you feel like you need to take care of the restaurant as a way to take care of me and honor your father. And I have appreciated that help every single day since your dad died. But I want you to live *your* life. Not mine, and not your father's.

"I've seen all the sacrifices you've made to keep the restau-rant running. I know you're the reason we're not in danger of closing every other month. I see all the work you've done, but honey, I don't want you to have to work like that forever. You're so smart and talented. You deserve to find your own way."

Find my own way. *My own way.* My own way *where?* Where am I going if not down the stairs to Marino's every day?

I stand there on the hot pavement and let the reality of my future settle over me. The problem is, that future is dark and shapeless, just a big blank. When I open my mouth, my words come out on a sob. "But I don't even know what that looks like for me," I say.

Mom pulls me in, my chin resting on her shoulder as she strokes my curls. "You'll figure it out," she says. "You're smart and driven and resourceful. And the money will give you time to search. I know there's a path out there for you, Pippin. I'm just trying to help you find it."

"Okay," I sniffle, trying not to get snot on my mother's linen shirt. I pull back and wipe at what I'm sure are mascara tracks underneath my eyes. "I'm sorry for yelling, it's just...it's a lot."

My mother nods and gives me a sad smile. "I know, Pip. It's okay to be sad. But be open to change, okay?"

I try to smile, but the lie of it is all over my face. Change? I'm good at a lot of things, but change has never been one of them. Not even when I was little. I've still never forgiven my third-grade teacher for going on maternity leave in the middle of the year. The only thing I like to change on a regular basis is the guy I'm dating. Still, I nod.

Then Mom levels me with a look. "As for the wedding, Polly is happy. It may not be what you would choose for yourself, but this isn't about you. Your only job here is to love her and help celebrate her happiness."

I sigh. "And help organize her shindig."

"*Her* shindig. It's *hers*. And if you don't think you can honor that, then you need to step aside now."

She's right, of course. But there's no way I'm going to tell my twin sister I won't help plan her wedding. If this thing is happening—and I really need to stop saying "if"—then I'm all in.

"Now, promise me that for the next four months, you will not sigh, roll your eyes, or perform mental math as Polly celebrates her love."

"I promise."

"Hand in the air or it's not a swear," Mom says, invoking her favorite tactic from when we were kids and Polly and I got into some knock-down, drag-out fight. She called them our "solemn vows," and we took them very seriously...when we were six. But I'm twenty-six now, and standing on the sidewalk, it feels a little ridiculous. But I raise my hand anyway.

"I swear," I say, letting out a whoosh of breath. "I'm sorry."

Mom nods, satisfied by the sincerity of my solemn vow. "Forgiven. Though you owe Polly one of those too. Now, are you coming to lunch?"

The thought of sitting at a table and trying to be a person in front of my family and a restaurant full of strangers while this bombshell that incinerated my entire life smolders in front of me makes my stomach do seven cartwheels.

I shake my head. "I think I still need a little space, if that's okay."

Mom pulls me in for a final hug. "Going for a run?"

"Yeah," I say, already yearning for the feel of my feet on the pavement, the city rushing by.

"Be safe," Mom says. "See you back at home."

As I walk away, I try not to focus on the fact that *home* isn't going to be there forever, like I always thought. It isn't going to be there very much longer at all. It feels, in fact, like it's already gone.

Chapter 13

I took up running after my dad died.

I was eighteen, a week into my freshman year of college. It was the morning of the funeral, and I was standing in my bedroom, staring at two black dresses, trying to decide which one I never wanted to wear again. Because I knew that as soon as I followed my father's casket down the aisle of St. Michael's in this dress, I'd never be able to look at it again, much less wear it. I had taken charge of planning the funeral and was trying to step in to handle as much as I could at the restaurant, and still I was so full of itchy energy that if I didn't do something I was going to wind up standing in the middle of Charles Street and screaming until my lungs fell out.

Dad's death was something I couldn't plan for—none of us could. His heart attack came as a total shock. One minute he was serving plates, greeting customers, and teasing me, and the next he was gone. And for someone who'd gone through life with a checklist in hand and a plan in mind, I felt especially unmoored when he died at fifty-one. Running started as an escape—literally—from the sadness of his funeral and soon became my therapy. Now if I go more than a few days without a run, even a short one, I feel on the verge of emotional liftoff.

Back home, I slip out of my jeans and into running shorts and pull my stubby ponytail through the back of a Red Sox cap. I pop in my earbuds and fire up a playlist of seventies, eighties, and nineties rock to set my pace. Once my sneakers are tied, I'm out the door.

My run always begins as a game of human Frogger as I dodge the crowds in Beacon Hill, but once I hit the Esplanade, it usually starts to open up. Which is when I can finally relax, sync my pace to the beat of the music, and just run. I focus on my breathing, on the rhythm of my feet hitting the pavement, on not overstriding and giving myself shin splits (a lesson I learned in my early days of trying to sprint down the Esplanade like a gazelle on the savannah).

I breath in. *Ten million dollars.* I breathe out.

That's life-changing money. Were it not for the fact that Great-Grandpa Marino took ownership of the building nearly a hundred years ago under dubious circumstances, there's no way we'd be living on Charles Street today. I mean, not only could we never open Marino's now, we couldn't even afford to continue running the restaurant if we didn't own the building outright. It's why I had to make so many changes after Dad died. Sure, the building is free, but things like property taxes?

And maintenance on a building that's over a hundred years old? Those are definitely not. So the menu got smaller, the hours grew fewer, and we lived to see another day.

But with ten million dollars and no restaurant to run, all our lives will be very different. Mom and Nonna can retire, obviously. Nonna can watch her medical dramas and read her cozy mysteries and make pasta only when she actually wants to eat pasta. Mom can take up painting again. She can teach if she wants, but she certainly doesn't have to. Even Polly and I will reap the benefits. Sure, finding a place to live will be scary, but I'll be able to afford it with the money Mom will set aside for me. And I'll be able to take my time figuring out what I want to do after I'm no longer running Marino's.

I try to let the idea sink in. That I won't have to worry about the restaurant going under anymore. That I won't have to be the keeper of the family legacy. That'll be a relief, right? It's been hard trying to keep it going with the weight of my dad's—hell, with three generations of my family's hopes and dreams on my shoulders.

As I run, I try to picture my new life. I'll need a place to live. And a new job. I have a business degree and experience, so I'm totally employable, but what do I *want* to do? I've never done anything but restaurant work. The thought of running a different restaurant—someone *else's* baby—seems wrong, like putting on someone else's underwear. But if I didn't, would I miss being in a kitchen, slinging plates, greeting customers? Would I miss the regulars and the celebrations?

I blink and realize I've already made it down to the BU soccer fields, and I decide to turn back. I spend the return run trying to chart a course for my future, but I feel like I'm trying to sail a ship on foggy seas.

I'm almost back to the Charles Street T station when I see him.

Toby was never a runner when he lived here, so it must be something he picked up while he was in school. And watching him run—*shirtless*—next to the river, his tall, lean frame moving almost elegantly, I see that he's taken to it quite well. He looks like one of those guys who used to run cross-country and is now training for the marathon. He has a long, bouncy stride. He's wearing some kind of headband to hold back his thick curls, and sweat is glistening on his sculpted chest. A woman ahead of me passes him and then fully stops on the path to turn and stare.

Yeah, right there with ya, sister.

And then all of a sudden I'm imagining what it would be like for Toby to wrap those tanned, muscular arms around me, pull me close, his skin on mine and his lips moving down my neck and *oh my god stop it*. I've got to keep my mind from taking a swan dive directly into the gutter just because I saw Toby without a shirt on.

And I *really* have to stop thinking like that at this very moment, because he's getting closer, and I can't be caught ogling him, mouth agape. That would be hard to explain. *Sorry, Toby, I accidentally had a sex thought about you the other day, and you showing up in front of me shirtless is making those thoughts multiply like horny bunnies!*

I'm trying to make my eyes obey my brain and look the fuck the other way when an older man in Rollerblades and a neon-orange vest comes ripping around Toby at a speed that doesn't seem physically possible unless he has rocket boosters strapped to his ankles. He does a little hop and turns backward, his feet swizzling in and out for a few strides before he hops back around. I'm so dazzled by his moves (which include some artful arm motions) that I don't realize he's about to crash directly into me until it's nearly too late. I try to leap out of his way, which instead puts me directly in the path of a mom pushing a double jogging stroller, so I leap in the opposite direction.

A flash of dark green and the thought *This is going to hurt* are all I get before I collide headfirst with a lamppost. My last thought before I crumple to the ground is, *Polly will absolutely murder me if I'm missing my front teeth at her wedding.*

I don't know if I actually black out or if my soul just leaves my body for a moment so I can contemplate this absolute disaster, but all of a sudden I'm sitting up, Toby kneeling at my side, and when I reach up to my forehead, my Red Sox cap is missing and my hand comes away covered in red.

In blood.

And then I really do pass out.

When I open my eyes, I expect to see blue sky and trees and feel mud soaking into the butt of my running shorts. Instead I feel the rush of arctic air conditioning and see a harsh wash of neon bulbs and white-speckled ceiling tiles. And I'm not on the ground—I'm being cradled by a pair of strong arms.

"What the hell?" I mutter, but the effort required to produce words sends a spike of pain through my forehead.

"Oh, thank god," Toby says, pausing in the hallways to study me. Because they're *his* strong arms that are holding me up. "Pip, do you know what day it is?"

"Saturday. Do I still have my teeth?" I move my tongue over my front teeth and feel them all still firmly in place, thank god. "Where am I?"

Toby grins, then looks up, scanning the space. "Hey, Naseema, open curtain?"

A young black doctor in a hijab studies the tablet in her hand. "Three, but it's gonna be a while. Bachelor party of fifteen just arrived with either alcohol poisoning or norovirus. It's barfing frat boys as far as the eye can see."

"No problem. This'll just be a quick in and out, I think."

She arches an eyebrow at him, maybe because he's breaking the rules or maybe because he's standing in the middle of the ER shirtless. Whatever the reason, I'm pretty sure I like her. "Fine. But Hollister is attending today, so keep an eye out."

Toby nods—that apparently means something to him. "Will do."

"Wait, am I at the hospital?" I ask. "How the hell did I get here?"

Toby looks down and smiles, giving a little shrug that jostles me enough to make my head throb. "I carried you."

We arrive at what must be curtain three, and Toby sets me down gently on the bed, then immediately turns around and starts rummaging through drawers while I calculate the distance he carried me. Sure, we were basically right next to Mass General when I went down. But still, it was about two city blocks, which is not nothing.

"You carried me?" I say. "To the *hospital?*"

"Yeah. You went down like a bag of hammers. Blood was everywhere—it was pretty gnarly. It would have taken three times as long for an ambulance to get to us, and I'm pretty sure you only passed out at the sight of the blood. You probably only need a butterfly bandage. But better safe than sorry, so I scooped you up and ran for it."

He turns around holding a handful of gauze and one of those little pen light things. He presses the gauze to my forehead and takes my hand, guiding it up to hold it in place. Then he leans in so close to my face that I swear I can feel his warm breath on my neck. I'm going to attribute the way my insides light up to the potential head injury. Am I swooning because a well-muscled, shirtless Toby is close enough to feel his breath on my skin or because my brain is bleeding? Guess we're about to find out!

"Okay, follow the light." His voice takes on a sort of low,

smooth, authoritative tone that sends another zap of awareness straight into my running shorts. And that's *definitely* not the head injury.

"Yo, Dr. Baywatch, catch." A guy in a white coat tosses a blue scrub top at Toby as he passes by the opening of the curtain. Toby catches it and shrugs it on, looking way too much like one of the hot new interns from *Grey's Anatomy* (I'll never be able to watch that show the same way again, dammit). I studiously ignore my pang of disappointment as his tanned, toned chest disappears from view. *Best friends*, I repeat to myself like a mantra. *No benefits.*

"This is very sweet of you, but I'm fine." I start to sit up, carefully leaning away from him, but I pause as a dull thud begins pounding a rhythm in the front right quadrant of my skull.

"Hey, what hurts?" Toby asks, once again close to my face. His hand rests on the back of my head as he helps me lie down in a motion that looks entirely too much like one of Nonna's romance novel covers.

"My brain," I say. "Also my dignity."

"Be serious for a sec, Pippin. I'm trying to evaluate you for a head injury."

I glare at him. "Who died and made you a doctor?"

"No one died. That's why I'm a doctor, ya ding-dong," he says, and even though my eyes are closed tight as I wait for the wave of pain to pass, I can hear the grin in his voice. This is good—the gentle teasing I'm used to. Like brother and sister. More of that.

"Well, it definitely feels like I injured my head," I say. "The blood was the first clue."

"Yeah, I see you've still got your fear of blood. Let's get that cleaned up," he says. He reaches up and pulls back the gauze, then sets to work gently cleaning up my forehead. He applies some kind of solution that causes me to hiss in pain, which helps with the whole *don't have weird thoughts about Toby touching your face* thing. He blows gently on the wound, which works shockingly well to ease the sting but immediately undoes whatever progress I've made. Because suddenly I'm hoping for Toby's warm breath on other places.

"Is that hygienic?" I ask.

"Not standard procedure, but I like you, so I don't want you to suffer," he says with a wink. Ugh, he *has* to stop winking if I'm going to have any hope of not picturing him naked.

It takes him another minute or so to poke at the wound, treat it with something antiseptic, and determine that I don't need stitches. When he's done, he places two butterfly strips over the cut and covers the whole thing with a square of gauze and some medical tape. Then he stares into my eyes with that serious doctor face again.

"Any blurred vision?"

I squint at him and see that his brown eyes and long lashes are in crystal-clear focus. "Nope."

"Nausea?"

"Only when I think about the fact that I ran headfirst into a lamppost in front of a bunch of strangers." *In front of you.*

"Hey, that wasn't your fault. That Rollerblade dude was a menace," he says. He sits back on one of those rolling stools, his arms crossed over his chest, and yup, there it is. There's season-one George Clooney from *ER*. Damn, Evie really hit the nail on the head with that one. And I really need to stop watching so many medical shows. "Okay, no blurred vision, no nausea, no slurred speech or confusion. But you did lose consciousness for a minute, so you'll need to be monitored for a concussion."

"Here?" My stomach roils, and this time it's not my head wound; it's the possibility of a bill and also of having to spend any actual time in the hospital where they brought Dad when he died. I haven't been in the Mass General emergency department in eight years, and I have no interest in staying here any longer than I have to now.

"No, you can just have someone watch you at home. But—"

And then suddenly I'm crying. Hard. Like, end of *My Girl* when Vada screams about Macaulay Culkin needing his glasses, an ugly cry that comes from deep in my chest and pours tears down my cheeks.

"Pip, are you okay?" Toby's voice is trying really hard to retain that cool, calm doctor-in-charge thing, but I hear a little squeak in his voice like when we were twelve years old and I cut my knee open falling out of a tree on the common.

"I don't have a home!" I bark out mid-sob, my mouth operating independent of me, because if my brain were working, I'd suck it up and stop being a walking drama case right now.

"Is this...confusion?" Toby asks. He reaches for his flashlight thing, and I realize he thinks my brain is melting because I ran into a lamppost. But actually my brain is melting because my mom is selling our family home and our family business and basically putting me out on the street with no job and no place to live. And even though I tried to run off the pain and confusion of that, it's still with me in a big way.

"No," I say, working to hold back some of the tears. I take a deep, shuddering breath and manage to calm down a little bit. "Mom just told us that she and Nonna are selling the building and Marino's so they can retire and I can finally live my dream, whatever the fuck that means."

Toby's jaw drops fully, which—*thank you*—is the proper reaction. Of course Toby gets it. "Are you serious?"

"Yeah. They're going to retire to Nantucket, and Polly is getting married and becoming a professional art history nerd, and I'm getting fired from running a spaghetti joint, and oh yeah, also I'll be homeless." I lean back on the sad excuse for a hospital pillow and stare at the neon lights flickering above my head.

"Jeez, Pip. That really sucks."

It's the exact right thing to say. I don't want to hear about how it'll all be fine, even though that's rational. I don't need rational right now. I need to sob like Vada and have someone commiserate. And the fact that Toby knows that makes my heart swell in my chest. It reminds me of how precious my friendship with Toby is and how much I don't want to lose it. Especially not when I'm about to lose everything else.

Suddenly, beyond the curtain, I hear a gravelly voice talking about a CT scan, and Toby jumps off his stool. "Okay, I think you probably have a mild concussion but nothing serious. So why don't we get out of here before someone takes your insurance information and charges you five hundred dollars for that Band-Aid on your head. Can you walk?"

I blink at him. "Wait, is this illegal?"

"I mean, not really? Sort of? It's not like I gave you IV antibiotics or an X-ray. You literally sat on a bed and I put some alcohol and a Band-Aid on your cut, then determined that you're probably not bleeding into your brain."

My mouth drops open. "Wait, *probably?*"

Toby smiles and reaches for my hand to pull me off the bed. "Hey, I'm new, and this is free. You want me to perform a craniotomy?"

I shake my head. "I've seen enough medical shows to know that the answer is *absolutely not.*"

The voice that was rambling about CT scans suddenly goes quiet, and we hear footsteps. I suspect this is the feared/dreaded Dr. Hollister, and while part of me is eager to find out what *Grey's Anatomy* character he most resembles, the other part—the part that knows my insurance falls into the "solidly meh" category—is happy to motor.

I stand up from the bed and am thrilled when I don't feel a

zap of pain in my noggin. That's got to be a good sign regarding any potential brain bleeds. "I'm good, let's go."

Toby takes my hand and pulls me through the emergency department, and even though there's a blond guy in a Wicked Pissah T-shirt barfing into a pink plastic bucket, and even though I just moments ago resolved to stop thinking about it, I smile a little at the spark that ignites where our palms meet.

Chapter 14

TOBY

Singing in the shower is fun until you get soap in your mouth. Then it's a soap opera.

PIPPIN

How did you get into medical school?

The garden apartment of Toby's parents' Louisburg Square town house is a barely contained mess.

It wasn't always this way, of course. When Toby and I were growing up, the space was mostly reserved for visiting grandparents or friends of the family, with shiny antiques, a heavy leather sectional, and an assortment of art that could have been valuable or left over from a hotel decor fire sale—I could honestly never tell. But upon Toby's return to Boston for residency, Mr. and Mrs. Sullivan offered the space to him so he could save him money on rent and be close to the hospital.

And in return, he has turned the place into a nerd frat house.

Immediately inside the door is a pile of discarded shoes, T-shirts, and sweatshirts, the whole heap topped with the backpack he usually carries to the hospital (and I don't even want to *imagine* what kind of germs live on that thing). There are scrub tops and pants discarded throughout the living room like light blue confetti, and there are half-full glasses of water left behind on nearly every surface. Part of me wonders if I need a hazmat suit just to walk in the door.

Once a disorganized slob, always a disorganized slob, apparently. This is just a larger version of what Toby's room looked liked growing up, except back then it was an array of Dropkick Murphys T-shirts and *Call of Duty* posters instead of scrubs. He also had a penchant for hiding junk food all over his bedroom like an overgrown Claudia Kishi. The only difference now is that he doesn't have to hide it, as is evidenced by the family-size bag of Cool Ranch Doritos open on the kitchen island and the pile of fun-size Snickers bars. Apparently four years of undergrad, four years of med school, and one long-term live-in girlfriend couldn't change any of his habits.

Bypassing at least four half-empty water glasses, Toby races into the kitchen and pulls down two fresh ones, filling them and passing one to me. Because this whole misadventure began with a run on the Esplanade, and yeah, I'm a little dehydrated after four miles and a header into a light pole.

After downing half my water, I look at Toby, still in his running shorts and a scrub top. I immediately flash back to the sight of him jogging down the Esplanade in all his shirtless glory and nearly choke on a mouthful of water.

"You okay?" he asks.

Yeah, just picturing you half naked. "When did you get into running?" I ask instead. "Because back in high school, you said you'd only run if a tsunami rose out of the Charles River and made it the quarter mile inland through Beacon Hill to your house."

"And even then I probably would have just let the water take me, I know," he says with a laugh that brings out his dimple. All of a sudden I want to reach up and run my finger over it like this is some kind of soft-core porn.

God, I really need to get laid; otherwise I'm going to wind up turned on by the thought of Toby's sweat socks. Maybe I should have kept Everett around a little longer. It would be worth it to eat chicken at a restaurant if it meant I could stop having blush-worthy sexy time thoughts about Toby.

Thankfully, Toby cannot see into my thoughts, so he just flops onto the couch. "It was Jen. She ran cross-country in college, and at that point I was basically living on pizza and General Tso's chicken, so I figured I'd better attempt some kind of physical activity before my arteries filled with rocks."

"Is that a medical term?" I come around and take a seat next to him and find myself unsure of exactly where—or how —to sit. Before I started finding Toby attractive, I would have flopped down right next to him, head at one end of the couch, legs sprawled across his lap for maximum comfort and stretchi-tude. But Toby's entire being suddenly feels like a sex magnet, and if I get too close to him I might just be sucked in with enough force to try to shove my hands up his scrub shirt. Instead I take a seat a respectable distance from him, leaving a full cushion between us, and lean back.

Toby gives me a sarcastic laugh. "Speaking of, how's your head?"

I reach up and feel a goose egg forming beneath my bandage. I'm dreading looking in the mirror for sure. My bruises usually look like Jackson Pollocks, and I am not psyched for one of those to form on my face. One time I cracked my head on the pass-through in the restaurant, and the next week my gynecologist asked me if I felt safe in my relationship. At least the throbbing has ceased, so thank god for small favors. Hopefully the wedding is far enough away that I won't still have a mark, because I'm not talented enough with makeup to hide something like that. "Fine," I say, letting him change the subject away from Jen, as he always does. "My bigger problem is that I'm starving."

"Unfortunately I have neither the ingredients nor the skills to make you anything, but I can Postmates whatever you want," Toby says. He whips out his phone and fires up the app. "So what's your fancy? Thai? Pizza? Thai pizza?"

"Burgers," I say, because I haven't eaten anything since breakfast, and I've had at least two full breakdowns since then. That requires some red meat for sure. Good lord, was wedding dress shopping really just this morning? My stomach immediately constricts at the memory of Polly in that dress while I melted down in the salon. "Make mine a double, please."

"Lettuce, tomato, ketchup, mustard, and cheese?" Toby asks, tapping at his phone. It's been my order since I was twelve and discovered that mustard is good, and I'm pleased that he still remembers despite all those years on the West Coast eating burgers with strangers.

"And cheese fries and a Coke the size of my head, please," I add.

"On it." Toby enters the rest of the order, and within minutes he's tracking it to his door. "Twenty minutes. Can you hang on that long, or should I dig out that brown banana I chucked in the trash this morning?"

I swat at him, though I'd be lying if I said my thoughts don't linger on the banana for a moment. I lean back on the couch and take a deep breath, my nostrils filling with a noxious mix of sweat and hospital cleaner.

"Ugh, I smell disgusting," I say. "Sorry, I hope this scent isn't leaching onto your couch."

"This couch is older than I am, so no worries," Toby says. "But you can hop in the shower if you want. I've got some sweats I can loan you."

Which is how I find myself standing in Toby's shower, surreptitiously smelling the amber bottle of shampoo he apparently uses now that has notes of eucalyptus, pine, and cedar—or at least that's what it says. To me it just smells like sex, the good kind that's lazy and lasts all afternoon and ends with a big meal and a glass of wine. Which is not a thought I need to be having while standing naked in Toby's shower, the suds of his new sex shampoo running down my naked body. Goddammit, I'm definitely going to have to call Everett and un-break up with him. Or download Tinder again, even though I think I'd rather eat my own hand. Anything to kill this case of the hot-and-hornys I've developed for *Toby*.

Of course, despite his fancy-man shampoo upgrade, Toby still uses the same old Irish Spring bar soap I remember from when we were kids. As I scrub it over my skin, I have a rush of sense memories—everything from shivering in a tent with him over spring break sophomore year, cursing him for dragging me on the camping trip, to the time he made me watch a double feature of musicals from the Golden Age of Hollywood at the Brattle and I fell asleep on his shoulder during *Singin' in the Rain* (people romanticize those movies, but hoo boy, are they boring). Sure, a lot of the time teenage Toby smelled like a walking armpit, as most teenage boys do, but when he wasn't rank, he smelled like Irish Spring, and I can't help but smile, the spray of the shower lingering on my lips.

I didn't realize how much I missed him while he was gone. Sure, we texted and FaceTimed and hung out over every holiday break, back when he actually came home for them. But it's never the same with that much distance. He had a whole life without me, first at USC for undergrad, then at Stanford for med school. He had friends and classes and favorite bars. He had a whole relationship with Jen that I still know barely anything about. Hell, he became a runner and I didn't even know it. Having him back in my life now, seeing him regularly and getting to have that bond again…it feels good.

And I certainly don't want to fuck that up by picturing him naked. It's clearly just a by-product of Polly planting the idea in my subconscious and then shaking up my entire brain with her fast-track nuptials. It's not *real*, because I don't want to have sex with Toby. I mean, my hormones do, because he's tall and beautiful and makes me laugh. Fuck, it would probably be phenomenal. But then it would be terrible, as most decisions made by my hormones tend to be.

So I don't want to do it.

Or think about it.

Dammit, I can't stop thinking about it.

I use the dude sex shampoo and help myself to his face wash, carefully navigating the bandage Toby applied to my forehead. When I step out of the shower and wrap myself in a towel, I have to stop myself from opening the medicine cabinet to snoop. Then I step out of the bathroom into Toby's bedroom and find that he's laid out a pair of basketball shorts and a Boston Marathon T-shirt for me. I have to go commando, and the pants are a little big, so I make a mental note not to make any sudden movements lest I accidentally take a flying leap past the "just friends" line by putting on an impromptu striptease. Luckily, my tender forehead ensures that sudden movements are not in my immediate future.

"Hey, Toby, do you have any ibuprofen?" I call as I pull the shirt over my head, careful not to tug on the bandage.

"Tylenol only," he says, appearing with a glass of water and two pills in his hand. "Ibuprofen can increase the risk of brain bleeds if you have a concussion."

"Yeah, we get it, you're a doctor," I reply, tossing back the pills and praying for them to work quickly. "Fancy medical school and everything."

Toby ignores my sarcasm. "Food will be here in ten, do you

mind if I hop in next?" He points to the open bathroom door, and I nod. I move toward the living room, but not fast enough to avoid seeing Toby peel off the blue scrub top out of the corner of my eye, giving me another glimpse of the definition of his muscles, this time the taut ones across his back. I nearly swallow my tongue and bolt for the door before he gets too comfortable with his old best friend and starts peeling off his shorts.

Which is a good reminder that while I seem to be having a series of impure thoughts about Toby, he is definitely not having the same thoughts about me. I'm still Pippin, best friend of twenty years, knower of all secrets, seer of all embarrassing moments, and practically his fifth sister.

The only thing worse than trying to start something with Toby would be trying to start something with Toby and having him reject me.

Toby's shower is so fast I barely have time to settle into the sofa before he's emerging in a loose pair of lounge pants and a Boston Duck Tours T-shirt, his wet curls dripping on his shoulders.

"Okay, I have to ask," I say, pointing at the overtly touristy shirt that I don't remember ever being in his collection. "Do you have some kind of deal with the Boston Chamber of Commerce? Or the tourism board? Are you going to start calling it Beantown?"

Toby looks down as if he doesn't even realize what he's wearing. "Oh yeah. I amassed this ridiculous collection during undergrad, but I never wore them when I was visiting home. But now I *live* at home, and I can't let all these perfectly good T-shirts go to waste." He flops down on the couch next to me and grins. "See, when I got to California, I discovered that Californians are just so fucking *proud* of being from California and have to remind you of the state's virtues at all times, as if they personally grew all the avocados and regulated the climate. I sort of went ham on the Boston freshman year in retaliation. Like, full Ben Affleck. It started with me just wearing the ones I had—you know, Dropkick Murphys and that Wicked Pissah one you bought me as a joke before I left. But soon people started giving them to me for, like, every occasion, and then my entire wardrobe became a walking postcard for the Bay State."

"It's good to honor your roots," I say.

"Yeah, my mom was apoplectic the first time she called and realized her son had developed a Southie accent in Los Angeles," he says, laughing, and I can only imagine Mrs. Sullivan's reaction. Her ancestors came over on the Mayflower, and she still speaks with a slight Brahmin accent like a Kennedy.

"Why do I remember none of this?" I ask.

Toby opens his mouth and sucks in a deep breath, then shrugs and sighs. "You had other stuff going on," he says, and then the timelines align in my brain, a little light of grief illuminating the answer. All that would have been right after my dad died, when I wasn't paying attention to...well...anything. Unless that thing was Marino's. And while I did eventually emerge from my grief haze and become a person again, I still spend most of my mental energy on the restaurant.

Or I did, anyway.

Before I can stumble too far down *that* particular rabbit hole of emotion, the door buzzes, and Toby hops up to grab the food and sets everything up on the oversize steamer trunk that serves as his coffee table. My mouth waters as he unpacks the burgers, fries, and Cokes, along with a pair of frappes that he stows in the freezer. I wait as patiently as I can, but as soon as he sits back down on the couch, I leap upon the food, shoveling handfuls of cheese fries into my mouth, leaving my fingers greasy and salty and cheesy. I reach across him toward the little pile of napkins on the couch.

"Gimme? Please?" I ask.

"Down, girl, nobody's gonna take your dinner away," he replies, laughing. He passes me a napkin, his fingers brushing over the back of my hand and lingering on a jagged pink scar on the back of my middle finger. He grips my hand and pulls it close to examine the raised flesh. Once again, that inconvenient zap of damn electricity shoots through me at the point of our connection.

"How's my first-ever act of medical treatment holding up?" he asks.

"Honestly, I should sue. The scar still looks gnarly," I say, jerking my hand away so I can sever the connection that feels a little too close for comfort.

"Well, you get what you pay for," he says. He points at my forehead. "Lucky for you, I've learned an awful lot since then."

The scar is almost exactly eight years old. It came from a tuna can. Dad always kept a stash of tuna packed in olive oil in his desk drawer. ("The good stuff, Pepperoni, not that water-packed cat food shit.") It was his go-to quick meal when the smell of pasta turned his stomach after a long weekend shift ("Don't tell Nonna I said that") and he was too tired to walk upstairs or actually cook anything for himself. On the day of his funeral, overwhelmed with sadness and sick of the platitudes and prayers and sad looks from everyone around me, I went to hide out in there, sinking into his giant rolling desk chair that still smelled like him. I opened the drawer and found the little stack of cans and, realizing I'd barely eaten a thing since he'd died three days prior, I pulled one out and tried to wrestle it open with the little pop-top tab. The lid snapped back, and the sharp edge caught my knuckle with a jagged slice.

It was at that moment that Toby walked in, knowing just where to find me. He'd flown back on a red-eye as soon as he'd gotten the news, though I knew his parents had urged him not to come. He was barely a week into his first semester at USC and already had a punishing premed schedule, but he'd put the ticket on his emergency credit card and was at my side as soon as he possibly could be, rumpled and sleepless and ready to hold my hand through it all.

When he saw me staring wordlessly at my bloody finger, he pulled down the first aid kit my dad kept on the wall, knelt in front of the chair, and started tending to the wound without asking a single question.

That was the first time I cried after Dad died. I sat there as Toby silently cleaned the cut on my finger and let out three days' worth of tears and a lifetime of tears to come. And after the wound was disinfected and covered with a Band-Aid, Toby pulled me to him and let me sob all over the suit jacket he'd worn to graduation just three months prior.

I still run my finger over the scar all the time. It reminds me of that horrible day, yes, but also that Toby has always been there for me. Even when he was supposed to be on the other side of the country.

But now the feeling of Toby's finger lightly drifting back and forth across the scar makes my heart squeeze in extra beats. Slowly, silently, he lifts my hand and brushes his lips feather-light over my knuckle.

I suck in a breath, my heart stopping right along with my lungs.

Toby pauses, his eyes on that scar, and then he drops my hand and reaches for his burger.

And we eat.

We eat until all that's left are greasy wrappers, spotted paper boats that held fries, wadded-up napkins, and a sprinkle of stray salt.

He doesn't say anything about the fact that he kissed my hand, and I don't either. Mostly because I'm not entirely sure that it actually happened. I have suffered a head injury, after all. And if it did happen, it was probably just him being a friend. Remembering that day, and how broken I was, and offering me some comfort. He placed a kiss on the Band-Aid back then too. It's just another memory from our long friendship.

Toby clears away all the trash and returns to the couch with his iPad in hand, plopping back down next to me, and finally he speaks.

"I asked Turner to email me her wedding planning shit so you could look at it. You wanna check out some budget spreadsheets?" He turns and meets my eyes, no trace of any awkward moment there. Because it apparently wasn't awkward for him. He's not the one having sexy thoughts.

That's all in *my* head.

Chapter 15

TOBY

How do you make a tissue dance?

You put a little boogie in it!

PIPPIN

NOPE

Three days after my bridal salon meltdown, I still haven't seen Polly. When I got back to the attic in Toby's clothes, she was gone, along with her suitcase. Mom said she was at Mackenzie's and that I should give her time, but I've never been a patient person. Three days has felt like an eternity, and on Tuesday morning I finally pull out my phone and tap out a text:

PEPPERONI

I'm sorry. I was an enormous asshole. Please come home so I can apologize for real.

The three dots pop up almost immediately, and I suck in a breath, waiting to see what kind of response comes.

PIZZA

> The biggest asshole. Bigger than Tom Brady's ego. Just massive.

PEPPERONI

> Let me make it up to you. Mani/pedi?

PIZZA

> But you hate when strangers touch your feet

PEPPERONI

> That's how much I love you

Polly was right. I really do hate pedicures.

As the woman at my feet scrubs my heels with some kind of cheese grater, I grip the armrests on the chair until my knuckles are white, teeth gritted to keep from laughing. I cannot believe there are people who can sit through this without feeling on the verge of peeing their pants the whole time. Could never be me.

"You know you can ask them not to do that part, right?" My sister glances over from where she's serenely having her feet tickled by an industrial feet-tickler, and she's not even cracking a smile.

"It's...fine..." I grind out, then huff out an enormous exhale when the woman lowers my foot back into the hot water. To be fair, my feet are probably in desperate need of attention. I haven't had a pedicure since the last time Polly forced me, which was when she graduated from Harvard and told me nobody in the Yard wanted to see my "troll toes." That was four years ago. Four years of being on my feet in the kitchen, four years of running off my stress, and four years of wearing flip-flops on city streets.

It goes without saying that I will tip this nail tech exorbitantly.

The woman at my feet raises my left leg and starts in on her next round, and this time I cannot manage to hold in the bark of laughter.

"You don't have to torture yourself for me," Polly says, rolling her eyes. Apparently sensitive feet aren't genetic, because my carbon copy over there is perfectly calm.

And anyway, I think I do need to torture myself a little, because until this moment, Polly has barely said four words to me. This is one of those "shut up and relax" pedicures, with her scrolling on her phone and me stewing about how I'm going to fix things with her. And I guess now is the time to bite the bullet.

"I know," I tell her, melting into the backrest when the cheese grater finally disappears. "But I thought if I got you in the pedicure chair, you'd be a captive audience for my apology."

Polly puts her phone in her lap and turns to me, the corner of her lips quirking up. "I'm listening."

I suck in a deep breath, deep enough to fuel the monstrous apology I owe my sister. "I'm so, so sorry, Polly. I took what should have been a special moment and ruined it by shouting at you. I never should have said that Dad wouldn't want this for you. I was absolutely wrong, and that was next-level shitty."

"Thank you," Polly says, and the way her voice drops to a whisper is just a reminder that what I said to her was a cheap shot.

"Dad would have loved that dress on you," I tell her.

"I think he would." Polly smiles. "And I'm sorry that I wasn't more sensitive in the moment. I know that Mom selling

Marino's is less jarring for me. Of course you melted down, what with everything changing in your life. Lord knows you're not the most flexible member of our family."

"Hey! In my defense, literally every part of my life is being uprooted. I'm losing my home, my job, and my sister all in one foul swoop."

"It's one *fell* swoop, Pepperoni," Polly says. "And you're not losing me. I'm getting married, not leaving the country. Nothing has to change between us."

"It does, though. You're moving in with Mackenzie."

Polly sighs. "Did you think I was going to live in the attic with you forever?"

"No." *Maybe.* "But now Mackenzie will be your person."

"And Toby is yours."

My mouth drops open. "No he's not!"

Polly shrugs. "Well, Toby's always been the one you call in a crisis. The one you tell all your secrets to first. I get them, but only after you've workshopped them with him first. We're sisters, and we'll always be sisters, but Toby's your person."

Okay, I guess maybe she's right about that. Polly is my twin sister and I love her, but Toby is my best friend. He's the one I told when I failed AP calculus. He's the one I turned to when Nick Furman dumped me a week before prom. He was my first call when Dad died. Polly is the friend I was born with, but Toby is the friend I chose.

"Unless he's something more?" Polly's voice rises, her eyebrows right along with it.

I groan. "You've got to stop that, Pizza. Seriously. All the teasing and innuendos are really screwing with my head."

Polly grins. "How so?"

I stare into the bubbling water, wiggling my toes. I have always gone to Toby first. But I can't go to Toby with *this*. And maybe that's part of my issue at the moment. This is one problem I can't spill to him, and so I'm left with it swirling around in my head, stewing in my bones and infecting every part of me with these pesky thoughts. Maybe pouring it out to Polly will help me exorcise these dirty thoughts I'm having about Toby.

Or maybe it'll just add fuel the fire.

Either way, I need to do something, because my dirty dreams of him are only getting more vivid.

"Toby is a salad," I say finally. And then I explain my salad theory to her, about pictures of salads and how they're messing with my head. I tell her about the zap I felt when he held my hand in the hospital. About how he kissed my knuckle just like he did when we were eighteen, but suddenly it felt different.

And I tell her—not in too much detail—about the dreams.

"But it's obviously all just a mental mindfuck," I say, "because Toby is a salad, and I want a *steak*. I've *always* wanted a steak. And this is where my metaphor breaks down, I'm sorry, but in this instance, a salad would be very bad for me."

Polly blinks at me, her brow furrowed. "Let me get this straight. You seriously think your feelings for Toby are just your brain misfiring due to the power of suggestion?"

"Yes."

"And it has nothing to do with the kind, smart, funny man who is hot as shit and, oh yeah, adores you?"

My mouth presses into a firm line, then I grind out, "As. A. Friend."

"Are you sure you're not using the whole salad thing as an excuse?"

I throw my hands up, then panic that I've ruined my fresh manicure. "An excuse for what?"

"To feel your feelings!"

I shake my head. "I don't have feelings for Toby."

Polly's phone vibrates, a text from Mackenzie appearing on the screen. She picks it up and swipes to read.

"You have feelings for Toby, Pepperoni. Just not the feelings you think," Polly says as she taps out a reply. "Now, before I fully accept your apology, there's one more thing you have to do."

—

I'm sitting at a table outside Bartley's in Harvard Square across from my sister and an investment banker.

Okay, I know she's not *actually* an investment banker, but I truly have no idea what her job really is. Maybe today is the day I'll figure it out.

Polly is in a casual, brightly colored sundress while Mackenzie is in a navy pencil skirt and a white Oxford, a pair of leather loafers on her feet. She looks like her next stop after this lunch is a meeting of the Harvard Debate Club. I feel wildly underdressed in a pair of ripped jeans and a T-shirt with Harry Styles's face on it, even though my outfit fits in a lot better at Bartley's than Mackenzie's. We chose this lunch spot because Polly has a meeting with her dissertation advisor, who's at Harvard for a conference, and Mackenzie has an office over in Kendall Square by MIT.

That information? That's the extent of what I've learned from our conversation in the five minutes we've been sitting here. I have eaten half my burger and damn near all my fries in an effort to distract myself from the crushing silence that is our table. I'm going to have to go back for seconds if this continues. I can see Polly starting to fidget, and I know if I don't make serious headway soon, whatever goodwill I garnered with my apology will fade away.

"So Mackenzie, did you go to Harvard too?" I ask. I hate myself for going straight to the old *where did you go to college* question like this is some kind of job interview. But I'm desperate, and also not ready to listen to a bunch of technical jargon while Mackenzie tries to explain her job to me. I need more caffeine for that. Or maybe some alcohol.

"No, I went to MIT to study computer science and engineering. I did my MBA at Harvard, though," she says.

And then the conversation dies a quick death again.

I glance at the table next to us, where there's a couple who is almost certainly breaking up. She keeps dabbing at her eyes with a greasy napkin, and he keeps sighing. And I'm fucking *jealous* of them and their level of social interaction. That's how awkward our table is right now. Then I glance at Polly, who is definitely not yet feeling kindly enough toward me to rescue me from this conversational abyss. And I don't blame her. I told her Dad would be ashamed of her while she was wearing her future wedding dress.

Jesus, I'm such an asshole.

But then I remember the dress, and I grab at the idea like a lifeline.

"Hey, I'm sure Polly told you, but she picked out a killer dress. It looks incredible on her. Have you picked one out yet?"

Polly lights up, and even Mackenzie seems to brighten, which surprises me, since I wouldn't have taken her for a fashion girlie. But then again, she is always impeccably put together.

"I did, actually! My mom and I went over the weekend. It was the first thing I tried on, which was surprising, because I've seen enough episodes of *Say Yes to the Dress* to think it was going to take a really long time," she says. Which, okay, she watches *SYTTD*. *That's* definitely a surprise. Mackenzie strikes me as the kind of person who refers to reality television as "trash," but this is a good sign. What's *not* a good sign is that she's pulling out her phone and flipping through her camera roll, a flash of white appearing on the screen.

"Hey hey hey!" I cry, flinging my hands over the screen.

"You can't show off the dress before the wedding! It's bad luck!"

Mackenzie shoots me a look, which she then turns on Polly, who's covering her entire face lest she catch a glimpse of said dress.

"Are you two serious? You can't possibly be that superstitious," Mackenzie says.

"We're Italian, are you kidding?" Polly says. "Dresses stay secret until the wedding! I'm not starting this marriage cursed!"

Mackenzie rolls her eyes, a semi-spicy reaction I appreciate even though we're disagreeing with her. At least it seems like this lunch is showing me a slightly looser side of my future sister-in-law. An eye roll and a *Say Yes to the Dress* name-drop? Maybe she doesn't actually plug in at night to recharge her batteries. Maybe she actually *is* a human woman. I'm still curious what Polly sees in her, but there's a blurry little wave of recognition there.

"Speaking of the wedding, I thought we could use this opportunity to go over a few of the bigger details. Knock some items off the old I-To-Do list." I pull out my phone and open the app and the email Toby forwarded me on Saturday. "Toby sent me the master checklist and budget spreadsheet Turner used when she got married last year. I thought we could use it as a bit of a guide."

"Didn't Turner have a full Catholic mass at the Cathedral of the Holy Cross? And a reception at the Boston Public Library?" Polly asks.

"Yes, but we can obviously scale down all her stuff for our own use," I say. *Way* down, because even with Polly's trust money, there's no way we could approach what I'm pretty sure was a mid-six-figure wedding. The Sullivans do not fuck around when it comes to ceremony. Toby's eighth-grade graduation party was held at the JFK Library, and that wasn't even that much of an achievement.

"Who's Toby? And Turner?" Mackenzie asks.

"Toby is Pippin's best friend since they were kids, and Turner is his older sister," Polly says. "Well, one of them. Doesn't he have, like, five?"

"Four," I say. "Siobhan, Rowan, Riley, and Turner, and Toby's the baby of the family."

"The Sullivans are *rich*. Like, Mayflower rich," Polly says. "They have this enormous brick town house on Louisburg Square that's been in their family for generations. Toby's dad is a federal judge, and his mother is a tenured professor of biochemistry at MIT with, like, a dozen patents, and all the kids are genius overachievers."

Polly's not wrong. Siobhan, the oldest, is a partner at a ritzy New York law firm; Rowan is a venture capitalist in Silicon Valley; Riley followed in her mother's footsteps and is a medical researcher at Cornell; and Turner is a speechwriter for the First Lady. As in, the First Lady of the United States of America. I've spotted her in the background of four different events on CNN.

"Oh, I've heard of Dr. Sullivan," Mackenzie says. "But I avoided biochem at all costs. I can do computers all day, but as soon as nature enters the picture, I'm lost."

"Hard same," Polly says, which makes me laugh, because while Polly is being truthful about hating the natural sciences, I'm pretty sure she's also grossed out by computers. She actually wrote the first draft her dissertation longhand on legal pads and kept her research on index cards. She's still carrying around her old iPhone 7, and when I asked her if she was ever going to upgrade, she replied, "Why? It still makes calls."

"So Toby is *just* your friend?" Mackenzie asks.

"Ugh, not you too! Come on, you don't have women friends you have zero interest in sleeping with?" I ask.

Mackenzie shrugs. "I'm bisexual, but I guess I get it. It just seems less common between women and men. Friendship without attraction, I mean."

I ignore the fact that there has been, well, *a little bit* of attraction lately and instead just let out a big, dramatic sigh. "You *really* need to watch *When Harry Met Sally*. It seems right up your alley."

We spend the rest of the meal going over wedding details as college kids and tourists stream past us on the sidewalk. Because the wedding is so close, we opt to skip the save the dates and go straight to invitations. Which means we have to set times for the ceremony and reception so I can start getting proofs together. I show Polly and Mackenzie an Instagram account of one of our former sous chefs who left to start a catering business. I know Belinda will give us a good deal, and her partner runs a bartending business, so that's taken care of. We agree on an open bar, because there has never been a fun wedding in the history of the universe that didn't have an open bar. (I keep saying "we" as if I'm going to have any part in this marriage...but let's be honest, as the keeper of the I-To-Do checklist, I'm definitely a key player in this collaboration.)

"What about the rehearsal dinner?" I ask, looking up from my app, where a delightful number of boxes have been checked. I've never done hard drugs, but I imagine looking at all those baby-blue check marks is what heroin might feel like. "I was thinking we could do it at Marino's. We could cook ahead, so we wouldn't have to worry about staffing the kitchen or anything."

"Should we really be planning on that? I mean, it could be sold by then," Polly points out. She says it like it's a simple logistical note, but the comment stops me dead in my tracks. The wedding seems so *soon*, and the notion that the restaurant could be gone before then makes my stomach sink into my feet.

"Your mother mentioned that the restaurant company

can't get out here for another month, and a sixty-day closing could easily be put into the contract. You could even get ninety if you're willing to negotiate a little," Mackenzie says. Her lips press together in the firm line that I now know to be her smile. "I think we should do the rehearsal dinner there."

Sure, it was based in dry facts and logic, but I think my future sister-in-law just tried to cheer me up?

Polly smiles, then reaches across the table and grabs my hand, giving it a squeeze. "Mackenzie's right. I don't think it's all going to happen that fast, and even if it does, I doubt Mom will set a closing date anywhere near the wedding," she says. "I know this is going to be hard as shit, Pip. But I'll be right here with you, and I know that in the end, you're going to find some incredible opportunity you didn't even know existed. You're going to be all right."

Easy for her to say. She knows where her suitcases are going—right into Mackenzie's Fort Point condo. But me? I have nowhere to go. I feel tears well up in my eyes and quickly suck down a big gulp of Coke to distract myself. It would be a hell of a lot easier if I could believe that there's something special out there for me.

Chapter 16

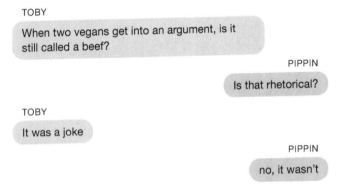

That night, I'm already exhausted by the time I roll into my bedroom to get ready to meet Toby for the rabies gala. (I still have no idea what it's actually for, and I'm not sure Toby does either.) I wasn't supposed to work tonight, but I made the mistake of popping in after lunch with Polly and Mackenzie just to see how prep was going.

Not well, as it turned out.

Justin, the new guy Fernando was training, quit this morning because his band got a standing gig at a club in Worcester. Which meant I had to jump in to help peel garlic and get the pots of sauce going for the evening. Then the linen delivery was late, which meant Evie would never finish rolling silverware in time if I didn't jump in to help there too. And Melinda misspelled *orecchiette* on the specials board, which meant it needed to be cleaned and re-lettered. Which I did.

By the time I finished all that, I had forty-five minutes before I was supposed to meet Toby. I'm sweaty and cranky and I smell like a meatball.

I jump in a quick shower, opting to leave my hair out of the spray and instead douse it with dry shampoo to mask the smell of garlic. I stumble out, pink and slick and wrapped tight in a towel, only to realize as I stare into my closet that I have absolutely nothing to wear to a fancy gala that's being held in a five-star hotel. I've never been very interested in fashion, preferring comfort in the heat of summer or the frozen tundra that is a Boston winter. And over the last few years, as I've spent more and more of my time at the restaurant, my closet has truly fallen by the wayside. Yeah, I date, but my dates tend to lean more toward burgers than consommé. If I can't wear jeans there, I'm not going, is what I'm saying.

But jeans will not cut it at a black-tie event.

I'm just about to reach for my senior prom dress when Polly finds me, blinking at the meager supply of clothes not meant to be worn on shift at Marino's—a few sundresses, a pair of black pants, and a blazer that I only pull out when I have to meet with the accountant or the health inspector.

"Help," I say, and the word is barely out of my mouth before Polly is pulling a dress from her own closet.

"Thank *god*, I was worried you were going to wear the dress you wore to Alma's wedding," Polly says, referring to our cousin, who got married in a traditional Catholic mass where we all had to cover our shoulders. That wedding took place when I was a senior in high school. The dress has long sleeves and a peplum. Very mid-2010s fashion. *Very* not hot now. I honestly forgot it was in there, and I'm glad Polly found me before I realized, because between that and the prom dress, the peplum definitely would have won out.

Unfortunately, the dress Polly is coming at me with is *very* not me. But I can't even get the words out before I'm being shoved back into the bathroom, the hanger in my hand.

"Just try it!" Polly calls through the bathroom door. "No complaints until it's on you, please."

I shimmy into the dress and climb up onto the toilet lid to try to get a glimpse of myself in the tiny mirror over the pedestal sink, but all I can see is boobs. Seriously, the dress performs a very impressive lift-and-separate that makes my chest look like it's on display, some artful boning holding it aloft. Maybe I should have waited until *after* the gala to make up with Polly, because now I'm going to have to go out like this, and while the prom dress is unfashionable, at least it fully covers the girls.

"Polly, I cannot wear this," I say, walking out to stand in front of the full-length mirror next to her bed. "I look—"

"*Hot,*" she says. She stands back and gives me a full up-and-down, then walks over and spins me around, adjusting seams so they fall in the right place on my full hips and fastening the hook over the zipper that I couldn't reach because I am not a member of Cirque du Soleil.

"Like a hooker, is what I was going to say." I eye the knee-length dress, fitted around my round hips with a fitted waist and a sweetheart neckline, tiny spaghetti straps serving as mere ornamentation because the built-in corset is really what's doing all the work of holding it up. Polly reaches back and pulls on the zipper, sucking me into the thing like it's been painted on my body. "Polly, it's red."

"So?" She's still behind me, so I can't see her face, but it's clear from her tone that she's only half paying attention to me. Her sole focus is the fashion.

"I don't wear red," I reply.

"Why not? You look amazing in it."

"Red makes people look at you. I don't…" I say, eyeing my reflection. "I just want to blend in."

Polly sighs and reappears in front of me, grabbing me by the shoulders and giving me a little shake. "Come on, Pippin. Please? Just this once, let yourself shine. You look fucking amazing in this dress."

I do a half turn in the mirror, looking at the way the dress hugs my butt and makes me look like a pin-up girl. I definitely don't look a thing like *me* right now. But maybe that's a good thing. Frankly, I could use a little vacation from being me.

"Look, you're going out with a friend who didn't pay for the tickets, and both of you are just in it for the free food. You won't know a single other soul there except him," Polly says. She steps back and shrugs. "The stakes couldn't be lower. For once, wear the damn dress."

I turn and square my shoulders in the mirror, taking it all in. Polly's right. I should wear the damn dress. It's absolutely not me, but maybe that's the point. "Me" is the person who spent the last two hours in the kitchen putting out fires before dinner service. "Me" is the person who has given nearly every waking moment to the restaurant for the last eight years only to *still* have it pulled out from under her. "Me" is the person who's confused and scared and stressed. I need a break from that person. And this red dress and an open bar might just be the perfect opportunity.

My smile must give me away, because Polly grins, letting out a squeal.

"Toby is going to swallow his tongue." She claps and jumps up and down a little. I give her a look to remind her that I've told her ten thousand times that Toby and I are just friends and don't look at each other like that, and while she doesn't stop grinning like the cat that ate the canary, she *does* at least stop jumping up and down.

"At least we'll be in a room full of doctors who can help him retrieve it," I say finally.

"Interesting…" Polly cocks an eyebrow at me, which is one expression that, though we are identical, I've never been able to master. Which is annoying, because it would be so *useful*.

"What?" I snap.

"It's just that usually when I make comments like that about you and Toby being attracted to each other, you shut me down so fast I nearly bite my cheek. But tonight you just let that one sail right by. Maybe Toby's finally starting to look a little more like a steak?" She grins and shrugs like she knows something I do not. But the joke's on her, because I know exactly how much I've been picturing Toby naked lately, and it is 100 percent more than I want to be picturing Toby naked.

"The dress is so tight it's constricting the blood flow to my brain," I reply. But the truth is there is a little part of me that wonders if maybe the dress will give Toby thoughts about me that are even a fraction as intense as the ones I've been having about him lately. Not that I *want* him to want me. Because I don't. But it would be nice to know that the whole thing is no big deal. He goes running shirtless, I temporarily swoon. I step out in a sex dress, he swoons. Fair's fair, right? That would only confirm that the feelings are unimportant and normal and we're still just friends.

"Okay, we've got to figure out how to cover that wound on

your forehead," Polly says, reminding me that, oh yeah, I still bear the mark of having run headfirst into a lamppost.

"Can't I just wear a bandage over it?" I ask. The swelling has gone down, and the cut is actually pretty small, but just as I feared, my forehead is an abstract painting of purple, blue, and even a little yellow bruising.

"I can definitely cover up a lot of it with makeup," Polly replies. "And then we'll do shoes!"

From the way her grin grows to double its normal size, I know I'm in for some real trouble.

⊏⊐

I didn't want this to seem like a date, so I told Toby I'd just meet him at his house. Him picking me up felt too weird. But now that I'm wearing this dress and strutting through Beacon Hill in the strappy heels my sister loaned me, my hair sprayed within an inch of its life, my makeup subtle but smokey (all courtesy of Polly, who took one look at the compact of Clinique powder foundation that's been sitting on my dresser for going on five years and legitimately looked like she was going to hurl), I kind of wish I'd told Toby I'd meet him at the hotel. I know as soon as we walk into the event, the lights will be low, the music will be loud, and the crowd will be dense, which will make it easy to focus on why we're there: lobster tails and an open bar. But if we're crammed into the back of an Uber together, I fear I'm going to lose my nerve and do a tuck and roll out the door somewhere on Boylston Street. Assuming this dress will allow for such moves. After two blocks of walking, I suspect I won't be going anywhere fast.

My fear only grows tenfold when the door of Toby's apartment swings open to reveal my best friend, all six foot something of him, clad in the best-fitting black suit I've ever seen outside a David Beckham ad. His hair looks freshly cut and is styled in a way I've never seen him wear it before. It looks like it's ready for an Instagram photo from the barber who did it. The sides are smooth, the curls on top mostly pushed back, though they still flop slightly over his left eye. I have to swallow the *unfgh* that starts to exit my mouth at the sight of him and his brown eyes that seem to smolder—when did Toby learn to *smolder*?

I catch the exact moment when he registers the sight of me —all of me, especially the parts in the dress, because his eyes go wide as dinner plates and his jaw drops so low I can see the filling in his back molar. Suddenly that smolder is replaced with something else entirely.

"Holy shit, you look amazing," he says, his eyes roving all over me as a deep red blush blooms on his cheeks. "I mean, well...*wow*." He drags his eyes back up to meet mine in an effort not to ogle me like some roadside construction worker.

"It's Polly's," I say, shifting on my borrowed heels. "I don't usually wear red."

Toby makes a sort of understated *hmmm* sound whose meaning I can't decipher, then pivots quickly on his heel and marches toward the stone steps up to the front door of the main house, beckoning for me to follow.

"Hey, before we go, my mom needs help with a light bulb. Come in?"

I follow him past the stairs, down the hall, and into the kitchen, where Dr. Sullivan is standing at the counter, a slice of pizza in her hand, her laptop open on the counter. There's an open box of light bulbs on the island in front of her.

"It's the third one," she says, pointing at the pendant lights over the island but not even looking up from her screen. Not even when she adds, "Oh, hello, Pippin."

"Good to see you, Dr. Sullivan," I reply, because she's never been an *oh, just call me Erin* kind of mom. Toby's parents have always been incredibly formal. I'm surprised his dad has never made me call him Judge Sullivan. But he's always been Mr. Sullivan, never John. They're kind, good people who have always been welcoming to me, but I'd never for one second call them warm.

Toby reaches up and dislodges the burnt-out bulb in the pendant light, replacing it with a new one, not even needing to rise up on his toes. I feel envious, as I always do when I see him reach for high things. Being five foot two is rough in the normal world, but in a kitchen, where you're always trying to reach the high shelf in the walk-in or the overhead pot rack or the top of the spice rack, it sucks extra. The number of times I've nearly taken a header off a step stool during the dinner rush is…well, let's just say it's a common occurrence.

"Oh, honey, I got an email from Dr. Foley," Dr. Sullivan says, finally looking up from her laptop, but only to lock Toby in a tractor beam of a *look*. "He said they had a dropout, which means there's a spot open in the lab if you want it. Same fellowship, same funding. He'd love to have you. And Jen is still there. It's not too late."

Wait, what?

Toby pauses, his jaw clenching. "*Mom*," he says, the word loaded with all kinds of warning.

But if Dr. Sullivan clocks the tension in his voice, she ignores it. "What? I just thought that maybe after a month of this, you'd have come to your senses. Surely you can't want to keep this up for four full years of training plus, you know, an entire career. I just can't believe you really threw away a fellowship like that to stay up all night getting covered in bodily fluids. It's not a great way to spend your time."

The set of Toby's jaw is razor sharp, and I notice he steps awfully hard on the pedal for the stainless steel trash can. Its lid slams hard into the wall tiles, and the clatter makes me jump and wobble on my heels. "Tell Dr. Foley no thank you, and please stop interfering on my behalf," Toby says. "You're my mother, not my academic advisor."

Dr. Sullivan sighs, but she clearly doesn't see this as the end of the discussion, no matter how much Toby obviously wants it to be. And since this is apparently a conversation that has happened more than once, Toby seems to know what's coming next and heads for the door before his mother can say anything else. "We're going. I don't want to be late."

And then he's gone, leaving me standing there in the kitchen, where I finally catch the eye of Dr. Sullivan, who seems less impressed with my dress than Toby or my sister.

"Good to see you," I say again, like an idiot. I've never really known how to talk to Toby's parents. Every interaction feels like a job interview combined with an oral exam, and I never get the job or pass the test. So before I can say anything to embarrass myself, I turn and trot after Toby, stumbling slightly in my borrowed shoes.

I find Toby standing out on the street, tugging at the cuff of his shirt beneath his jacket. I don't know if I've ever seen him look this pissed off before.

"What was *that* about?" I ask, but by either luck or design, our Uber pulls up and keeps him from having to answer, which he seems pretty pleased about. He opens my door, and I slide into the back seat, a move that takes a little bit longer and requires a lot more coordination than normal in this dress. He walks around the front of the car and slides in next to me, and I decide not to let it lie. Because Toby and I are friends who have always vented our problems—parental, educational, and otherwise—to each other. And what better way to get my subconscious back to *just friends* than to let him unload his problems on me? "Seriously, you going to tell me anything about what just happened back there?"

Toby lets out a long, deep sigh that makes his shoulders drop a good two inches, and then he leans his head back against the headrest and stares out the front window. "I got a fellowship at a lab at Stanford doing biomedical research—full funding, prestigious, working with one of the preeminent researchers in the field—but I turned it down because I want to be an emergency medicine doctor. My parents are...not pleased."

The car lunges out onto Charles Street, knocking us back against our seats. "Why? Doesn't having a kid who's a doctor mean you won parenting?"

"Nah, not in the Sullivan family," Toby says, his jaw set so tight I can see a muscle twitching just below his ear. "Matching at one of the top programs for emergency medicine isn't prestigious enough, apparently. My mom thinks I'm wasting my talent and intellect."

My stomach turns at the venom, yes, but also the hurt in the voice of my brilliant, caring best friend, who has always wanted to help people and who, though exhausted by his first few weeks of residency, also clearly *loves* being a doctor. I would make it through maybe a day and a half of what he's doing before deciding no matter what the job, I'm out. Toby regularly stays longer than he needs to look after patients, help out his fellow residents, or polish his skills in the lab. I don't know what it takes to be an ER doctor, really, but whatever it is, it seems pretty clear he's got it. And the fact that his parents can't see that makes me sad for them. And for him.

Toby looks away out the side window, but I can feel the tension radiating off him like heat from a campfire. I hate how miserable he seems, my eternal optimist of a best friend. It's not right seeing him like this.

"Well, joke's on them, because you don't have talent *or* intellect," I say, trying to keep my tone light, and it works. Toby's shoulders shake as he barks out a laugh.

The tension eases just in time for us to pull up to Copley Square and climb out of the car. As the Uber drives away,

Toby crooks his arm, and I thread mine through his, mostly because I worry I won't make it across the cobblestones without eating shit in Polly's shoes.

But also a little bit because I'm wearing this dress and letting myself be Not Pippin tonight, and Not Pippin really wants to hold on to the hot guy in the fit suit who's getting stares from women passing by on their way into the library. *Look all you want, ladies. Tonight he belongs to…well…Not Pippin.*

I can't shake the memory of the scene in the kitchen, though. Especially the part about Jen being in Palo Alto. Does Dr. Sullivan not know that they broke up? And why *did* they break up?

Toby has never talked very much about his relationship with Jen. I mean, he told me when they met and when they moved in together. She was always present in his stories about his day or their travels, but he never talked about their *relationship*. We've always told each other everything, but with Jen he implied that there was nothing to tell. Which was fine because, like I said, she never seemed like a very big personality. I was always half surprised it went on for as long as it did. To me, Jen was mostly smiling photos on Instagram and a few awkward meals filled with stilted conversation when they visited Boston. It didn't seem weird, really, that I didn't have details. It's not like I ever wanted to hear about the nitty-gritty of their relationship. I didn't expect him to talk about sex with me or anything—ugh, just the thought of it makes me squeamish. Toby and I have talked about a lot of things in our lives; there's basically nothing he doesn't know about me. But the nitty gritty of our sex lives? It's never come up.

And because I've been tangled up in my own shit since Toby's return, I haven't pushed him to talk about the breakup. He said he wanted to move on, and I went with it. But something is not right.

With just a few minutes left before we disappear into the

hotel with its aforementioned dim lights, loud music, dense crowds, and open bar to ease any remaining tension, I ask the question I've been dying to ask ever since Toby showed up in Boston and told me he and his girlfriend of four years were no more.

"Is that why you broke up with Jen? Because she wanted to stay and you wanted to come here?" I ask.

The toe of Toby's shiny leather shoe catches the corner of a raised brick and he stumbles, but he quickly catches himself, then keeps walking. "Um, yeah? I guess?" he says, though it hardly sounds definite. And that's all I get.

"*You guess?*" I ask. "Toby, what happened between you two? You've been so cagey about it. I'm starting to think you discovered some hideous secret about her. Is she in the Illuminati? Does she run an illegal squirrel fighting ring? Does she prefer Pepsi to Coke?"

Toby laughs, as I wanted him to, but I also want an answer. But he just shrugs. "Yeah, that was a big part of it, I guess—me coming here. She's doing a postdoc, and I've got four years of residency. It's an awfully long time for long distance."

"Did you consider staying in California? Or did she consider coming here?" I ask.

"Not really. I mean, I guess, but…I don't want to talk about Jen tonight. I'm here with you, and you're in this amazing dress, and I'm wearing a *tie*, so can we just…be here together?"

There's an intensity in his eyes that makes my breath catch in my throat. I'm not sure what he's asking, exactly. Be here together…*together?*

But I wasn't kidding about this dress cutting off blood flow to my brain. With my tits hiked up to the heavens, I can barely think, so I just smile.

"Sure, of course," I say, reaching over to rub his arm just above where mine is tucked into it. "Let's go get drunk and eat lobster."

Toby smiles, the first genuine one I've seen since I arrived at his house. Which is a long time for Toby to go without smiling.

"Yes, please," he says. He holds out his arm to usher me through the open door, and we step into the hotel, leaving that conversation, and probably others, behind us.

Chapter 17

TOBY

What do a tick and the Eiffel Tower have in common?

PIPPIN

Don't do this ...

TOBY

They're both Paris sites!

PIPPIN

I'm going to reach over and smack you with this phone

Four glasses of champagne, a lobster tail, a filet mignon, and the most decadent parmesan mashed potatoes I've ever put into my mouth later, I think we've more than gotten our money's worth out of these free tickets. This gala is celebrating a multimillion-dollar gift the hospital received to fund cancer treatments, I've finally discovered.

The room is cavernous and ornate, the lights artfully dimmed, the linens a tasteful combination of ivory and champagne. A jazz band has been playing quietly for most of the evening, and while there's a small dance floor set up in front of the low stage, only a few elderly couples have taken advantage of it. This doesn't seem like a *get down* kind of crowd, for which I'm grateful, because dancing is not totally my thing. And dancing in four-inch heels and a sex dress? Yeah, not happening. I make a mental note that my maid of honor dress is going to need more leg room than this if I'm going to help pull off Polly and Mackenzie's reception properly.

Speaking of the wedding, I take out my phone and aim it at the floral centerpiece. It's a gorgeous blend of blue hydrangeas and pink peonies, and while those flowers definitely won't be in season come October, the square glass vase with the gold rim would fit well with Polly's industrial boho theme… I think.

"What are you doing?" Toby asks. He leans in close to my ear, and the warmth of his breath raises goose bumps along my neck. The food and champagne seem to have helped him unwind from the scene with his mom.

"Polly might like these," I say, checking to make sure I got a good shot in the dim light of the ballroom. I don't want to turn on the flash and draw attention. "You know, for the wedding."

Toby nods, and his curls bounce, having freed themselves slightly from the styling gel. His hair has always had a mind of its own, and now it falls roguishly over his eyes. "Ah, so you've decided to get on board with the wedding? Or did your addiction to planning things just finally take over?"

"I've always been on board with the wedding," I say, giving him a look, but he just volleys back a cocked eyebrow. "The *wedding*. The marriage I'm still a little less sure about."

"I don't think you get one without the other," Toby replies.

"I know, I know. I just need to figure Mackenzie out. Polly is clearly smitten, so there must be *something* in there that's interesting. But so far she just seems like an uptight businessbot."

"Well, you've got three and a half months to get to know her," Toby says. "Better embody your best Nancy Drew and solve that mystery."

"I think I'm more of a Veronica Mars, marshmallow," I say. "And I'm working on it."

At the front of the ballroom, on a raised stage surrounded by black and champagne bunting, a stagehand in black with one of those pop star monitors in his ear steps out and sets up a mic stand and a stool, studiously adjusting them.

Toby leans in, his voice lowered so his words go only in my ear, and not to the six strangers picking at their plates at our table. "Okay, so I think there are about to be some awards and a lot of really long, really boring speeches."

"Wow, fun night you've planned," I say.

"I'm just saying, if we want to slip out, this it might be our only chance."

An acoustic guitar on a stand has appeared next to the stool, which can only mean that some very earnest singer/songwriter shit is about to happen. No thank you. The only thing I hate more than earnest singer/songwriter shit is improv of any level, with slam poetry performed by white teenagers coming in at a close third. Toby knows this about me, of course, which is why he's also gesturing to the stage with his head. Man, why does anyone go to things like this with anyone other than their best friend?

"Yeah, I think it's time to make a quick exit," I say.

"I knew the acoustic guitar would do it," he replies with a wink.

We push our chairs back and try to make it look like we're just heading for the bathrooms, giving warm smiles and nods to the rest of the guests at our table, none of whom have spoken to us. Either they're awkward introverted donors or they have correctly assessed that we're young and broke and just in this for the free food. Either way, given that they didn't speak to each other either, I'm thinking we didn't miss very much.

As we head for the door, Toby's hand goes to the small of my back, his fingers pressing lightly but firmly as he leads me out of the ballroom. I tell myself my unsteadiness on my heels and my champagne-fizzy head are why I lean into his touch.

But I'm lying.

Out in Copley Square, the sun has gone down, and since it's a Tuesday, most of the traffic is people leaving nearby office buildings late or people coming from dinner. Toby and I definitely stand out in our gala finery. So much so that I get an honest-to-god wolf whistle from a guy in a velour tracksuit standing near the church. Toby shoots the man a venomous look that I guess would be scary if you didn't know Toby. But I *do* know Toby, and I know that one of his greatest fears is getting into a fistfight, so I just laugh.

"Where to now, boss?" I ask, trying not to think about the fact that I'm wearing this dress and these heels and Toby looks like…well…*that*.

Toby takes in a long breath of summer night air, which is only partially tinged with the smell of hot asphalt and exhaust. "It's a nice night. Want to just go for a walk?"

A light breeze picks up my hair, and I instinctively turn my face up and breathe in the cool air.

"My heart says yes," I say, lifting one leg to show off the four-inch heel, "but my shoes say no fucking way."

Toby's eyes linger on my leg, his teeth scraping across his lower lip, and I get those zaps that run up my thighs and down from my belly. My legs start to feel sort of gelatinous from the heat of his gaze, but then he breaks the spell by pointing to a nearby bench.

"Sit there. I'll be right back," he says, his eyes sweeping over my body one more time. "And don't talk to strangers." Then he turns and disappears around the corner at a light jog.

I sit and watch people go by, glaring at a few business bros who openly stare at me sitting here in this dress. Unlike Toby, I'm very much *not* afraid of a fistfight.

Ten minutes later, Toby reappears, slightly breathless, the top buttons of his shirt open to the night. His tie is folded in one hand, and there's a Walgreens bag in the other. He quickly shoves his tie into his pocket, then reaches into the plastic bag and pulls out a pair of cheap black rubber flip-flops.

"For you, madam, so the night doesn't have to end prematurely because you wore irresponsible footwear."

"First of all, what was I supposed to wear with this dress, Birkenstocks?" I reach for the flip-flops, which Toby has helpfully freed from the little plastic ring tying them together. A ring I'd usually have to cut with scissors, but he has snapped it open with merely a flex of his biceps, *mother of god*. I slip them on and find that they're a perfect fit. "And second, how did you know my size?"

Toby shrugs. "You used to borrow Siobhan's old skates when we'd go to the ice rink," he says. "I figured your feet couldn't have grown *that* much in the last eight years."

I loop my finger through the backs of my heels and stand in the flip-flops, letting out a delicious sigh as my feet sink into the soft rubber. I swear, these things feel like memory foam slippers after wearing those awful shoes for two hours.

"Here, I'll carry them," Toby says, holding the Walgreens bag open and nodding at my shoes. I drop them in. "Now, how do you feel about ice cream?"

And even though I just ate my weight in lobster, filet

mignon, and the creamiest, richest parmesan mashed potatoes on the planet, my stomach lets out a growl of assent.

"I feel amorous of ice cream," I say with a grin, and try to ignore the fact that ice cream isn't the only target of my amorous feelings at the moment.

⸺

Twenty minutes later, we're leaving J.P. Licks with our treats (a brownie batter waffle cone for me and a peanut butter cookies 'n' cream waffle cone for Toby) and heading toward Comm Ave, where we can stroll down the tree-lined greenway in peace.

Our walk is quiet at first, since we're both mostly focusing on sucking down our dessert before the warm summer night air sends it dripping down our wrists. But by the time I'm popping the gooey, crunchy bottom of my cone into my mouth, I realize that I still have questions. That conversation we started before we walked into the Fairmont? It *was* waiting outside, at least for me.

"So you really never considered staying in California? With Jen? I mean, they have emergency departments on the West Coast." I don't know why I'm pushing this. I just thought…I mean, after four years together, I'd think they would try to stay together. They seemed happy enough. He never complained about her to me.

"No," he says. That's it. Just…no.

We step off the curb to cross the road, and a cyclist playing Cannonball Run comes whizzing around the corner. Toby throws out his arm to keep me from stepping into its path. I crash into it with an *oof*, his fingers brushing my hip in a way that makes me blow out a deep sigh. Luckily, I can mask it with the whole *oh my god, I almost got flattened by a cyclist* thing.

"You okay?" he asks.

"Yeah, fine," I say, like I nearly get run over by bicycles every Tuesday night. "Why?"

"Well, you seem to be breathing pretty heavily there," he says, his eyes dropping to my cleavage, which is literally heaving.

His gaze makes me feel warm all over, and I need to distract him before he notices the flush I can feel climbing up my body.

"I mean, *why* didn't you want to stay in California?" I ask.

"Oh, that." He blinks, then looks back at his cone. Finishing the last bites, he tucks his hands into his pockets, looks both ways twice, and then steps out into the street. It's not until we reach the next block that he finally answers. "I wanted to be here."

"At Mass General?"

"Yeah," he says, but it seems like his mind is elsewhere. It appears the breakup with Jen was not as smooth as I thought. Toby still seems very much caught up in it.

"And you didn't think about maybe doing long distance?"

"It didn't seem like a good idea," he says.

There's something he's not telling me. And man, does he seemed determined to keep it to himself.

We've reached the end of Comm Ave, the gates of the Public Garden before us. Toby crooks his arm just as he did before we entered the hotel, and I take it, letting him lead me through the stone gates, past the hulking statue of George Washington atop his trusty steed, and onto the bridge that traverses the pond. During the day, tourists drift slowly around it in the famous swan boats. But the swans are tucked in for the night, and because it's a Tuesday evening, the park is pretty quiet. We're alone on the bridge with only a busker playing a violin at one end. I listen closely to a few bars before the nagging familiarity of the song finally pings in my brain.

"Is it just me, or this a weird song for violin?" Toby asks as she starts sawing away at another chorus of "We Didn't Start the Fire."

"It certainly is an impressive arrangement," I say, and then we both mouth along as she gets to the "rock 'n' roller cola wars" line, one of the few *everyone* knows from that song.

I can't help but think about the last time we were on this bridge together. Right before Toby left for freshman year at USC, I planned an entire day of Boston fun, of being tourists in our own city. I bought us stiff new Red Sox hats and cheap, boxy Wicked Pissah T-shirts at Faneuil Hall and demanded we rock our matching duds all day. Then we set out on a Duck Tour, followed by clam chowder at Union Oyster House (which, for the record, is not an appropriate dish for a steamy August afternoon). We stood in line for cannoli at Mike's Pastry. We walked the Freedom Trail and took the Green Line out to the Gardner Museum to stare at the empty frames. Then we watched the sun start to set over Fenway Park before wandering along the Esplanade back up to Beacon Hill. And we took pictures at every stop to document this last day of our old lives. Several of those pictures still adorn the corkboard over my little desk back home.

We ended up on this bridge, me trying not to cry at the thought of him boarding a plane to fly to the other side of the country. I didn't know then that the four years would turn into eight. I didn't know my dad would die and my own college plans would change so drastically. I didn't know that eight years later, we'd be standing here in fancy clothes, leaning over the stone railing, staring down at the dark water below while my mind whirls with a tornado of thoughts about the warmth coming off the man standing next to me and the responses my body is having in return.

"I'm sorry things didn't work out with Jen," I say. "But I'm glad you're back. I missed you."

I glance sideways and see his brown eyes looking back— really *looking*—at me. A shiver goes through me, and I bite my lip to try to keep still. But I can't stop the smile that forms on my face. At his warmth, at his gaze, at having him *here*.

With *me*.

Finally.

"I missed you too, Pip," he says, the nickname coming off his lips with such ease and care, and it's not enough that he's back. It's not enough that we share secrets and ice cream and jokes. I want him.

I *want* him.

Maybe it's the champagne, or the ice cream, or the dress that's making me feel like Not Pippin. Or maybe it's the chorus of voices that has been telling me for years that Toby and I belong together. I never believed it. But suddenly I'm leaning toward him, my hand rising to his forehead to brush back a curl. My calves flex as I rise up on my toes. His eyes widen, then narrow, his lips parting just before I brush them with mine.

The bolt of heat is instantaneous and so strong it nearly knocks me back. But before I can stop, I feel him lean into the kiss, his lips firmly on mine. Soon he's rising to his full height, his hands going to my cheeks, pulling me closer, higher, *taking*, and I want to give and give and give. I reach up and wrap my arms around his neck, his hands going to my hips as he pulls me flush against him, and I feel his want, his very real desire, through those snazzy suit pants. Thank god for his tailor, because I can feel all of him, and oh my god, Toby is *all* grown up.

I let out a sigh that he swallows with a gravelly little sound from deep in his chest. It turns me into a puddle of desire. His lips part, and I feel his tongue brush my bottom lip, his teeth nipping before his tongue sweeps inside to meet mine. There's a tiny voice that sounds an awful lot like thirteen-year-old

Pippin Marino shouting *You are French-kissing Toby Sullivan!* But I just high-five that girl and go right on losing myself in Toby's kisses and the hard length of him that presses into my abdomen.

Toby grasps my hips and turns us so my back is against the stone railing of the bridge, boxing me in with his tall body. His hand comes up to tangle in the curls at the nape of my neck, angling my head so he can taste even more of me. When his hips press me against the stone, I let out a little gasp that makes the corners of his lips turn up in a grin even as he keeps kissing me.

And then the sound of a siren rips through the moment. But it's not a police car or a fire truck. No, it's my stupid phone, alerting me to a text message that had better be the single most important piece of information I've ever received, otherwise I'm chucking this phone directly into the pond below.

I step back from Toby like we've just been hit with a cattle prod. I stare at him, mouth parted, little huffs of breath coming out of me as if I've just run a marathon. And from the way his brown eyes flick down to my chest, still very much on display in this dress, I know my breasts are heaving right along with the rest of me.

"Pippin—" Toby says, his voice lower than I've ever heard it, but then my phone beeps again, and without thinking, I pull it from the tiny purse Polly loaned me. The screen lights up with a text from her.

PIZZA

> Mom says pick up Windex on the way home if you can. Real estate agent is coming by to look at the place tomorrow and mom wants the windows spotless.

A real estate agent. Who is coming to look at the place so they can sell it to strangers, who will probably turn it into some insufferable tapas bar and rent my attic bedroom out for thirty-five hundred dollars a month. My stomach turns somersaults just thinking about it. Suddenly Pippin returns from vacation and tells Not Pippin to take a fucking hike.

"Everything okay?"

I glance up and see Toby, who, for a split second, I forgot existed. Or that I just kissed him. Like, *a lot*. I kissed my best friend. Hell, that felt like more than a kiss. Or at least it was going to be.

And then it hits me: I did the one thing you're not supposed to do in a friendship. I crossed a line, and I don't totally know where I've ended up. It's like I walked up to the Massachusetts border and stepped across, only to find myself in Canada. Are people speaking French? Is it snowing? *What is happening?*

Everything everything *everything* is changing. Polly. Our little attic bedroom. Marino's. My whole life. Toby, my one constant, is standing there looking at me, his cheeks fiery red, and I've gone and rocked that boat too.

What was I thinking? I don't do relationships. My string of ex-boyfriends and the hours worth of jokes at my expense in the kitchen have proven that. What makes me think it would be any different with Toby? And if I do the thing I *want* to do right now, if I go home with him, if I follow that kiss where it felt like it was going, what then? In five or six weeks, will I wake up and discover the flaw about him that drives me crazy? Will I wake up and realize that he was a great friend but we're not meant to be? Will I wake up and realize I have to *break up with my best friend?*

No. That can't happen. Not with everything else that's

going on. I only got through the horror of my father's death because Toby picked me up and put me back together. The thought of going through what's coming without him by my side makes me want to pull open the Earth with my bare hands and dive into the gaping hole. I can't—I *cannot*—lose him.

What do I do?

Immediately I start to panic, and then immediately after that I try to hide the fact that I'm panicking. All I can think is that I need to get out of here. Before I ruin things more, break them beyond repair. I need to retreat so I can figure out what to do and how to fix this.

And so I start backing away slowly.

"Oh, it's just Polly. Mom asked me to pick something up at the drugstore. So, um, I should probably go do that," I say, trying to quell every instinct in my body to take off running. I shake my phone like a visual aid, as if it's proof that my escape right now is no big deal. I'm not running, see? It's just a text message! On my phone! I look like a flight attendant demonstrating in-flight emergencies! And anyway, everyone knows that when faced with a problem, the worst thing you can do is to run away from it. So I'm backing away from it slowly, which is way better, right? It's totally different. This is *fine*.

"Do you want me to walk with you?" Toby's brows knit together. There's a whole host of emotions in his eyes, but I can't bring myself to look at them long enough to figure out what they are. I'm not ready to find out what I've done. I'm not ready for the consequences yet.

"No, no, it's fine. You just, you know, you head on home, and I'll catch up with you later," I say. "I had a lot of fun tonight! Thanks so much for the invitation!"

And those are my parting words before I turn on my flip-flops and walk away as fast as I can with my legs encased in this skintight dress. I manage to keep myself from breaking into a full sprint as I leave the bridge and start down the winding path through the garden that will take me to Beacon Street, then to Charles to get Windex, then home. I can practically feel the heat of his gaze as I go.

But I don't look back.

Chapter 18

TOBY

Why did the cookie go to the doctor?

It was feeling crummy.

Are you okay?

I was hoping a morning spent Windexing, vacuuming, and polishing the restaurant would distract me from last night's kiss.

It doesn't.

All it does is make my hands work as hard as my brain, which is consumed by an ever-rising sense of panic. That I kissed Toby. That I ran away after I kissed Toby.

That I haven't texted him back because I have no idea what to say.

Instead I'm scrubbing fingerprints off the back banquette for maybe one of the last times ever because a real estate agent is arriving any minute and then my entire life as I know it will be gone.

"Oh, Penny, it's just lovely. It'll be gone like that."

I turn to see a woman with blond hair and even blonder highlights snap her fingers, flashing her red-polished nails. My mom is standing next to her, smiling nervously.

"Pippin, this is Wanda Barnes. She's going to be listing the building," she says, a smile on her face but a look in her eyes that says *Please act in the manner in which I raised you.* "My other daughter, Polly, has a meeting, so she can't be here."

"It's so nice to meet you, Pippin," Wanda says. "Your mother tells me we're standing in your inheritance. You're about to be a very rich young lady!"

I can give her only the tightest of smiles. The mention of the money does little to calm my anxiety. I'd rather have my home.

"Do you think there's anything we need to do to get it ready to list?" Mom asks Wanda.

"Oh, I wouldn't touch it. A buyer for a property like this will want to make their own changes. The only thing they care about is that the bones are good and the location is prime."

The bones. My life, my family's history, reduced to a withered skeleton. How apropos. I glance over at the smear of red paint on the doorframe outside the kitchen, and my heart grows heavy. I know this is what Nonna and Mom want. It's what they *need.* I've seen the way Nonna limps up the stairs, the way Mom looks tired by lunch.

But that doesn't mean I have to stay here and watch it happen.

"I need to go run some errands," I say. "For the wedding."

"Oh, okay," Mom says. I can tell she was hoping I'd stay, but I think she understands why I can't. I try to conjure up a warm smile to let her know that what she's doing is okay, even though every single part of my life is upside down.

"Wanda, it was nice to meet you," I say. And then I step

out the door, trying to get used to the idea of leaving my whole life behind.

Of course, I don't actually have any wedding errands to run. Which means I have to come up with something, because otherwise I'll be forced to wander around with only my thoughts for company, and frankly I'd rather lay down on the Green Line tracks.

I need a task.

I pull out my phone and scan through I-To-Do until I find the perfect thing. Then I open a text window and fire one off to Polly. She had an early-morning meeting with her dissertation advisor, which is why she wasn't at the clean-a-palooza at the restaurant, but she should be done by now.

PEPPERONI

We need to get measurements at the Bryan house for the tent and table rental. Want to meet me over there?

PIZZA

Can't. Meeting is going long, but you can head over. I'll text Nora to let her know you're coming

Fine. I'll do it myself.

Which is how I wind up standing alone on the stone stoop of the Bryan family mansion, being welcomed in by Dr. Nora herself. Today she's got a pair of cobalt-blue reading glasses tucked in her sleek black bob, and she's wearing a flowy pair of matching blue linen pants and a floral kimono. How does she look chic even in loungewear?

"Pippin! Good to see you again. Come in, come in." She flings the door wide and ushers me into the main hall. She picks up a heavy tape measure from the hall table and hands it to me. "I was just about to hop on a Zoom with my editor, otherwise I'd help you. If you need anything, just holler. Oh, and don't use the downstairs bathroom. Something's wrong with the toilet. I've called the plumber, but he can't come until next week. There's one right at the top of the stairs on your left."

And then she's hustling down the hall to her meeting, leaving me alone holding my phone and a tape measure in an otherwise empty house.

I let myself out the French doors and set about my task, measuring the space in the backyard where the tent will go and calculating the square footage of each of the three patios—one for the ceremony, one for the cocktail hour, and one that will be a quiet space with chairs where people can relax away from the reception. This distracts me better than the cleaning did, mostly because it requires me to do math. I never thought I'd be so grateful for basic geometry.

An hour later, I've got a neat little drawing of each space on my phone with dimensions and estimates of how many tables it can fit. I'm about to go wave goodbye to Nora in her office and head out when I remember the long walk to the Green Line and the shaky train ride ahead of me and decide I might as well make a quick pit stop first. I turn and head for the upstairs bathroom. Only when I get to the top of the stairs, I can't remember—did she say right or left? Not willing to interrupt a discussion of Dr. Nora's next bestselling book, I shrug and turn right. Either I'll find a bathroom or the skeletons in the Bryan family's closets.

I find neither.

What lies behind the heavy wooden door with its antique brass knob is Mackenzie's bedroom, apparently unchanged since she left for college. At least I assume it's unchanged—I doubt Mackenzie recently hung a One Direction poster over the head of her brass bed using unicorn washi tape. It's frankly hard to believe that *any* iteration of Mackenzie did that, and yet here lies proof that my future sister-in-law once had a personality.

And a lot of it too. The walls of her room are covered with posters, photos, stickers, prints, and greeting cards, all stuck to the wall with brightly colored, sometimes glittery tape and thumbtacks. I count two more One Direction posters, plus a vintage Lilith Fair poster. There are some printed-out memes from *The Office*, both the American and British versions. There's a LESLIE KNOPE FOR PRESIDENT poster and a front-page *Boston Globe* article, yellowed and curling but still triumphantly announcing Obama's first win. I have to step closer to see the photos, one of which shows a grinning Mackenzie on the back of an auburn horse, holding two blue ribbons next to her smiling face. There's Mackenzie in a group of girls at what appears to be summer camp, arms thrown around each other, all in blue face paint and clothes. There are several of that group, actually, photos that follow the girls through years of summers and multiple growth spurts. There's a snap of Mackenzie at a protest, making a peace sign with one hand while the other hoists a handmade BLACK LIVES MATTER sign. There's a rainbow flag over her dresser and a whole collection of photos from various Pride parades. In one, Mackenzie is wearing gold sequined hot pants and hot-pink roller skates.

Apparently I have seriously misjudged my future sister-in-law.

But the photo that really gets me, that knocks the breath clear out of my lungs, is one in a silver frame. It's new, and it sits on the bedside table. It's of Mackenzie and Polly. They're leaning out of one of those red phone booths they have in London. Mackenzie has her arms around Polly. Polly is grinning at the camera, but Mackenzie is grinning at her. They both look so happy, love oozing out of the frame at such a high intensity that it warms even *my* cynical heart. This isn't Polly being infatuated. This isn't some passing feeling. These are two people who love each other. Two people who want to stand up in front of their friends and family and the federal government and say, "I pick her. Forever."

It's both a comforting and terrifying realization. It means that my sister really has found love.

And it means that I really am losing her.

Chapter 19

"The bathroom's across the hall."

I whirl around, barely keeping the silver frame from tumbling to the floor, and find Nora leaning against the doorframe, arms crossed and a kind smile on her face.

"Yeah, I opened the wrong door, and then I just kind of…" I trail off, gesturing to the walls of Mackenzie's room. It's a visual explosion, one that would have been hard to walk away from even if Mackenzie weren't marrying my sister.

"There are layers underneath too," Nora says, striding into the room to peer at a photo of Mackenzie with a gold medal around her neck, a banner for high school math bowl behind her. "She's being doing this since she was a kid. I'm pretty sure there are third-grade art projects under here somewhere. And probably a few spelling tests. My strong girl always did need a soft place to land."

"It's like a scrapbook in museum form," I say.

"It is. Which is why it'll be here until we leave this house in body bags," Nora says with a laugh. Then she turns to face me, her eyebrows knitting together. "You look like something's troubling you."

Now it's my turn to laugh. What *isn't* troubling me, Dr. Nora? And while my usual instinct would be to blow past the concern, maybe make a joke, I find myself *wanting* to respond. Maybe I feel like I can be honest with her because she's a stranger, sort of like how I could kiss Toby last night because I was Not Pippin. Or maybe it's that she's Dr. Nora, who once made Barbara Walters cry and confess her deepest fears on her podcast. A mere mortal like me is no match for her powers.

Whatever it is, I find myself replying, "A lot of somethings, actually."

Nora pulls out Mackenzie's desk chair and takes a seat, gesturing to the edge of the double bed, where I sit.

"Well, you can't solve anything if you try to solve everything, so why don't we start with *one* something."

Since kicking things off with the admission that I've been assuming her daughter was a personality-free drone and not good enough for my sister seems like it's not the move, I decide to start with my newest problem.

"I kissed my best friend Toby last night, and now I'm afraid I've ruined our friendship forever. And I need him if I'm going to deal with all the other somethings in my life right now." The words rush out of me, but they don't make me feel any lighter. In fact, hearing the whole thing summed up so succinctly just makes me freak out even more. My problem may be simple, but it's also enormous, and I have no idea how to solve it.

"Was the kiss good?" Nora asks.

A laugh whooshes out of me, first because that is *not* the question I was expecting. And second because it sends my mind straight back to the bridge, where just last night I had Toby's arms wrapped around me, his lips on mine. I feel a hot blush creeping up my neck and into my cheeks.

"Y...*yes*," I say finally.

"Oh my," Nora says, fanning herself, because I have apparently just imbued that one word with all the heat and intensity

I felt when my lips met his. Hell, that I *still* feel just thinking about it a day later. "And after the kiss, what happened?"

I figured Dr. Nora would bathe me in her sage advice, not walk me through a play-by-play of one of the single most shocking and confusing and, well, *hottest* moments of my life. But she doesn't sound like she's prying for a sexy story. She sounds matter-of-fact. And so I answer.

"I ran away."

"That's it? You just ran?"

"Well, I got a text from Polly asking me to pick up Windex so we could clean the windows for the realtor who was coming to sell our family home and livelihood," I explain. "So I said I had to go to CVS. And *then* I ran."

"I see." Dr. Nora nods, and I get the sense that she really *does* see. Not in a supernatural way, but in a way that shows that she's really listening. That she's connecting threads I don't even see as loose. "And did he give you any indication that he didn't like the kiss?"

And now I'm back to the blushing and fidgeting and nervous laughter. Because, um, *quite* the opposite, Dr. Nora. I felt *exactly* how much he liked the kiss.

"Okay," she says, not forcing me to get graphic while I sit on her daughter's childhood bed beneath a torn, peeling One Direction poster (although I get the sense that the spirit of Harry Styles would be more than happy to hear the dirty details). That's why Dr. Nora earns the big bucks—because she knows when to ask questions and when to listen. "But you're *sure* nonetheless that this kiss will ruin your friendship."

I pause on that for a moment, because it does sound like a giant leap to a very specific conclusion with not a lot of evidence. Then again, Dr. Nora doesn't know me that well.

"Eventually it will," I say. "I mean, I've never had a relationship last very long. I'm restless. And focused. And busy."

"Yes, Polly told me that you basically saved your family's

restaurant by taking charge of it," Nora says. "But as I under-stand it, soon you're going to have an awful lot of free time."

"Yes! A lot of free time to fill with a whole host of other problems! Like where I'm going to live and what I want to be when I grow up! I'm twenty-six—I didn't think I'd need a new answer to that question at this point! And if I ruin things with Toby, then I'll be friendless too."

Nora sits back in her chair and stares me right in the eyes for what feels like an eternity.

"First of all, Pippin, I don't know the specifics of your situ-ation, but I know what a building like that in Beacon Hill can go for. You're about to be sitting in a really good financial posi-tion from which to search for answers to all these questions."

My entire body feels tingly, and twin flames of shame bloom on my cheeks. "You're right. I've been...well...I'm sorry."

"Oh, honey, when we're in it, none of us can see the forest for the trees. You're not a bad person just because you lost sight of your privilege there for a minute. Your problems are very real to you, and I won't diminish them. I just want you to remember where you're starting from."

I nod. "Absolutely. You're right."

"Second, I'm still not willing to concede that starting some-thing with Toby means you'll automatically lose him. But you know your relationship better than I do, so I'm going to have to trust that you're being honest with yourself." She gives me another long, intense look that makes me swallow hard. "You also need to be honest with Toby."

"What do you mean?"

"You need to tell him how you feel. Why you ran away. If you truly don't want anything to come of that kiss, you need to tell him that. Otherwise your friendship is broken no matter what happens."

Ugh. I was afraid of that. "Do I have any other options?"

"You could ask him how *he* feels first and use that information to inform your decision."

No. Nope. No. Because if Toby tells me he doesn't want me, I don't know if I'll ever recover from that. I have to be the one to say it first. Not that I don't want him, because—since Nora is forcing me to be honest with myself, fuck it, let's go—I *do* want him. Toby is amazing, and that kiss was incredible. I bet whatever could've come after it would have been too, at least in the short term.

But that doesn't mean wanting him is the right thing.

The right thing is for us to go back to how we were. And in order to do that, I have to tell him that I want my friendship with him more than I want…anything *else* with him. Even if I might want that other thing a whole goddamn lot.

Now, finally, I do feel a little lighter. I mean, don't get me wrong, I'm absolutely dreading this conversation. And also a little bit disappointed that Dr. Nora's advice wasn't more along the lines of "Take some space, let things settle, it'll all work out." You know, the *just ignore it and it'll all go away* strategy that's apparently not at all popular amongst therapists. But I sure as hell would prefer it.

"Thank you," I tell her, and despite how much I don't like what she said, I mean it.

"But I also think you need to interrogate this idea that because everything in your life is changing, you need to cling harder to the things you feel you can control," Nora says, rising from her chair. "Because your feelings are not something you can control, and the more you try to, the more volatile they'll get."

Chapter 20

For a week I take the coward's way out.

I wait for Toby to just show up. But he doesn't. I tell myself it's because his program at the hospital is so demanding that he doesn't have a spare moment. But that doesn't account for the lack of calls or texts, either. By Friday, I've taken to lurking around outside the Mass General ER like a fucking creep, but even then I can't seem to manufacture a chance encounter with him, and I can tell the security guard stationed out front is starting to think I'm up to no good.

Toby is either pissed that I ran or, worse, pissed that I kissed him in the first place. Or he's trying to figure out how to let me down easy. Or maybe he's ignoring the whole thing and hoping it just goes away, which is an option I would've been *very* on board with had I not talked to Dr. Nora. Damn her and her thoughtful, mature advice! Who needs a guru anyway?

When another weekend has come and gone with no sign of Toby, I realize I'm going to have to hike up my big-girl panties and reach out. Every day that passes is just another step away from our friendship, which is exactly what I'm trying to preserve.

So I guess it's time to go ahead and preserve it.

It's also time for the one wedding task I've actually been looking forward to ever since I downloaded I-To-Do. And I think I might be able to kill two birds with one stone here.

Polly, who has very strong opinions about the cake (no shade, baked goods are important), has selected a baker known for beautiful, avant-garde creations at a price that makes her dress seem reasonable. But because I vowed not to detract from my sister's happiness, I am choosing to focus on the fact that when I googled the Merilee McDonald Cakery, the top review called her creations "sinfully delicious."

After I apologized for my shit fit at the bridal salon, Polly decided to move back into the attic with me. She stays here most nights, and while I'm insanely grateful to have her company this one last time, I also know that part of the reason she's back is because she saw a mouse at Mackenzie's and the exterminator can't come seal the place for another two weeks.

"Hey, Polly, would you mind if I invited Toby to the cake tasting?" I ask.

"Huh?" Polly is on her bed, her knees tucked up and her laptop balanced on top. As the wedding approaches, so too does her dissertation defense, and just as she did in high school whenever a big exam or paper was coming up, she's beginning to slip into full-on study-hermit mode. Soon she'll abandon her collection of sundresses, opting instead for only leggings and this one oversized beige wool sweater I like to call Gladys. Polly found it at a vintage store and paid three bucks for it, which was $2.50 too much.

Despite my direct question, she continues typing, squinting through her glasses.

"Toby. Cake tasting. Please?" In my experience, when Polly is fully down the nerd rabbit hole, it's best to keep things as simple as possible.

"Yeah, sure," she says, finally tearing her eyes away from the screen to blink at me.

Excellent. I can reach out under the guise of inviting him to go cake tasting, which, who wouldn't want to do that? And on the way there, I can do the whole telling-him-the-truth-about-my-feelings thing that Dr. Nora suggested. It's a perfect plan. But I need the perfect opening, and after just a moment, I have it. I pull out my phone and tap out a text.

PIPPIN

What concert costs just 45 cents?

I wait an absolutely torturous four and a half minutes before the three dots appear, followed by Toby's reply.

TOBY

Are you attempting a joke?

PIPPIN

Yes. Play along.

TOBY

Okay. What concert costs just 45 cents?

PIPPIN

50 Cent featuring Nickelback

TOBY

... Damn, that's a good one

PIPPIN

It's not, but thank you. Do you want to come cake tasting with us? Tomorrow at noon. All you can eat, all the flavors you can imagine. Polly needs opinions. Meet me at Starbucks and we'll go together.

The three dots blink, then disappear. Blink, then disappear. This little digital choreography continues long enough that my stomach has time to claw its way directly into my throat, and by the time his reply finally appears, I'm wound so tight that the little ding nearly causes me to send my phone sailing across the room.

TOBY

Yum. I'll be there.

I let out a breath I absolutely knew I was holding.

"Toby's in. We'll meet you and Mackenzie at the bakery," I say, and Polly just grunts in response. I swear, if she doesn't come up for air soon, I'm going to have to pry her jaws open and start chucking garlic knots into her mouth to make sure she gets enough sustenance.

I haven't told Polly about kissing Toby. Partly it's because I don't know if I can drag her out of her academic coma long enough to get the whole story out. Partly it's because I don't want a steady stream of *I told you so*s and smug looks whenever the three of us are together.

But mostly I think it's because if I tell Polly, I'll have to tell her all the details, and if I relive what happened, I may not be able to go through with the next part of the plan. Sure, Dr. Nora lightly suggested that I "interrogate" my desire to friend-zone Toby, but she doesn't know me. She doesn't know Toby. She doesn't know *Toby*. It was easy to tell her what I felt. Polly would make me work for it, and frankly, I don't want to.

I just want to rip off this Band-Aid and then go back to how everything was before, when Toby and I were friends who had never kissed and I didn't know how fucking good he is at it.

Toby's waiting outside the Starbucks when I arrive, leaning against the wall with one leg bent, his foot pressed to the brick. There's no novelty T-shirt today, just a well-worn pair of jeans and a loose button-up, the sleeves rolled to display his corded forearms. I press my lips together, worried that if I'm not careful, my tongue will fall out of my mouth and unfurl down the pavement like a cartoon character's.

"I went ahead and ordered," he says, pushing off the wall, two coffees in his hands. Well, *mine* is a coffee; Toby's is the beverage equivalent of a stripper who calls herself Coffee. He passes me my drink.

"Venti sweet cream cold brew with caramel drizzle and whipped cream," I say, reciting his usual order while staring in horror at his sweating cup. "There's, like, a hundred grams of sugar in that, by the way."

Toby shrugs. "I don't do drugs. Caffeine and sugar is basically my speedball."

"Lord be with you," I say, holding up my cup.

"And also with you." He clinks our plastic cups and then takes such a long pull from the straw that it makes *my* teeth hurt.

"Don't judge. I once saw you smear rainbow chip frosting on a piece of cinnamon toast," he says.

"In my defense, I ate an edible half an hour before I did that," I reply. I point to his sugary, creamy cup. "That right there is a sober choice."

"I am what I am," he says with a smile so warm it reignites Tuesday night's fire in my bloodstream. If I don't do what I came here to do—and fast—I'm going to accidentally trip over a cobblestone and fall directly into Toby's lips.

"Hey, so, I don't know how to, like, ease into this conversation, so instead I'm just going to Kool-Aid Man my way through it." I glance at him over the rim of my cup.

"I wondered if we were going to talk about it," he says. His shoulders noticeably tense, and in that instant I imagine at least fourteen ways *he* might want this conversation to go. But before I can get too far off track, I bring Dr. Nora's words to the front of my mind like a mantra.

Be honest with Toby.

Okay, then, here goes nothing.

I point toward an empty bench at the edge of Boston Common, and after giving it a quick once-over for obvious signs of bird poop or barf, we sit. I want to turn my body toward him, try to look him in the eye, but in the end all I can do is stare down at my coffee cup.

"We need to talk about the gala," I say.

"Okayyyyyy," he replies, as if drawing out the word will give him time to gather his thoughts. I search his tone for any indication of what he might be thinking, but he's doing that serious doctor voice I recognize from when I ran into the lamppost. It betrays nothing. Do they teach that in med school? Like, do they bring in theater teachers who have worked with the cast of *Grey's Anatomy*?

Focus, Pippin.

"We kissed," I say, as if he wasn't there when it happened, but I can't keep dancing around it. *Be honest.* "And it scared the shit out of me."

Now I finally look up and meet his eyes. His curls are blowing back in the light breeze, and his eyebrows are knitted together, though I can't tell if it's with worry or concern or what. I pause for a beat to see if he's going to jump in and save me, but he just keeps his eyes locked on mine, waiting to hear what's coming next.

Shit.

"Toby, you're my best friend in the whole world. You mean

more to me than anyone outside of my family. Hell, you *are* my family. And the thought of doing anything that could fuck that up terrifies me," I say. I glance down at my hands, which are gripping my plastic cup so tightly I'm running the risk of popping off the lid and showering myself in coffee. I blow out a breath and try to calm myself. "It was a mistake. I'm sorry. I shouldn't have done it."

Toby finally pulls his eyes away from mine, letting his gaze roam over the cobblestone sidewalk. He hasn't touched his rapidly melting drink, and if he's feeling anything like I am right now, he'd rather pitch the whole thing in the trash than take a single sip.

His gives this little bob of his head, a nod, like he's agreeing with whatever conversation is happening in his head. Then he finally turns back to me, his eyes soft. "So why did you kiss me?"

Oh. So he *is* going to make me talk about it. Dr. Nora didn't prepare me for this part, but I guess I'll just keep going with the honesty thing. Which is good, because I don't know if I could stop the words that burst forth.

"Because you looked liked a young James Bond if he were modeling for Gucci, and I was high on champagne and ice cream! Because we were standing in the moonlight and talking about old times and I got carried away! Because I *wanted* to!"

I pause and watch Toby's cheeks flush all the way to the tips of his ears.

"But when I thought about it after—when I think about it *now*—I realize that I love you too much as a friend to do anything to mess that up," I say, getting to the most important part. "I need you, Toby."

He's silent for a long time. Long enough to hear the entire chorus of Toto's "Africa" blaring from a minivan stopped at the corner of Charles and Beacon. Long enough that I have to fight my instinct to leap up from the bench and sprint home and hide under my covers forever. Long enough that I think maybe Dr. Nora is absolutely full of shit and I should figure out how to contact Oprah and tell her that. Honesty is nonsense, clearly.

But then Toby turns to me with a little half smile, his one dimple appearing.

"Was the kiss good at least?"

My mouth drops open, then closes, then opens again as I blink at him like a freshly hooked fish. Am I hallucinating right now? Is this all a dream? Was the kiss good? Was the kiss *good*?

"Yes!" I shout, as if the blush on my cheeks hasn't answered that question for me. It was the best goddamn kiss I've ever had, but I manage not to tack *that* part on at the same volume that I hear it in my head. Dr. Nora asked the same thing. Man, everyone is really obsessed with Toby's making out skills.

Toby nods, his half smile cranking up to the full meal deal. "Okay," he says. "As long as the kiss was good."

Then he stands, takes a long sip of his disgusting drink, and reaches a hand down to pull me up off the bench. Which I take, even though I feel like that can't possibly be it. Can it?

Toby starts walking toward Park Street, and I follow him for about four steps before I say, "Wait, are we okay?"

Toby pauses, glancing over his shoulder. "Yeah, we're okay. I mean, I guess it was something that had to happen eventually, right? Now we've done it. And we're fine." He cocks his head, indicating that I should catch the hell up, literally and figuratively.

"We're fine," I repeat. I can hardly believe what I'm hearing. And that this conversation hasn't been nearly as painful as I anticipated. Shit, maybe Dr. Nora wasn't just right—she's a damn *genius*. Should I be honest all the time? Is honesty really the best policy? I always assumed that was a thing we *said* but that it really only applied to, you know, not cheating on your spelling test or sneaking out of bed for extra dessert. I thought adult life was far too complex for actual honesty all the time. Honesty all the time seemed like a one-way ticket to getting punched in the face.

"I can't believe you asked me that," I say.

"Asked you what?"

"If the kiss was good."

"Hey, it's been a long time since I've kissed anybody new," he says as we descend into the T station and tap our Charlie cards. "I deserve to know if I'm repelling women with my lips alone. I mean, you dumped that one guy just because he was a bad kisser."

"Derek. And he wasn't just a bad kisser, he was a *horrible* kisser. Abominable. It was like having an encounter with a mastiff. I needed *napkins* after that kiss, Toby." I watch him laugh and try not to remember the saliva pyrotechnics of Derek Easterly, a guy from my macroeconomics class at UMass. "You're no Derek, trust me."

"Good," he says, leveling me with a wicked smirk that banishes all thoughts of Derek Easterly, leaving behind only thoughts of how good Toby's lips felt on mine.

The train comes whooshing into the station. As the doors open, Toby steps aside and holds his arm out like he's welcoming me into my own personal subway car. "Shall we go taste some cake now?"

Still mildly shell-shocked that I both fixed my friendship with Toby *and* confirmed that he's an incredible kisser (and also wondering if I can ask *him* if *he* thought the kiss was good, which I haven't so far because I need to put the whole kissing thing behind me as soon as possible starting *now*), it takes me a minute to step inside the car. But I hear a woman waiting behind me loudly clear her throat, jolting me out of my panic. I step into the train and realize that I got what I wanted. I wanted us to move past this, to pretend like it never happened.

And that's what I got. If I don't start putting one foot in front of the other, I'm going to undo all that good hard work I just did.

Still, as I situation myself in the subway car, my forgotten coffee, now more water than ice, sweating in my hand, I can't help continuing to focus a little too much on the incredible kisser part.

I sit down on the empty bench next to Toby. "Hey, so now that that's out of the way, do you want to help me figure out what I should do with the rest of my life?"

He laughs. "Do you want to be a doctor?"

"Fuck no," I reply.

He shrugs. "Then I'm out of ideas."

Well, shit. I guess we can't solve all my problems in one day.

Chapter 21

TOBY

I'm about to make a joke about cake. You butter believe it.

PIPPIN

Stop texting me, this baker looks like she could Sweeney Todd us easy.

First Birgit at Vow'd, and now this? I thought people in the wedding industry were supposed to be founts of joy, the kind who cry at Hallmark commercials and whose priority is to "make your day oh so special." Where is Polly finding all these dour purveyors of wedding foofaraw?

Merilee McDonald is anything but merry. She seems to approach cake decorating with the kind of intensity usually reserved for MMA fighters and corporate litigators. We've been in her bakery for fifteen minutes, and she has not smiled once.

But looking around the shop, at the displays in various cases and the framed photos on the wall, I can tell why people look past Merilee's bitter facade. Because her cakes are truly works of art. I'm especially impressed by one that appears to be covered in charcoal-colored linen with delicate white dahlias cascading down one side, all of it edible. I just hope they taste as good as they look, because thanks to my nerves over talking with Toby, I skipped lunch, and now I'm starving.

Mackenzie and Polly were waiting for us when we arrived, and Polly immediately took control of the appointment. It was clear that Mackenzie had ceded all decision-making authority about cakes to her betrothed.

We sit at a round café table while Polly rattles off her ideas, Merilee nodding and her assistant furiously typing on an iPad.

"No fondant," Polly says.

"Of course, we want people to eat this," Merilee says curtly.

"I want fresh flowers," Polly says. "And I don't want any colored frosting. I don't want to see purple tongues and teeth in photos."

"Has she been like this about all the plans?" Toby whispers in my ear, earning a sharp look from Merilee.

"This and the dress are literally the only things she cares about," I reply, my voice as low as I can make it without being silent. Still, Merilee shoots me a look like she wants to send me to detention.

It's true—Polly has been, for the most part, the opposite of a bridezilla. She has really let me run with my ideas. In just a few weeks, I've confirmed a caterer who is going to serve a Haitian Creole/Mexican fusion menu that I honestly cannot wait to eat. After reading a few horror stories of DIY DJs in a Reddit thread, I convinced Frantz to acquiesce to a DJ, promising he could provide an extensive track list of requests. I've finalized the tent rental in case of bad weather, along with tables, chairs, linens, and patio heaters. The photographer is booked, thanks to one of Evie's art school friends. The flowers are so close to being finalized that I can taste it, and then it'll all just be small details until the actual wedding day. I even ordered my dress from Birgit at Vow'd. Polly let me have free rein so long as I stayed in the "color palate."

I'm sort of owning this whole wedding planning thing, honestly, and the cake tasting feels like my reward. Well, that and the actual wedding, but I think I might be looking forward to the cake tasting more.

After taking more design marching orders from Polly, Merilee disappears to retrieve the samples for tasting, her assistant hot on her heels. This is why we're all really here, as is evidenced by the loud gurgling coming from my stomach.

Merilee returns, and her assistant sets a silver tray on the table. In front of us are a half dozen small cakes about the size of large cupcakes.

"I made the two flavors you requested on our phone call last week," Merilee says, gesturing to two cakes on the left side of the tray, "and the other four are flavors I think you might also enjoy based on the sense I got of your palate."

I don't know why "the sense I got of your palate" sounds like an insult, but it really, really does.

Merilee's assistant—whose name I still have not gotten, as it seems she is of the "seen, not heard" variety—passes out forks.

"Pippin," Toby whispers.

"Shhh," I reply, trying to focus on Merilee's descriptions as she explains what's inside of each cake.

"Pippin!" This time his whisper sounds more urgent.

"What?" I mutter.

"This cake isn't good." His words are muffled because his mouth is already full.

"What?" I ask.

"This cake," he says, pointing his fork at a small white cake with a bite out of it. It looks like the inside might be red velvet, but it's super crumbly, and the frosting looks sort of...cracked?

189

It's also *not* on the silver tray. "Something's wrong with it. It's not good!"

Merilee whirls on him. "That cake is a *display*. It's been there for two *weeks*. I don't imagine it would taste very good."

Toby freezes, his mouth held in the international signal for *I need to spit this out*. But nobody moves to provide him a napkin or a trash can or any kind of spittoon substitute. His eyes dart around at us, and then I watch his Adam's apple bob ominously as he swallows the entire bite with all the enthusiasm of a kid who's been forced to eat boiled Brussels sprouts.

I glance up at Polly, whose eyes are wide, and Mackenzie, who is trying very hard not to laugh.

"Okay, well, who wants to eat *fresh* cake?" I ask, and we all grab forks. Merilee, keeping a wary eye on Toby, explains the rest of the flavors. Then she leaves us to taste in peace.

I decide to start with the one Polly's most excited about, a lavender chamomile cake with a lemon ginger curd and lavender buttercream. That's an awful lot of flavors for one cake, but Polly seems to really know her shit, so I figure why not.

I fork a large bite into my mouth.

You wouldn't think you'd need different words for "this is a well-made cake" and "this cake tastes good." But as soon as the bite of Polly's cake hits my tongue, I know immediately that those are two very different things. The cake itself is moist and delicate on my tongue, but the flavor is...well, it's *bad*.

"Ugh, I love it," Polly says, digging her fork into her slice. "Merilee is a genius."

Mackenzie, I notice, doesn't echo the sentiment. Next to me, Toby just smiles.

"What do you guys think?" Polly asks.

"Ummmm..." Toby says, clearly worried Merilee will end him right then and there upon hearing any critique from him.

"It tastes like Nonna's perfume," I say finally.

"I think my mom has a candle that smells like this tastes," Mackenzie says, placing her fork down gently on the edge of the tray.

"Seriously?" Polly says. She turns to Toby, her last chance to get someone on her side.

"I'd rather eat the display cake," he says, and I think I agree with him.

"Sorry, hon, it's just…cake should taste like sugar. Maybe chocolate. Fruit is okay under some circumstances, but this is just…a disappointment," I say.

Polly glares. "Well, what do you suggest? And don't say rainbow chip!"

"I love rainbow chip!" Mackenzie says, and for the first time I see the girl with the collaged walls in her childhood bedroom sitting in front of me.

"Thank you!" And, wonder of wonders, Mackenzie holds up her hand for a high five, which I provide.

Polly stares at her fiancée with her mouth agape, but Mackenzie just shrugs. "What? Boxed cake is classic for a reason," she says.

"I don't want our wedding cake to taste like kindergarten cupcakes!"

"We could do a version of rainbow chip, but elevated," Merilee says, reappearing from the back. I'm guessing she was hiding right outside the door, waiting to swoop in for a victory lap. She scoops up the plate of lavender laundry soap cake and hands it to her assistant, whose nose wrinkles in distaste. Apparently Merilee, ice queen that she is, also believes the customer is always right—or should at least get a chance to taste how very, very wrong she is. Merilee is a Machiavellian boss bitch, and she can sneer at me all she wants, because making that cake was a genius move. "It could be fun and retro, but without all the chemicals."

"Does rainbow chip even taste good without all the chemicals?" Mackenzie asks, and I huff out a laugh.

Merilee looks at Mackenzie like she's something she stepped in.

We taste the rest of the cakes while Merilee disappears into her kitchen, then—through what I'm assuming can only be some form of witchcraft—reappears with a small cake that looks like a very classy version of rainbow chip.

"I had to use sprinkles, but I can make rainbow chips myself using white chocolate. I can mix them into a classic buttercream frosting, and for the cake itself I recommend alternating layers of vanilla bean cake and devil's food," she says, gesturing to two cake options.

"Wow," I say, biting into the devil's food. "Okay, *this* is what cake should taste like."

"I'm shocked to say it tastes better than Duncan Hines," Mackenzie says.

"Seriously, Polly, do this one. I want to eat this again," Toby says.

Polly sighs, but she tastes both cakes. I can tell she wishes she could have the one that tastes like champagne-scented dish soap, but even she has to admit that these cakes are delicious. "Fine," she says, forking another bite into her mouth. "Not my first choice, but these do taste pretty epic."

"Wonderful," Merilee says. She snaps her fingers at her assistant, who pulls out a small pink invoice detailing the cost. And when I see the number next to deposit—just the *deposit!*—it takes everything in my body not to react. Guess Dad is going to be buying the cake for this wedding too.

And he would have *loved* this one.

Chapter 22

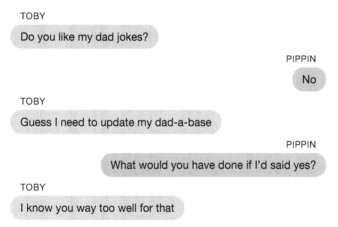

TOBY
Do you like my dad jokes?

PIPPIN
No

TOBY
Guess I need to update my dad-a-base

PIPPIN
What would you have done if I'd said yes?

TOBY
I know you way too well for that

As July fades into the steamy heat of early August, everything actually goes back to normal. Toby and I have not spoken of the kiss again. He was right—we *are* fine. Granted, I haven't gotten to see very much of him in the last few weeks. Residency has completely swallowed him whole.

He's always either at the hospital or sleeping, and I only get to see him for fleeting moments when he's on the way to one or the other. As much as the dad joke texts make me want to roll my eyes into space, at least they mean there's still a bit of him in my day. I missed him something fierce those eight years he was gone, and I'd be lying if I said I don't still miss him. But he keeps assuring me that once he gets "into the swing of things," it will be better. I remain skeptical, but then again, I'm not the one who wants to be an ER doctor when I grow up. Which is apparently now. We're grown up now, which—let's be honest—is fucking wild. Sometimes when I'm with Toby I still feel like I'm seventeen, my whole life and the whole world laid out before me.

As for me, my life has returned to its normal state, which means living and breathing the restaurant for as long as it's mine. I work so hard that I'm able to ignore the question of what will happen when this work disappears entirely. I'm sure Dr. Nora would have thoughts about this coping mechanism, but she's on a book tour for the paperback release of her latest self-help book, *Future to Come*, so I haven't had a chance to run it by her.

Queen's greatest hits are blasting through the kitchen during the lull between lunch and dinner. Ladles, spatulas, and wooden spoons have all been employed as microphones as we lip-sync and work. Evie uses a mop to do some very impressive Freddie Mercury mic stand work as she scrubs the floor.

We're all gathered back in the kitchen prepping for a busy Friday night. Nonna is pressing her thumbs into fresh pasta dough to make orecchiette, Evie rolls silverware when she's done mopping, and Mom is making the base for pistachio gelato, which will be served with her house-made pizzelles as tonight's dessert special.

And I'm standing at the prep table, chef's knife in hand, mincing my way through a crate of garlic.

"It was so bad, Evie," I tell her as I smash cloves beneath

the flat of the knife. "I'm serious, it was like if you marinated Jolly Ranchers in lemon Pledge and then used the sludge to bake a cake."

"I told her I'd make her millefoglie," Nonna says.

"Nonna, we want you to just enjoy the wedding," Mom tells her for the millionth time. Dissuading Nonna from cooking for any event is nearly impossible, but Polly was adamant that our grandmother not spend the days leading up to the wedding making hundreds of sheets of puff pastry from scratch, even if her millefoglie is heavenly.

"Bah, I *do* enjoy baking." She waves us off like bad vibes and goes back to her pasta.

"You vetoed the flowery fruit cake, right?" Evie asks. "Because I'm not saying I won't come if the cake is bad, but if the cake is bad I'm going to have to hunt for a date to distract me."

"You're not bringing a date?"

"I'm thinking about flying solo and picking someone up there," Evie says. "All those businessbots on Mackenzie's side? Surely there'll be someone rich and hot who I'll want to go home with. As long as the cake is good."

"Never fear," I assure her. "It'll be layers of vanilla and devil's food with a luxe version of rainbow chip frosting."

"Thank god. A bad wedding cake has got to be bad juju for the marriage."

"That's true," Nonna says.

"There will be no bad juju for the wedding *or* the marriage," I say, and then reach into the salt cellar for a pinch to throw over my left shoulder for good measure.

The door to the alley clangs open, and a rumpled beanpole clad in light blue scrubs stumbles in.

"Carbs. Lots of carbs as soon as possible, or I'll fall asleep and won't be able to make it all the way home," Toby says. He collapses in a heap on a stool across from me. He doesn't even bother to take his backpack off, just lays his shaggy head on the table.

"Toby, you live two blocks away," I say, never breaking my stride with the garlic.

"I worked all night. And all morning," he mumbles into the cool steel of the table. "And all afternoon. Peds ER rotation. So much crying. So tired."

My face contorts into the expression I get whenever someone tells me my dinner will include beets. "Residency seems like hazing." I decide not to ask if the crying was him or his patients.

"I'm too tired to formulate a rebuttal at the moment."

Fernando drops a plate of orecchiette Bolognese and a fork on the table in front of Toby. He moans like he's just been rescued from the island Tom Hanks was marooned on. After only three bites, he begins to perk up, though he still looks like hell. There are prominent dark circles underneath his eyes and a shadow of stubble across his jaw, and his curls, usually more jaunty, hang limply around his face.

"You're my hero," Toby says between bites, then turns back towards the front of the kitchen, saluting Fernando with his fork. "Thank you."

"De nada, mi amigo. Just promise me that if I ever show up at the ER, you'll point me toward the most well-rested doctor?" Fernando says with a wink.

"You got it," Toby replies with a thumbs-up.

"So how's your checklist going?" Evie asks.

I drop my chef's knife and reach into my back pocket for my phone to open the I-To-Do app. When it fills the screen, I can't help but smile at the row of check marks. Unfortunately, when I scroll down, there are still *so* many more. Including one highlighted in yellow, indicating an upcoming appointment.

"Oh shit, I totally forgot that I'm supposed to go try on my maid of honor dress today," I say, glancing at the mountain of garlic that still needs chopping. "They have to start the alterations if they're going to be done in time for the wedding, otherwise they're going to slap me with another rush charge on top of the original rush charge."

"You go. I can take care of the garlic," Mom says. She pours the simmering gelato base from the pot into an enormous bowl and covers the whole thing with plastic wrap. It'll sit in the walk-in for a few hours until it's perfectly cooled and ready to be loaded into our ice cream maker.

"I'll go with you," Toby says. He's scraping his fork along the empty plate, trying to get the very essence of the sauce off the porcelain. Knowing my best friend as I do, I'm sure that if he were alone right now, he'd absolutely be licking that plate.

"Toby, you're barely conscious right now," I say.

"That's not true. The carbs did their job. I'm practically bright-eyed and bushy-tailed." He tries to illustrate by wiggling on his stool, but he only succeeds in knocking his fork onto the floor with a clatter.

"You gonna get that?" I ask, because he's staring down at the fork like it's fallen into a Mt. Everest crevasse.

"I would, but I think there's still barf in my socks," he says.

"Toby, you're a health department violation waiting to happen. Get out of my kitchen," Mom says, waving her spatula at him.

"I scrubbed!" he swears. "C'mon, Pip, let me come. I feel bad. I told you I'd help you with wedding stuff, and I've barely done anything."

"And how is coming to the bridal salon to watch me try on a dress helping?"

"I don't know, moral support?"

I roll my eyes, but the truth is that I'm excited to get to spend a little time with Toby. I have to take what I can get these days. There have been no film festivals, no lunches in the garden over the last few weeks. The texts are all I have of him, and that's making me almost start to like the jokes.

Ugh, curse the thought.

"If you insist," I say, and he gives a tired first pump and muffles a yawn.

━━

"Eet ees lovely dress." Birgit turns to Toby, who is swaying slightly on his sneakers as he stares around at the mountains of white tulle surrounding him. I bet he's questioning how well he scrubbed all that barf right about now. Birgit points at him. "You like."

As Birgit turns to march us toward the dressing room, Toby leans in and whispers, "Was that a question or a command?"

"I believe it was a fait accompli," I reply.

Birgit leads us past the bridal dressing rooms with their expansive wood floors, round pedestals, and gorgeous lighting to a back hallway lined with more typical dressing rooms, each blocked off by a heavy canvas curtain. Birgit pulls back the curtain on the first stall, where my dress is hanging on a cardboard dress form and zipped into a garment bag, which makes the tableau look like a very elegant crime scene.

"You try on, I come back and mark for alterations," she says, snapping her fingers toward my chest. "You bring correct bra?"

Oh shit. "Uh, I…no?"

Birgit sniffs. I have already failed at this appointment. Her eyes flick down to my chest, which is restrained by a very old Lululemon sports bra that I often wear when I'm working in the kitchen because it absorbs sweat and keeps me from accidentally dipping my tits into pots of sauce when I'm leaning over the pass-through.

"Take zat sing off for alterations," she says, as if she possesses laser vision and can peer through my stained T-shirt at the ratty undergarments beneath. "You have young, perky breasts. Let zem be free."

Toby snorts.

"I...thank you?" I say, but Birgit is already striding back toward the shop floor.

"Is she related to the cake baker? Because they both give off big headmistress energy," Toby says, sinking down onto the bench opposite the dressing rooms. "And not in, like, the naughty fun way."

"I don't need to know your kinks, Toby," I say, stepping into the dressing room. He slumps back, his head hitting the wall with a dull thud. "Just wait there. I'll be done in a sec. And try not to fall asleep."

"I make no promises." He yawns.

I go into the dressing room and slowly unzip the garment bag to reveal my dress. I yank my T-shirt over my head and shimmy out of my jeans. Because I'm the only attendant on Polly's side, she told me I could pick out any dress I wanted in her color palate, which (as clearly stated on our first visit to Vow'd) includes navy and gold. I opted for a rich golden color that works well with my hair and doesn't make my skin look like I've been locked away in a Bulgarian boarding school for a long, cold winter. The dress is made of layers of delicate, gauzy fabric with a deep V at the neck, thin straps, and a nipped-in waist. As I step in and slip the straps over my shoulders, I realize that Birgit it correct. My breasts do look pretty perky, although if I go sans bra, I'm going to have do something about my nipples. It's cold in here, and the fabric is thin enough that I'm putting on a bit of a show. I make a mental note to add pasties to my I-To-Do checklist.

The delicate straps of the dress crisscross over my back, a hidden zipper to close it up. I reach back to pull up the hidden zipper; it takes a little bit of warming up and stretching to even get close, and when I start to pull, it quickly snags on the fabric.

"Fuck," I mutter, trying to gently tug the delicate, gauzy material out of the teeth of the zipper. If I rip it, I'm absolutely screwed. There's not enough time to get another dress in and get it altered, and this material isn't the kind you can just sew up if you rip a giant hole in it.

"Toby?" I call through the curtain.

"Yeah?"

"Are you awake?"

"What do you need?"

"The zipper's stuck. Can you, um…help?"

There's a pause, and then the curtain slides to the side enough for Toby to slip inside. I do my best to hold the back of the dress together. He freezes as he surveys the dress and me in it. His eyes pause at the neckline, and my nipples pebble even more. His gaze quickly flicks back up to mine. He looks like he's working to hold himself very still, his only movement the hard flex of his fingers at his sides.

I glance down at the bright fabric of the dress, then back up at Toby. "Is it…okay?"

Toby's lips part, then press closed. He swallows hard, the cords in his neck working. When he opens his mouth again, a little huff of a sigh escapes. "Yeah. It's…damn, Pip. It's incredible."

My cheeks heat. "It's just a dress."

"You look beautiful. I mean it." His eyes drag down the length of my body, then back up again, his teeth scraping over his bottom lip, his mouth tugging up into a shy grin. "You're radiant."

My cheeks heat, and I can't help but laugh, a nervous tic. "Thanks," I say, trying to shake off the weird feeling that's coming over me. This is no different from when he complimented my prom dress senior year. We went together. As friends.

"Can you..." I nod over my shoulder at the stuck zipper at the small of my back.

There's a pause where I wonder if he's going to say no. If he's going to turn and go find Birgit, who will use her ice-cold fingers to solve this problem. But then he nods, a quick little motion that sends one of his curls over his forehead, his brows knitted together as if I've asked him to go into battle with me.

I turn around to show him the zipper, which leaves me facing the full-length mirror. I can watch him as he watches me. Watch him as he steps up close, his eyes raking down my back. Watch him as he lifts his hands to the zipper, one of his fingers brushing along my exposed skin. Am I imagining it, or is his finger shaking?

My heart is pounding so loud I worry he can hear it. I feel the heat of him everywhere. He works the zipper a little, wiggling it until it lets go of the fabric, and then he slowly—*so* slowly—raises it. His knuckle traces a soft line up my spine, leaving a trail of sparks behind that forces me to swallow a gasp. I watch him every moment. I can't look away. But his eyes stay on my back, on his hands, on the way he's just *barely* touching me. And when he reaches the top of the zipper, he releases it, his hands ghosting across my shoulders and down my arms as he towers over me. They pause at my hips, so close to touching me that I can practically feel the weight of his palms, but then he drops his hands to his sides.

Finally—*finally*—he meets my eyes in the mirror. His deep brown eyes simmer like warm chocolate, his gaze rooting me to the floor. I can barely breathe as I watch him watch me.

"Good?" he asks finally, his voice low and ragged.

It's the exhaustion, I tell myself. He's so, *so* tired.

"All good," I reply.

He nods again. "I'll go get, uh, what's-her-name so she can

do the measurements or whatever." His eyes drop down to the dress once more, and then he turns, slipping back through the curtain.

My heart is in my throat.

I'm breathing so hard I worry I might bust a seam in this dress.

What *was* that?

The curtain flies open, and Birgit stands in the opening, a pincushion tied to her wrist, her eyes appraising every inch of me, and not a bit like Toby's did. I look for him on the bench in the hall, but I don't find him before she whooshes the curtain shut again.

"Not many alterations. Ees good." Birgit starts to pull and pin, and I swear to god she could stick me right in the ass with one of those straight pins and I wouldn't notice. At one point she pinches my side and says, "Breath normal. You suck in, dress will not fit right." And that's when I realize I've been holding in a deep breath, my muscles taut.

From *need*.

"Hey, Pippin, I'm really beat. You mind if I just head out?" Toby calls from the other side of the curtain. The sound of his voice, still rough and just a little off, sends a bolt of heat to my lower belly. So much so that it takes me a moment to process that he's leaving.

"Yeah, okay," I croak out. He's leaving. Shit. What is going on? What the hell *was* that? I'd try Dr. Nora's honesty tactic and straight-up ask him, but it's too late. All I can do is listen to his retreating footsteps.

Chapter 23

TOBY

> Dogs can't operate MRI machines. But cats can.

> Autocorrect really kills that punchline. CAT scan. Cats can. Get it?

I stare down at the text, Toby's first sign of life since he left the bridal salon and—I assume—passed out for a solid twelve hours. I'm comforted by the fact that it's one of his usual ridiculous dad jokes, even if this one is particularly awful.

But also—he's sending me a typical dad joke after he looked at me like that? After he touched me like *that*?

I read and reread the text as I climb the stairs to the attic, having just finished checking in on Saturday lunch prep down in the kitchen. Fernando found another new guy, this one a girl named Kylie whose knife skills are ninja-level and who showed up for her shift a solid fifteen minutes early. She seems more than competent, meaning I can leave lunch in their hands and head upstairs to go over wedding tasks.

I'm buried in the I-To-Do app as I climb the stairs. I shove open the door to the attic and step inside to find Polly and Mackenzie wrapped around each other in Polly's bed, Mackenzie's hand kneading Polly's ass cheek at they make out like one of them is about to ship off to war.

I groan and fling my hands over my eyes, thunking myself in the forehead with my phone. "Come on, you guys. You have a whole-ass condo to yourselves. Why would you want to hook up in a twenty-year-old twin bed?"

"Because it's hot," Polly says, sitting up. Her cheeks are flushed as she smoothes the back of her hair. "Plus, this is one of our last chances."

The ball of lead that appears in my gut whenever I'm reminded of the impending sale starts rolling around, disturbing the tomato sandwich I ate for lunch.

"Can we not talk about it?" I ask.

"Pippin's still in denial," Polly says to Mackenzie.

"I'm not in denial. I know it's happening. I'm just choosing to ignore it for now, while I have eleventy billion other things to deal with. Nonna always says don't borrow trouble."

I can practically hear Polly's eye roll. I drop my phone down on my bedside table and flop down onto my back, the mattress creaking beneath me.

"You're tense. I thought the new girl seemed good," Polly says.

"It's not the new girl," I mutter, then regret the utterance. I'm not in the mood for follow-up questions. But my sister has never been one to let a juicy secret lie.

"Then what is it?" Polly asks.

My phone vibrates with another incoming text.

TOBY

> I'm off Monday and Tuesday. That's two days off. ***In a row*** Come over? Make a list of wedding tasks. We can knock SO much shit out.

"Arghughugh," I groan.

"Ooooo, is it Toby? Did you two finally bone down?" Polly asks.

"No! God, no," I say, but it's too late. The image of Toby on top of me, pressing me into this narrow, squeaky mattress, is blooming in my mind. I can practically hear the headboard banging into the wall. And I like that thought way too much. The only way to distract myself from it, obviously, is to barf out every fragment of thought in my head, whether it makes sense or not. So that's what I do.

"Please stop. We talked about this. You and I, I mean. And also Toby and I. Everyone talked, and everyone came to an agreement that the kiss was a mistake and we're moving on. And then Toby starts changing the conversation with his sexy eyes and his not touching and my *nipples* were hard, and he was looking! He was! And now *you*! Please don't talk about boning Toby. I can't take it. I *can't*. I don't want Toby. I *don't*."

There's a solid fifteen seconds of silence, though the look Polly and Mackenzie exchange is awfully loud.

"Pippin," Polly says, her voice gentle like she's talking to a tantrumming child.

I take a deep breath and try to not freak out again.

"Okay, maybe I *do* want him," I say, trying to slip into logic mode. Problem solving mode. I'm good at this stuff usually. I can figure out how to stretch ingredients when a delivery is short. I can figure out how to Tetris all the reservations in when we're overbooked. And dammit, I can figure out what the hell my feelings for Toby are. "But that doesn't mean it's a good idea. It's like when I was nineteen and I wanted to get those John Mayer lyrics tattooed on me. You talked me out of it."

"And I was right," Polly says.

"Well, hooking up with Toby would be like getting the lyrics to 'Your Body is a Wonderland' tattooed on my forehead."

"You know you can get tattoos lasered off," Mackenzie says.

"Yeah, well, there's no laser for undoing the damage of turning your best friend into your fuck buddy."

Polly wings a pillow at me. Her aim is improving—it glances off my shoulder. "Who said anything about a fuck buddy? I still contend that you love him," she says.

I sit straight up in bed and hit myself in the face with the pillow. "That's worse! What, we start dating, and when everything goes to shit, I have to break up with him?"

Polly crosses her arms and levels me with a look. "What makes you think everything will go to shit?"

I've had this conversation before. I recognize that tree.

"Because it always does," I say. "You've seen me in relationships."

"Did it ever occur to you that maybe your relationships don't work because whatever energy you have to give to a partner, you already give to Toby?" Mackenzie asks.

"Ooooo, that's good, babe," Polly says.

My mouth drops open, because this is new. Man, those Bryan women sure do know how to see through bullshit. "That's not good! Because if it's true, then not only can I not date Toby, I need to back off of my *friendship* with Toby if I ever hope to have a functional relationship."

Polly groans. "My god, Pippin. You will crawl through a mile-long drainpipe filled with horseshit in an effort to miss the point."

"That's…descriptive," I say.

"You should just be honest with him," Mackenzie says.

"Yeah, that's what your mom said, and I did that, and I'm still here."

Mackenzie shrugs. "Honesty isn't a one-stop shop. You have to keep at it."

"Ugh, so I have to talk to him about my feelings *again*?"

"If at first you don't succeed…" Polly singsongs.

I flop back on the bed and growl at the ceiling. "If you guys don't watch yourselves, I'm going to make the DJ play Nickelback at your reception."

"Frantz will wrestle you to the ground before he lets that happen," Polly says. Then she waggles her eyebrows at me. "Now, would you do us a favor and find someplace else to have your breakdown? We were sort of in the middle of something."

Chapter 24

TOBY

What did the pizza say when it went out on a date

I never sausage a beautiful face.

PIPPIN

I don't get it.

TOBY

Say it out loud.

PIPPIN

I'm in line at Whole Foods. I'm not going to tell myself jokes out loud in public.

TOBY

I question your commitment, Pippin.

PIPPIN

As well you should, Toby.

I trudge down two flights of stairs and knock on Nonna's door. God, it's going to suck when my entire family isn't fourteen steps away from me at all times.

Nonna flings the door open. "Oh! Pepperoni, come in. I was just about to switch the DVD!"

I step into the small apartment, closing the door behind me. "Nonna, I showed you how to pull it up on Netflix." I drop my purse on the table by the door and walk into the living room as she slides a DVD out of the season-two box set of *Grey's Anatomy.*

"I like my DVDs," she says, popping it into the player. "Does the Netflix have the bonus content? It does not."

I know she's referring to the extended "steamy scenes" advertised on the box, and you know what? That's fair.

I settle onto the worn leather sofa and pull one of Nonna's embroidered throw pillows into my lap. Her apartment has always been a cozy little haven. The one bedroom, which is located directly over the restaurant, always smells like lasagna and is full of the ambient sounds of Charles Street that filter through the tall front windows. Nonna's furniture is all perfectly worn and molds to your butt for maximum comfort, and there are always good snacks. She's also got a television the size of a Fiat mounted to the wall opposite the couch, which she purchased when her hearing started to go and the subtitles on her old set were too small to read.

"To what do I owe the pleasure, Pepperoni?" Nonna asks as she settles in beside me. She gestures to a plate of Boursin cheese and crackers on the coffee table, and I help myself.

"Can't a girl just want to visit her grandmother?" I ask between bites, little cracker crumbs raining down onto my lap.

"Sure, but you look troubled, cuore mio." She presses play on the remote, but I know she's still inviting me to talk. We've seen these episodes so many times we could perform a community theater version of each one. Throwing on *Grey's* in our family is the same as playing Beethoven. So even though the bright lights of a Seattle Grace operating room fill the screen, I decide to unload.

I tell Nonna everything. About how everyone kept telling me Toby was attractive and I should want him. About my salad theory. How he asked me to be his plus-one because he said the gala was more of a friend thing. How I got high on champagne and ice cream and kissed him in the Public Garden. How we agreed it was a mistake and then he turned around and looked at me in my bridesmaid's dress like I was a king-size Snicker's bar after a long shift.

"Dr. Nora told me I needed to be honest with him, so I told him I just wanted to be friends," I say. "I thought we agreed."

At that, Nonna reaches for the remote and pauses the episode. Then she fully turns on the couch so she's looking me straight in the eye. "But why do you want to be just friends, my darling?"

"Because everything is changing! Polly is getting married and moving in with Mackenzie, we're saying goodbye to the restaurant and our home, I'm going to have to find a new job. It's all too much," I tell her. "I can't lose Toby too."

Nonna sighs and pats my knee. "I think Dr. Nora gave you very good advice. Being honest is always the right move," she says. Then she reaches for another cracker and sets about piling it high with cheese. "There's just one problem."

"What?" I ask.

"You *weren't* honest," she says, then pops the cracker into her mouth.

"What do you mean?"

"You said you didn't want to be with Toby, but you lied, cuore mio," she says, patting my knee. "You clearly have feelings for him. You *want* to be with him. You're just too scared."

I open my mouth to protest, to tell her it wasn't a lie. I *don't* want to be with Toby, but I see immediately the distinction she's made.

"You're not playing fair," I grumble.

"If you were hoping I'd lie to you—or let you lie to yourself —you should have known better, Pepperoni," she says, then drapes her arm around my shoulders and pulls me in for a hug. "I love you too much for that."

"Well, what the hell am I supposed to do now?" I ask.

"I think Dr. Nora was right," Nonna says. "You need to be honest with Toby. But first you need to be honest with *yourself*."

Chapter 25

TOBY

Why did the Star Wars movies release in the order 4, 5, 6, 1, 2, 3?

PIPPIN

I don't want to watch Star Wars

TOBY

Because in charge of sequence, Yoda was

PIPPIN

Okay. But I still don't want to watch Star Wars

It's the end of August, the wedding now just six weeks away. All the big things (venue, dresses, flowers, food) are done, which leaves just the worst parts of project management: all the nitpicky little things like programs and playlists and making sure that evil great-aunt is seated as far away from everyone as possible. Luckily, I have Toby and his *two whole days off* (emphasis his, every time he brings it up, of which there are many) to help.

Before I knock on his door, I take a deep breath in through my nose and blow it out through my mouth. It's meant to be steadying, but I wobble from the effort, which isn't a good sign.

Since the *incident* in the bridal salon (as I've taken to calling it when it enters my mind, which is *a lot*), Toby has kept up his steady stream of jokes, and I've kept up my steady stream of disdain for them. Which hopefully means I'm just walking into my best friend Toby's apartment today and not the apartment of smoldering lust-monster Toby.

If he's just best-friend Toby, I won't have to confront my feelings about smoldering lust-monster Toby. But if smoldering lust-monster Toby is at the door, well...then I'm going to have to try that honesty thing again.

But I won't know until I knock.

So I do.

And I brace myself.

Toby answers the door in a pair of gray joggers and a paper-thin black V-neck T-shirt that stretches across his well-muscled chest. His hair is wet, and he smells like Irish Spring. He flashes me a wide, goofy smile that threatens to take over his whole face. He's not smoldering, but that's cold comfort when he looks like this. I wish he had at least gone with a pair of his novelty pajama pants. I *know* he's got a Bruins onesie in there somewhere. Couldn't he have thrown that on? It might have lowered his hotness factor a smidge.

"What's in the box?" he asks, opening the door and welcoming me in. "Hopefully not Gwyneth Paltrow's head."

"Aww, you finally worked up the courage to watch *Seven*?" I feel like I'm on steady ground, being able to do friend banter with him. Toby *hates* scary movies. On Halloween our freshman year of high school we tried to watch *The Exorcist*, and Toby got so scared that he cried and we had to switch to *The Emperor's New Groove* to calm him down. Memories like that help me remember that I'm walking into the apartment of my childhood best friend. They help me not picture Toby pulling me in for a kiss and then seeing where things go. I cling to the memory of fourteen-year-old Toby's snotty tears and vow to make sure my brain stays on that level all night.

"Nah, I got spoiled," Toby says.

Of course. The more things change and all that. "And only thirty years after the movie came out," I quip.

"I've got a solid streak going."

"Well, you'll be pleased to know that this box is full of programs for the wedding, along with a dozen spools of navy grosgrain ribbon and a hole punch so we can tie a bow at the top of each program. Assuming you're capable of tying a serviceable bow. I brought some extras so you can practice."

"You know I do stitches on actual people every day, right? I think I can handle tying a ribbon."

"We'll see, Sullivan," I say, following him into the apartment. "We'll see."

Inside, the apartment is a wreck. The coffee table is covered with notebooks and folders, photocopied handouts, and a scattering of highlighters, half missing their caps.

"Sorry, I was doing a little studying," he says, gathering the papers into a semi-tidy stack in the corner of the table. "They give us these fake case studies, and we have to present them in seminar. This one attending, Dr. Hollister—he's brutal. This guy got so nervous presenting that he developed an uncontrollable case of the hiccups and Hollister dropped a DSM-5 on the floor to try to scare them out of him."

"Did it work?"

"I don't know, he ran from the room," Toby says. "Should I throw on a movie while we beribbon some programs?"

"Sure. How about *Seven*?"

"Pippin. Come on. Not in front of the programs." He lifts a heavy piece of cream card stock and strokes it like a kitten. "How about something on theme?"

"*Bride of Frankenstein*?"

Toby rolls his eyes. "I was thinking more along the lines of *The Wedding Singer*."

Once there's a decent space cleared on the coffee table and I'm sure there aren't any coffee rings or errant crumbs hanging around to stain the paper, I drop the box and flop back onto the couch. "That works. Hey, maybe we should do Sandler for our next film festival?"

"I vote Drew Barrymore. I mean, can you imagine going from *ET* to *Ever After* to *Never Been Kissed*? She's got incredible range."

We continue to debate movie selections as I unpack the box. Toby proves himself a capable bow-tier while I try to convince him that *Firestarter* isn't *actually* scary. He argues that *Music and Lyrics* is the best Drew Barrymore rom-com while I set up our system for finishing the programs. We both agree that *Fever Pitch* is underrated (and that's not just the Boston talking).

And just like that, the sexy thoughts of Toby slip out of my mind. Just like that, he's my best friend again. Just like that, the world rights itself.

Until an appointment invitation from Mom pops up on my phone.

"Ugh, *fuck*," I groan, swallowing the acid racing up my throat as I press accept.

"I-To-Do disaster?" Toby asks.

"Worse. The guy from the restaurant company is coming next week," I say. "To check things out and make sure they're still interested."

Toby drops the ribbon he's fiddling with, turning to face me on the couch. "And how does that make you feel?"

"Don't psych rotation me, Toby," I say, giving him a shove. "Mom and Nonna are thrilled. And I looked into it. Kelleher is great. They don't have a reputation for destroying the restaurants they acquire. But…I still think I hate them."

Toby cuts a sidelong glance my way. "You're not going to do anything weird, are you, Pip?"

My nose wrinkles. "What does that mean?"

"It's just…well, you've made great strides getting comfortable with Mackenzie and the wedding. You haven't spit on a single one of these programs, for example. But I get the sense that you can't say the same for the sale of Marino's."

I let out a huff. "You mean the sale of my family's legacy and my childhood home, which will also evaporate my job?"

"Yeah," he says, his voice deadpan. "That."

"No, I'm not going to do anything weird." I sigh. "It's just going to be hard, you know? Trying not to imagine what dad would say while this slick corporate guy eyes the place his family built to see if it's worthy."

"I think your dad would be pretty psyched about it, so long as the company is a good fit," Toby says. "Your dad used to talk about selling the place and retiring all the time."

I blink at him. "No he didn't."

"C'mon, Pip, are you kidding? He brought it up constantly. He loved running Marino's, but he had plans to retire to the Cape someday. Eat his weight in lobster rolls and fried clams and breathe the salt air until the sun set. You don't remember that?"

It takes a moment for the image to emerge from the haze. It's always a bit of a gift when a new memory of Dad comes back. It's like being visited by his ghost. All of a sudden, I *do* remember him talking about retiring, about selling Marino's and eating lobster rolls and watching the snow fall on the beach in January. And as much as he loved having me help him out at the restaurant, he never talked about passing the place on to me. He talked about me going to college, having my own adventures, charting my own course.

We never got very far into what those would *be*, unfortunately. But staying at home and running Marino's certainly wasn't an option he considered.

I'm suddenly awash in all the things Dad never got to do. Never got to tell me. Things I never got the chance to ask him.

Being in that kitchen is the only way I still have to feel like I'm talking to him.

A lump forms in my throat. "It sucks that he never got to do that," I whisper, my voice catching. And just like that, it's time to press the release valve on my tears.

Without a word, Toby leans forward and pulls me into a hug, letting me bury my face in his shoulder, his shirtsleeve soaking up my tears. When I open my mouth for a sob to escape, he pulls me tighter, his fingers trailing up and down my back in a slow, steady rhythm. His other hand threads through the curls at the base of my neck, cradling my head. He lets me stay there until I've cried out all my tears, and then I sit up with a shuddering breath, my palms pressing against my cheeks as I attempt to erase the signs of my breakdown.

"It's okay, Pippin. You can be sad with me," he says, reaching out to grasp my wrists, pulling my hands gently away from my face. "You can be anything you need to be with me."

All the breath whooshes out of me at the way he's gripping my wrists, and then his fingers suddenly thread through mine so he's holding both my hands. My heart pounds out a symphony in my chest, and when I glance up, smoldering Toby is back.

My lips part, though I'm not quite sure what I want to say. Or ask.

But then Toby lets go. He sits back, giving the slightest little nod.

"Hey, pause the movie will you? I need to run to the bathroom," he says. I had forgotten there was even a movie on. I glance up at the screen, where Adam Sandler is on the plane befriending Billy Idol in first class.

I glance back at Toby, but he's already up and halfway to his room, his broad back retreating.

My hands are shaking as I reach for the remote on the coffee table, shaking so much that I knock over one of the three half-empty glasses of water he's left behind. The puddle starts creeping toward the stack of file folders full of his work for the hospital.

"Shit," I whisper as I frantically search for something to wipe up the puddle. When I find nothing nearby, I whip off my T-shirt and sop up the liquid. Luckily, because the glass was half empty, it's not much. I can probably just wring my shirt out over the kitchen sink and put it back on.

I scoop up my wet shirt and the other two glasses and head for the kitchen, gathering another three on my way. In the tiny galley kitchen, I drop my shirt on the counter and dump the glasses, then reach for a the dish soap. Might as well wash them—he's got to be on the verge of running out of clean glasses with this many dead soldiers left around his apartment.

I'm midway through the first glass when the hairs on the back of my neck stand up, half a second before I feel the warmth of Toby behind me. He leans forward and puts his hands on the sink on either side of me, his arms caging me in.

"What are you doing?" he asks, his voice low, his warm breath raising goose bumps on my neck.

"Dishes," I say, the word escaping on a shuddering breath.

"Shirtless?"

In that moment, I realize I'm standing at Toby's kitchen

sink wearing only a black bra with a lace overlay. Not my sexiest number, but definitely not my ratty old sports bra either.

"Uh, I spilled water and used my shirt to, uh——" I nod at the sopping heap on the counter. I can't believe I took my shirt off. I also can't believe it matters that I took my shirt off. I've whipped my shirt off in front of Toby plenty of times over the years, in dressing rooms and on camping trips and while executing a quick change in the back seat of a car.

But this feels different.

And as I feel the heat of his attention travel over me, I realize that I like it.

I like it a lot.

Toby grips my hips and spins me around, leaving me face-to-chest with him. I glance up and see that his gaze is rooted to the lace trim lying against the milky-white skin of my chest. His eyes narrow as he watches my breasts swell on a deep inhale. That breath catches in my throat when in one fluid motion, he grasps my waist to lift me and deposit me on the tiny counter.

"I can do my own dishes." His voice is gravelly, and he doesn't meet my eyes. He pauses, his hands pressing into the counter on either side of my hips, and I don't breathe as I wait to see what he does next.

When he turns and opens the freezer, I feel his absence as much as I feel the cold air wash over me. "Ice cream?" he asks, like he wasn't just staring at my chest with fire in his eyes.

"O-okay." This would be an ideal time to try that honesty thing, but I can't manage to form the words. I feel like we're dancing on thin ice here, and I don't know how close I want to get to the cracks.

"Mint chip, cookie dough, strawberry cheesecake, lemon sorbet, or chocolate brownie batter?" Toby asks, his head in the freezer.

"Why do you have so much ice cream?"

"I told you, sugar is my drug. And one of the perks of being an adult is that you don't have to limit yourself. Why choose?"

And somehow, in a matter of seconds, we've tap-danced right back into friend land. "Cookie dough, please."

Toby turns and levels me with a look, one eyebrow arched. It's not smoldering Toby, though—it's teasing Toby. Best friend Toby.

"Only if you promise you'll eat the ice cream part and not just go on a mining expedition for the cookie dough chunks. You always leave my ice cream looking like a squirrel has been in it searching for buried acorns."

I sigh. "Fine. Then I will also require the brownie batter and a big spoon."

"Deal." Toby grins, pulling out the two pints and popping the tops. He sets them down on the counter beside me, then rummages through a drawer until he finds a soup spoon.

Toby turns to the dishes, and I set about scraping my spoon through the cookie dough, then the brownie batter, crafting the perfect bite. But after a few swipes, since his back is to me, I let myself wedge the spoon deep in search of cookie dough gold.

"I know what you're doing," Toby says, never looking up.

"You do not," I reply, my mouth full of cookie dough.

"I could get you a bowl, you know."

"Nah, this is better. I can control the ratio in each bite, plus it won't melt into soup."

"Just don't make yourself sick. I'm out of the barf business when it comes to you."

"That was one time! And I was seventeen!"

"But it was enough barf for solid week. Seriously, Pip, I don't know who told you that melting Jolly Ranchers into Smirnoff Ice was a good idea, but they should be loaded into a rocket and fired into the sun."

My stomach roils at the memory. "Don't remind me. You're ruining my ice cream experience."

"Your punishment for ruining blue raspberry for me forever."

This is good. Toby is firmly in best friend territory right now. He's not smoldering, nor is he shooting me looks as I sit on his counter in my bra eating two pints of ice cream.

He finishes with the dishes and reaches for my shirt, wrings it out over the sink, then lays it flat to dry on the stovetop.

When he's done, he turns to me. "Can I get a bite?"

"Fifty-fifty?" I ask, waving the spoon over the open pints.

He cocks his head at me, his brows knitted together in mock outrage. "Pippin, you know me better than that."

I duck my head to hide the blush I cannot contain. I focus on scooping him a heaping spoonful of brownie batter, then dig out one nugget of cookie dough from the other pint. I hold out the spoon handle first, but he doesn't take it from me. Instead he dips his head and takes the bite directly off the spoon, his tongue swiping along the bottom of the spoon. I swallow hard, my eyes on the bob of his Adam's apple. I know I'm not controlling my face—my eyes have gone wide, my lips parting in surprise—but at least he can't tell that a rush of heat floods between my thighs.

Toby shoots me a wicked grin, like maybe he *does* know about my thighs and what's happening between them. Smoldering Toby is *back*, and my god, he's working for me.

"Don't get brain freeze," I stutter, a suggestion that must come directly from my own frozen brain. I have no idea what to do with a smoldering Toby, not when we're crammed together in this tiny kitchen, no one to interrupt us. Not when I'm wearing only a bra and my nipples are so hard I worry they're going to bore through the fabric. Not when I'm squeezing my thighs together with enough force to start a campfire.

"Cold is not my problem at the moment," Toby says. His eyes drop to my mouth, still sticky sweet from the ice cream. My tongue involuntarily swipes my lower lip as I pull in a shuddering breath.

Honesty. Might as well try it.

"Toby, it feels like…" My brain is swirling, working overtime to both form words and restrain my body. Toby is so close, and I want to touch him so badly. But…*honesty*. "Are you flirting with me?"

"For a while now," he says with a sly grin. "Is that okay?"

Honesty.

"Yes."

Toby reaches up and runs his knuckles down my arm, leaving a trail of goose bumps behind, his eyes on the swelling of my breasts over my bra as I try to keep my breath from coming in heaving gasps.

"Do you want me to keep going?"

I don't even need an honesty check this time. The *yes* bursts out of me with such force that it draws a low chuckle from Toby.

I don't know who moves first. It happens so fast. One minute we're looking at each other, the next our mouths are crashing together. Toby grips the nape of my neck, his other hand going to my hip. He pulls me close, my knees parting so he can step between them like he's always been there.

The first time I kissed Toby, I was caught off guard. Even though I was the one who started this whole kissing thing, at the time I was too busy being shocked and flustered to fully enjoy it. This time, though? This time I revel in the way he claims my mouth, his tongue demanding as it sweeps across mine. This time I moan against his lips as his hand creeps up from my hip, his thumb pausing at the lacy band of my bra, sweeping beneath the swell of my breast. This time I flex my fingers against the muscles of his back, this time I tip my chin up and tilt my head to take in more of him, wrap my legs around his waist and memorize the hard ridge of him, all too apparent in those gray sweats as I pull him closer.

"Fuck, Pippin, you feel so good," he says, his forehead pressed to mine. His hips roll against me, sending a ripple of pleasure through my core. His fingers tangle in my hair, gripping tight, the slight pull on my scalp so delicious I can practically taste it. "Can I touch you?"

"Yes," I hiss, answering with a hip roll of my own. We're already racing past just kissing, and there's a part of me that wants to ask if this is a good idea. But that part of me quickly drowns in the feel of Toby's thumb skating over my nipple. I drop my head back and sigh, giving him a chance to lower his lips to my throat, dropping a line of gentle kisses along my collarbone. His fingers gently tug at the cup of my bra, freeing my breast so he can roll my nipple between his fingers. *God*, just that alone makes the taut tension of an orgasm form low in my belly, and when he couples that with another thrust of his hard cock against my center, I nearly come apart.

Holy fuck, I have never felt anything like this, and I'm still wearing most of my clothes.

I reach for Toby's face and bring his lips back to mine. I need to give, because if I just sit here and take, I will lose it and this will all be over too fast. I busy myself with exploring his lips, his tongue. He nips at my lower lip, and I let out a low moan that would embarrass me if I didn't feel so goddamn good. But that's nothing compared to the sound that comes out of me when Toby dips his head and pulls my nipple into his mouth, his tongue laving across my pebbled skin, his hand kneading my other breast.

Holy *fuck*, honesty was a good idea.

"You are so...delicious," Toby says, his lips fluttering against my skin with each word. "The most goddamn gorgeous thing I've ever seen."

I could spend all night here, my head pressed against the kitchen cabinet as Toby lavishes my breasts with attention. Hell, I could come from just this.

But Toby's not done. His hands leave my breasts and float down to the hem of my leggings, grasping the waistband. He drops to his knees right there on the kitchen floor, then gazes up at me. Before he speaks, he leans forward and nuzzles his nose along the seam. I writhe against him, desperate for more.

"I want to taste you," he says, his hot breath causing me to move even closer to the edge of the counter, closer to his lips. His eyes flick up to mine, and his voice is low and husky, but sure. "Please?"

I have lost the power of speech, so all I can do is nod as I stare down at my best friend between my thighs. His cheeks are flushed, his brow furrowed, every muscle in his body taut and corded. He tugs on my leggings as I lift myself slightly off the counter, canting my hips so he can slide them down. He discards them on the floor, then places his large hands on my inner thighs, spreading me wide, the evidence of my arousal pink and glistening before him. Feather-light kisses dance up my left thigh. He crosses over to the right with the most torturous puff of air that makes my back bow, then kisses down that thigh. I'm nearly levitating by the time he returns to my center. The tip of his finger slides ever so gently down my seam as he gazes at me in wonder.

"For me," he says, and I can't tell if he's talking to himself or if it's a question for me. Either way, I'm unable to respond, all the breath gone from my lungs. He leans close, his curls tickling the insides of my thighs, and I groan in anticipation. I have never wanted anything as badly as I want Toby's tongue right now.

"Please, Toby," I gasp, arching to bring myself closer to him. My entire body feels like a live wire, tight and quivering.

The anticipation is no match for the feeling, though, when

he finally laps me up in one long, firm stroke. God, I hope these old brick town houses have good insulation, because I cannot suppress the guttural sound that explodes out of me when his tongue begins working in light circles around my clit. My legs tremble, and I tangle my fingers in Toby's curls so I don't rocket right off the countertop. He lifts my calves and rests my thighs on his shoulders, his hands going to my ass to steady me as he meticulously takes me apart. His firm grip, kneading into my skin, lets me tremble and shake without fear of falling.

Except I'm *definitely* falling.

But I shove that terrifying thought out of my brain, or maybe Toby's tongue banishes it, because as his fingers sink into the curve of my ass, his mouth works to bring me right to the brink.

"So sweet," he says as he devours me. "You taste so fucking sweet."

"Don't stop," I whine, pulling hard on his hair.

"Never," he says, and then he's silent because his mouth is busy holding me right at the edge of the biggest orgasm that's ever built inside my body.

"Fuck. More. Please. God. Right. There." I'm an explosion of one-syllable exclamations, all my brain can do as the coil of the orgasm tightens inside me. And when Toby releases one of my hips to slide two long, thick fingers inside me, I swear I nearly black out as that coil releases, flooding my body with sparks. I collapse over him, heaving, my thighs shaking as the reverberations of the orgasm flow through me.

Toby looks up, meeting me eyes, a smile on his face. "Good?" he asks.

"So fucking good," I reply through breaths so heavy I feel like I've just run a marathon.

I can't fucking believe we did that.

And yet, having stood at the edge of the pool and dipped

my toe in only to find that the water is *warm*, I suddenly want to dive all the way in. I want to slip my whole body inside this moment and float, enjoy. I'm not ready to get out just yet.

So I slide off the counter, gripping Toby's hips and walking him back a few steps, enough to give me space to kneel. The evidence of his arousal is thick and heavy against the seam of his sweats. I glance up at him to see his eyes dark, his pupils huge as he watches me on my knees, dipping my fingers into his waistband. He reaches out and grasps the counter behind me like his knees will buckle without the support.

It's not until I've freed his erection, long and thick and so fucking hard, that I take my eyes off him. My mouth waters as I stare at Toby's cock.

"Only if you want to, Pippin," he grinds out, his forearms flexing as he grips the counter like he's at the top of the first hill on a roller coaster.

I do not examine why the answer is an emphatic yes or if this is a bad idea. If we're going with honesty, then honestly I want his taste on my tongue. I want to feel Toby come apart the way he just made me come apart. I want to feel all of it. All of *him*.

"I am *made* of want, Toby," I say.

I grasp the length of him in my fist and give a gentle pull, causing him to suck in a breath through his gritted teeth. I can't help the grin that spreads across my lips at how much I want this and how much I like watching him want it too.

I guide the smooth crown of him to me, gently painting the bead of wetness across my lips, then swiping at the salty trail with my tongue.

"Fucking hell, Pippin," Toby groans. "I feel like I could die from this."

"But what a way to go." I grin, then lave the length of him with the flat of my tongue, circling around the head before sucking him into my mouth. His hips jerk when I rake my teeth across his velvety skin, then follow the scrape with my tongue. I suck and lick and tease until I feel his thighs begin to quiver and his breath comes in shuddering gasps, and when I grip him and pull him deep and hum, a tortured sound grinds out of him.

"I—Pip—I can't—I'm gonna come." He gasps, and when he starts to pull back, I hold him deeper, unrelenting in my attention to his cock. My fingers move over the length I can't take in as he twitches against my tongue. When his orgasm finally rips through his body, I swallow every drop until he collapses over me, his forehead on the countertop.

"Am I dead?" Toby mutters.

"You're the doctor, don't ask me," I say, rising to my feet, still reveling in the salty, heady taste of him.

Toby stands up and gathers me into his arms, his chin on top of my head. "Are you okay?" he asks. I feel his body brace.

And mine does too. Because Toby and I just had orgasms. Together. He came in my mouth. I came in his. I'm not freaking out, but I'm afraid that if I look too closely at this, I might.

"I'm not sure?" I say, sticking with honesty. It's worked for me so far, after all. I've never had an orgasm quite like that.

Toby is completely still, a feat for someone who just came so hard he nearly left finger indentations in the marble counter. "Do you want to talk about it?"

"Do we have to?"

"At some point we probably should," he says, planting a kiss on the top of my head. He yanks up his sweats and moves back a few steps, releasing me so he can lean against the stove, arms crossed over his broad chest.

I nod. What just happened with Toby was incredible. I think I want it to happen again. There's a possibility I never want to do anything else.

But it's not that easy, and my reservations—despite all this honesty—remain the same. I mean, the look on Toby's face right now is so fragile, so fractured, that I can barely stand to look at him. I'm *terrified* of what comes next. We haven't just crossed a bridge, we've torched the motherfucker behind us. There is literally no going back.

But that doesn't mean I'm strong enough to go forward at this moment.

"Can we, um, get a rain check on that talk?" I finally ask, staring down at my bare toes on the tile floor.

Toby's hands go to his hair, pulling at it until it's standing up, and then he scrubs them down his face. He scoops up my leggings, holding them open so I can step in. He reaches for my still-damp T-shirt and tugs it over my head. Then he leans down and plants a feather-light kiss on my lips.

"I know you have a lot going on right now, so this conversation can wait," he says, pressing his forehead to mine as he floats his hands up and down my arms. "*We* can wait. Just promise me you won't go home and spiral. That you won't work yourself up and then avoid me. Promise me that when you're ready, you'll talk to me."

I nod, the tension in my body unspooling a little. "Thank you."

We pad back into the living room, where he helps me pack up the box of programs, then walks me to the door. I'm out on the stoop when he calls to me. I turn and see him leaning through the doorframe, his hands pushed deep into the pockets of his sweats, his curls falling over his eye. A part of me really wants to drop the box and leap into his arms, kissing him back into that apartment until we find his bed. Part of me want to know what Toby would feel like inside me. Part of me wants to be consumed by him. To consume him. To melt into him until all my insecurities disappear.

But my orgasm haze is lifting, my heart is pounding, and

my mind is noisy with fears and insecurities and persistent thought spirals that keep me rooted to the bricks.

I hate that I'm leaving right now, but I love that he's letting me.

Only Toby would.

He gives me a rueful smile, his dimple deepening. "Just don't take too long, okay, Pip?"

Chapter 26

TOBY

What's the best way to make a small fortune in the stock market?

Start with a big fortune.

PIPPIN

That one was kind of bleak?

TOBY

Sorry, I don't know any business jokes, and the google results weren't great.

PIPPIN

You mean those jokes don't all live in your head RENT FREE?

TOBY

Pay no attention to the man behind the curtain. Good luck at your meeting, Pip!

Toby is true to his word. Our twin orgasms have a pin in them, waiting for future discussion. In the meantime, he's been sucked back into the hospital, leaving me with only a steady stream of groan-worthy jokes.

Not that my brain will let me forget what happened for a single solitary second. I just keep replaying the scene over and over again like a mental porn video. I walk around in a constant state of arousal, blushes constantly climbing my chest and neck and settling high on my cheeks.

On Thursday afternoon while I'm layering lasagnas, I have a flash of Toby sucking my nipple into his mouth that's so intense I drop a spatula loaded with béchamel onto my foot. On Friday night while bussing a table of half-empty wine-glasses, I swear I can feel the way his tongue circled my clit, feather-light and steady. I wind up with a red wine stain on the white button-up shirt I've worn to work front of house. On Sunday morning as the sun starts to break through the windows, I roll over in bed and let out an embarrassing moan, having just woken from a dream of Toby coming in my mouth.

By Monday, I am so horned up I can barely function.

Which is a problem, because today is the day of our meeting with Charlie Bruce of the Kelleher Group. The fact that I have to welcome in the man who's going to take over my father's restaurant, give him a tour and show him all the things I love that he will probably change, all the symbols of my child-hood and the love of our family that are soon to be painted over and refinished? Well, that's enough to keep me from running back over to Toby's apartment and jumping into his bed.

I cannot deal with anything else while I'm dealing with this.

It's the first week of September, and the heat of the summer is starting to burn off, leaving behind the cool rustle of leaves. With just six weeks until the wedding, my I-To-Do checklist is nearly complete. This should make me happy. Giddy. Ecstatic.

Except.

The plans for Polly's wedding are basically the only thing I have under control. Everything else in my life? Still a disaster. If only I-To-Do made a similar app for planning everything else. I could certainly use a checklist for that.

- *Figure out what you want to do with the rest of your life*
- *Write your very first résumé*
- *Find a job (in this economy!)*
- *Find an apartment (in this market!)*
- *Pack up your childhood home and all your family's earthly possessions*
- *Say goodbye to the only home you've ever known*

And it all needs to happen very fast. Because Wanda Barnes was exactly right. As soon as our building hit the market, we were flooded with inquiries. But because Mom and Nonna are hoping the buyer will keep the restaurant open, we haven't accepted one yet.

That's what today is for.

If Kelleher comes through, they'll buy the building and the business, continuing to operate Marino's while they rent out the apartments upstairs to new tenants.

As I wait at the hostess stand, alternating between straightening the stack of menus for the seventeenth time and checking the time on my phone, I think back to Toby's warning not to do anything weird. I definitely don't plan to. I couldn't do that to Mom and Nonna. But that doesn't mean I have to smile while a business bro pokes through my restaurant like it's an estate sale. I don't need to be gracious when he shows up to my professional funeral.

I think I'm going to be sick.

Kelleher acquiring Marino's is actually a dream scenario. They're local, their restaurants are well respected, and they can certainly afford to buy the place. But if this meeting goes well, it means I'll be one step closer to saying goodbye to my childhood home. To all I have left of my Dad.

But if I fuck things up, Kelleher could pass and Marino's could wind up being some Chuck E. Cheese monstrosity that will forever taint our family legacy.

It's a real lose-lose for me, huh?

The door opens, letting in the light and sounds of Charles Street, and a guy a few years older than me ambles in. He's wearing a suit, but his jacket is draped over his arm, his sleeves rolled up to his forearms, and he's carrying a well-worn leather messenger bag. If he'd just come in to order the lasagna before everything turned upside down, I would've already be plotting how I could get his number. But I already have his number, printed at the bottom of the emails we've traded regarding the sale of my entire life.

Cool cool cool.

"Hi, you must be Pippin," he says, sticking out his hand and giving me a Kennedy-esque grin. "I'm Charlie. It's nice to finally meet you."

"It's nice to meet you too," I reply. A lie, of course, but I'm not going to fuck this up. If I'm going to arrange the transfer of my entire life into someone else's portfolio, then I'm going to do a damn good job of it. So I direct him to the back banquette. "I've got us set up back here."

I lead him to the booth, where I've set up my laptop as well as a stack of files and binders all hauled out from Dad's office. At the sight of all the paper, Charlie raises his eyebrows.

"I know, it's not the most environmentally conscious, but ever since Oyster Island got attacked by Russian hackers in that massive small business blitz, I keep paper copies of all my most important files. I print double-sided to keep the footprint small, two pages per side, and I've got it all color coded and organized for quick access," I say. "Don't get me wrong, everything's also saved on hard drives and backed up to the cloud, but you can never be too careful, especially when your business is in perishables."

Charlie sits down and starts flipping through binders, nodding appreciatively. "That's actually really smart. Kelleher got caught up in that same attack, and we ended up paying the hundred and fifty thousand they demanded," he says. "With payroll across all the restaurants, it was just too much data to lose. And insurance paid for some."

"Well, Marino's is prepared for that and more," I say, launching into an explanation of the ways in which I've streamlined back-end administration. As I talk, I forget that I'm trying to convince this guy to take my restaurant, because *this* is the part of the job I actually love. Don't get me wrong, the cooking is in my blood, but it's hard, dirty work. The organization, all the paperwork, all the stuff Dad hated most? That's where I live.

"I'm really impressed with your systems," Charlie says. "I can see the benefits right here in your accounts. You've certainly maximized profit for a restaurant this size."

"Well, it helps that we own the building outright."

"True, but even factoring that in, you're doing better than a lot of restaurants in similar positions, especially these days. I see a lot of family restaurants, even well-loved ones, that get run like hobbies. But you've really done the hard work here, and it shows."

"Thank you," I say, my cheeks warming. Nobody's really ever noticed all my paper nerdery before, much less complimented it.

"If you don't mind me asking, what are your plans for after the sale? Are you hoping to stay on and run the restaurant?"

"Oh god, no," I say, then quickly try to walk back the outburst. *Don't be weird, Pippin.* "I mean, I think Kelleher is a great fit for Marino's, and I'd be proud for the business to join your group, but I don't think…" I trail off, not wanting to blow the whole meeting by saying something rude.

"Once you've been the boss of a place, it's pretty hard to step back?"

"Exactly," I say, though it's a much more elegant way to put it than I probably would. I was thinking more along the lines of *I can't watch a stranger raise my baby.* "I'm still trying to figure out what my next move will be."

"Well, you have a real talent for this kind of work. I have a buddy, he runs this consulting firm that specializes in helping floundering restaurants. Sort of like Gordon Ramsey but without all the yelling. I think you'd be a really good fit. I could pass on your info if you're interested."

I start to decline as a reflex, but then I realize a couple of things. One, I need a job. And two, that sounds like a job I'd be really good at.

"That would be great," I say. "I don't have a résumé at the moment."

"That's okay, I'll just shoot him an email telling him about our meeting and sharing your contact info. I think he's going to be impressed by what I've seen here today." Charlie pulls out his phone and starts typing, apparently not wanting to waste any time.

"Thank you. Really. I appreciate it."

"Of course," he says, dashing off an email. "There, sent."

"Wow, okay. Thank you."

"Well, I wanted to get that sent off so that when I ask you out for a drink, you don't think it's in any way tied to the offer.

I don't want to be, you know, weird or coercive," he says, and he smiles.

He's unquestionably handsome, and in any other universe I'd be making plans with him right now. But I'm living in a very weird universe at the moment. One where I've seen my best friend's cock and am constantly thinking about the places he hasn't yet put it.

"That's really sweet," I say. "Unfortunately I've got a lot going on right now with the sale and the move, and I'm also planning my sister's wedding, which is in a few weeks. So I think I'm going to have to decline."

Not quite honesty, but pretty close. I think Dr. Nora would approve.

"I completely understand. Oh, and just so you know, I'm absolutely recommending that Kelleher acquire Marino's. I think it would be a great fit for us. So don't think…" He trails off, grinning again, and watching this sharply dressed, capable man stumble over his words is deeply gratifying if completely uninteresting to me. "I don't know, sorry, I think I just made it weird."

"You didn't, it's absolutely fine. You were a perfect gentleman, and I'm going to recommend that my mother and grandmother accept Kelleher's offer. We're all good," I assure him. *Damn, play hard to get, Pips.* But I just don't have it in me. I really think Mom and Nonna are right. This is not just what Marino's needs but what the Marinos need. Maybe even myself included.

"Thank goodness. I'd feel like a real ass if I offended you and messed up a deal on a place as good as this," he says, his cheeks reddening. "You know, I actually met your dad once."

I freeze, my head cocking. "You did?"

"Yeah. I was working for this godawful catering company, my first job out of Dartmouth. Think college dorm cafeterias and hospital food. Just absolute shit. I was miserable and hoping to find something new, and the National Restaurant Convention was in Boston that year. I think it was maybe eight, nine years ago? Anyway, I was at a networking event and ran into your dad in the beer line. He took one look at the company name on my badge and bought me my beer. Told me I was too young to be that miserable. He actually recommended I look at Kelleher. He knew our CEO from way back, I guess, said he was hoping to turn his place over to us when he retired. It took a couple of years for me to get my foot in the door, but I was glad he put me on the trail. I love this job."

I don't realize I'm crying until a tear drips off my jaw and lands on my collarbone. I gasp, reaching up to swipe the wetness away.

"I'm so sorry for your loss," Charlie says, pulling a handkerchief from his pocket and passing it to me. I use it to dab at my eyes, but I know my mascara is already a lost cause.

"Thank you," I say, and I mean it. Because he just gave me the gift of a new story about my dad. I can picture him towering over Charlie, two sweating plastic cups of beer in his hands as he muscled his way through some crowded industry event. Dad *hated* those corporate catering companies, called their recipes cat food and slop. Nothing would have made him happier than making sure a charming, talented young guy like Charlie ditched their corporate asses. He probably did it as much for his own amusement as for Charlie's benefit. And knowing he was already thinking about Kelleher, planning to leave Marino's to them…it's like he's sitting right beside me on this banquette, patting me on the shoulder, saying, "It's time, Pepperoni."

God, I miss him.

"Well, I should probably get going—I've got a conference call back at the hotel. But it was really nice to meet you, Pippin. And look for an email from Nate Hawkins about a job interview. He's definitely going to want to talk to you." Charlie gathers his bag, shaking my hand firmly before starting for the door.

"Thank you again. Really. I've been a little at sea trying to figure out next steps, so it'll be good to at least get the lay of the land."

"Of course. We'll be in touch," he says.

And then he's gone, and though the deal isn't done, it feels close. And I feel…well, I don't know how I feel. I mean, I *killed* that meeting. Certainly the adrenaline of having done a good job in an intense situation is making me want to jump six feet into the air. And while the thought of walking out of Marino's for the last time still makes me feel like I'm being pushed to the bottom of a pool, Kelleher is going to acquire it, which means it will keep being Marino's. I may have to leave, but it'll still be here for me to visit, if I can ever bring myself to do that.

And this is what Dad wanted.

I gather up the binders and start ferrying them back to Dad's office. Funny how I still call it Dad's office, never mine.

And now it never will be.

My eyes catch on the framed photo sitting next to a pencil cup on Dad's desk. It's of Dad standing in front of Marino's twenty-six years ago, a car seat in each hand and a giant grin on his face. Polly and I are in matching knitted hats as Dad welcomes us to our new home. Polly is snoozing, and I'm screaming like I'm being murdered.

I sigh.

I should call Mom and tell her the good news. She and Nonna have been perusing Zillow but have held off on actually looking at anything until they were sure the sale would happen. Now it looks like they can get with a realtor.

But before I can dial, my phone dings with a new email.

From Nate Hawkins.

Pippin,

I just saw the email from Charlie. I wanted to let you know that we have a position open now, and I'd love to talk with you about it. The most important thing you need to know, though, is that it involves a lot of travel. Mostly domestic, as that's where our clients are, but we do send our consultants overseas every once in a while to meet with producers and suppliers. Also, Charlie mentioned that you've worked in the kitchen at your restaurant, which is great experience, but keep in mind that the job here wouldn't involve much of that. You'd be meeting with restaurant owners, helping them assess their menus, their procedures, and their administration in order to help them achieve their goals. A lot of people have been interviewing for this job without a full understanding of what it is and isn't, so I wanted to get that out of the way.

If this position is something that sounds interesting to you, shoot me an email. I'd love to set up a phone interview. Charlie speaks really highly of you, so I'm already impressed. Kelleher doesn't acquire just any restaurant, so the fact that you've already run a place of that caliber speaks volumes.

Hope to hear from you soon.
Nate

Travel? Do I want to travel? I've certainly never done much of that. In twenty-six years, I've barely left New England. There was the one school field trip to Washington, D.C. and a cousin's wedding in Chicago in middle school. But other than that… There's so much of the world I haven't seen. So much I *want* to see. Even if it's just metropolitan Orlando.

Do I want to travel?

Absolutely the fuck yes I do.

And when you add that this is an entire job where I'd get to be (gently) bossy and comb through spreadsheets and menus and make checklists for other people? If I were praying person, I'd be running straight to St. Michael's to light a candle. But none of us have been very Catholic in years, and the last time I was in a church was for Dad's funeral, so instead I reach for a Marino's matchbook and light the little red glass votive candle on Dad's desk. It glows ruby red, and I close my eyes and send a wish up to the restaurant gods—or maybe to Dad—asking them to smile down upon me. Then I blow out the flame and write an email to Nate.

That sounds exactly like something I'd be interested in. I'd love to chat with you. Here's my number, just let me know what time works best for you.

Pippin Marino

Chapter 27

Did you hear about the restaurant on the moon?

Great food, no atmosphere.

PIPPIN

Get your ass over here before these jokes make me change my mind

"Knock-knock," Toby says, leaning against the frame of the office door. *Damn*, the man can lean. "How'd the meeting go?"

"What?" I ask, temporarily distracted by his forearms, which are crossed over his chest. But then I remember we've put a pin in that and shake it off. "Oh, yeah, it was good."

"Good like you think they're going to take over?"

"Good like I think they're going to acquire the restaurant and maybe I also have a lead on a job?"

Toby's eyebrows shoot up into his hairline. "Here? At Marino's?"

I shake my head. "No, the guy I met with from Kelleher told me about his friend who runs a consulting company and is looking for someone who can travel around helping restaurants figure out how to be more profitable."

Toby lets out a low whistle, then drops into the chair across from the desk. "Are you serious? That sounds great!"

I smile. "Yeah, it kind of does, doesn't it?"

"That would be the perfect job for you."

"It would, I think," I say. "Of course, I'm going to have to put together a résumé, which I've never done before, and I don't even know if he's going to think I can do the job once he talks to me. I've only got a first interview, and—"

Toby places both palms flat on the desktop, leveling me with a look. "Pippin Marino, stop talking yourself out of this before you've even had a phone call. You're smart and qualified, and this guy has no reason to blow smoke up your ass about what he's heard. So please let yourself off the hook and revel in the good news."

I let out a long breath and realize my heart is pounding. Because while I've been busy planning this wedding and orchestrating the sale, I've sort of set my future on the back burner. But now it's here, staring me in the face, and I'm a little bit scared. I'm scared that I'm not good enough. I'm scared that even if I am good enough, this isn't the right thing. And I'm scared that I won't know the difference.

"Pippin," Toby says, his voice a gentle warning. "I can still see you spiraling."

I nod and lock eyes with him. My best friend, who knows just how to talk me down. Thank god for him. Thank god I haven't messed that up yet.

"You're right. This could be a really good thing. And I think I would be great at it. And my résumé shouldn't be *too* hard to write, since I've only had one job."

"Damn right," Toby says, and starts to get up, but before

he can rise to his full height, I reach across the desk and grab a handful of his shirt, yanking him down until his lips meet mine. Fuck the pin—I feel too good right now. Toby's *made* me feel too good. And I want to chase that feeling.

I kiss him so hard that I rise out of my chair, climbing up on top of the desk so I can crawl closer to him. He's so tall that even kneeling on the desktop, I'm just barely at eye level with him, my arms around his neck as I tangle my tongue with his. He wraps his arms around my waist and pulls me close. As he licks a warm trail from behind my ear down my neck, leaving me sighing into his hair, he says, "I would fuck you right here right now if it didn't mean staring at several framed photos of your father while I took you."

Holy god.

I pull back, a grin on my face as I try to slow my breathing. "Yeah, we should probably stop," I say. "Sorry, I know we agreed not to do, uh, *that*, but—"

"No, no, climb over a desk to kiss me anytime you want," he says, smiling back. He lets me go and reaches down to adjust himself inside his jeans. "And congrats on the sale. Everything's going to stay the same? With the restaurant?"

"Yeah," I say, lowering myself off the desk and gathering a few papers. "I mean, I'm sure *some* things will have to change, and they're going to do some upgrades to the kitchen and bathrooms and stuff, but the staff will get to stay on, and Kelleher can pay better than we're able to, so everyone seems to be coming out on top."

"Well, congrats again. Want to go celebrate? I have to work tonight, so no champagne, but how about a slice of pizza?"

My stomach growls. "Pizza sounds great."

We walk back to the front of the restaurant so I can make sure everything's locked up when Charlie reappears.

"Hey, sorry, I left my jacket," he says. He smiles, then points to the back banquette, where his navy suit jacket is hanging over the back of the booth. "Thank god you're still here—I have a board meeting this afternoon, and coats and ties are required."

"Of course," I reply. "I got an email from Nate, by the way. The job sounds great. I'm going to talk to him about it."

Charlie grins, a real sixty-watt smile. "That's great! I think you'd really like the work. You certainly have a real talent for it."

I smile. "Thanks again for making the connection. I really appreciate it."

"Of course, Pippin. Happy to help. And let me know if you ever want to get that drink," he says. "As colleagues, I mean."

"I will, thanks."

The door swings closed, and suddenly I feel Toby next to me, very close and seeming extra tall.

"Who was that?" he asks, staring at Charlie's back as he passes by the front window.

"Charlie Bruce. He's the guy from Kelleher," I say. I lock the front door and gesture for Toby to follow me out the back, which will put us closer to our favorite pizza place.

"That guy? Handsome McSmileyface?" Toby says. His tone has a weird edge to it, so I glance over my shoulder to catch a glimpse of his face. I'm too slow, though, and Toby has already rearranged his expression into once of nonchalance.

"Uh, yeah. I guess."

"What did he mean, 'as colleagues'?" He hooks his fingers into the most sarcastic air quotes I've ever seen, which is really saying something.

"Oh, he asked me out."

"Like, on a date?" His eyes grow wide, as if I've just told him that Charlie offered to father my children.

"Yes. But I said no. I told him I had a lot going on with the sale and my sister's wedding."

Toby's hands flex hard at his side, his brows knitting together. "*That's* why you told him no?"

"Yeah," I say.

"You didn't tell him that you're, you know…" He gestures between us.

"I didn't think it was any of his business," I tell him, and when his brow furrows, a look of irritation flitting across his face, I throw up my hands. "What, was I supposed to go into a whole soliloquy about the nature of our relationship with a guy I'm hoping will drop ten million to buy my family's business? That seemed unprofessional, to say nothing of the fact that I have no idea what the nature of our relationship even is!"

I feel the sudden stillness of an oncoming storm, like the clouds are about to swoop in and make everything dark. The birds have stopped chirping, dogs are staring at the sky, and any minute a tornado siren will sound.

"Pippin, can we talk?"

There it is.

"I thought you said we could put a pin in it," I say, busying myself by wiping stray wax pencil marks off the hostess stand with my sleeve. There's a scratch over table twelve, and I really should try to get some rubbing alcohol to deal with—

"Well, I think maybe now's a good time to take the pin out," Toby says.

"But…I mean, there's so much going on, and I don't know…" God, I can hear myself sounding like an absolute fucking idiot, but I also feel like Toby is shoving me to the edge of a cliff in high winds. He's making me look down at the rocks below, and he's asking me to wiggle my toes over the edge while he points at the danger at the bottom.

Toby steps forward, grasping my arms as he dips his knees so he's at my eye level. "I know it's really scary right now, Pip. But let's rip the Band-Aid off. I don't think it's going to be as bad as you think. Let's just talk about it. It's pretty clear we can't keep our hands off each other."

I shake him off, my heart pounding. I'm scared about what's at the bottom of that cliff. I'm scared it's the wreckage of our very long, very incredible friendship. "I don't want to talk about it," I say, stomping away to straighten the silverware rolls on table four. "If we talk about it, everything will change."

Toby huffs out a laugh. "You think *talking* about it will change things? Pippin, you've had my dick in your mouth. Things *have* changed."

God, the sentiment crushes me. It destroys the fiction that because he let me run away, we are still Pippin and Toby, best friends and nothing else. Makes it crystal clear that this is just an illusion, that I broke things already. Maybe back when I kissed him the first time.

"I'm sorry, Toby. I just…I really liked being with you. Touching you. Feeling you. Can we just leave it at that for now?"

Toby shakes his head. "I can't be your best friend and your fuck buddy," he says, his voice filled with a bitterness I've never heard from him.

"We're not fucking," I say.

His head snaps up, and I can't tell if that glare is coming from a place of anger or hurt. "Don't try to play by Clinton rules."

I throw my hands up. "So, what, you want to be in a relationship?"

"You don't?"

"Not with you!" I cry, the words exploding out of me.

Toby stills. "Ouch," he says, his voice quiet.

"I don't mean it like that. I just…" I huff out a sigh. This is all going so badly. Fuck, this is why I didn't want to talk about it. And this is why I can't have a relationship with him. I'll fuck it up the same way I'm fucking up this conversation.

Toby lets out a low chuckle, but there's no joy in it. "I'm sorry I'm not some bland idiot who can't be bothered to get to know you well enough not to break one of your many unspoken rules. One of those guys who's so weak that you never have to worry about them breaching any of your carefully built walls."

Now it's my turn to glare at him. "Hey, that's not fair."

"Neither is this, Pippin. What you're doing to me. Leaving me hanging. It's not fair," Toby says. He crosses the worn carpet on the dining room floor and takes my chin between his thumb and forefinger, tilting my head so I can't hide from his searching gaze. "Pippin, this isn't just messing around for me. What happened the other day—I've never felt like that before. I want to feel like that again. I want you to be *mine*. I *want* you. I want *you*."

There's a lump in my throat, and when I speak, my voice breaks. "You mean so much to me, and I'm so scared of…well, I'm just scared. I didn't realize you'd already made it to this point, the relationship point. Everything happened so fast. I'm still getting used to the fact that you give me orgasms."

"Well, catch up, Pippin. Because you mean something to me too. You mean a lot to me, and I know you say you don't want a relationship because you're afraid it means you could lose me."

He leans forward and presses his forehead to mine, taking my cheeks softly in his palms. His thumbs rub across my cheekbones, swiping away the tears that are starting to fall. He sighs, his warm breath a whisper across my lips.

"I can wait for you, Pippin," he says, his voice low. "If that's what you need, I can wait. I can be your friend. But that's all I can be while you figure this out, okay? Because being with you the other day was too fucking good. It felt like *everything*. But we're operating without a net here, and I'm afraid any more might wreck me."

Then he brushes my lips with the softest kiss, just a whisper of contact that nearly breaks me. I feel the truth right there on the tip of my tongue, begging to get out. I desperately want to ask him to stay. To give him everything. To let myself just *love* him.

Instead I feel a fat tear roll down my cheek as he turns and walks out the door.

Chapter 28

TOBY

Good news. Successfully switched my shifts so I can come to the wedding. I look forward to hearing which of my jokes you're working into your maid of honor toast.

PIPPIN

See, was that so hard?

TOBY

Switching shifts? Yes. It was actually very hard.

PIPPIN

No, I meant texting me without a dad joke

TOBY

How do you get a country girl's attention?

PIPPIN

I'm blocking your number

TOBY

A tractor!

I'm not sure if it's by accident or by design, but for the next six weeks, all I see of Toby are those blasted texts. His residency is absolutely brutal, full of rotations and labs and lectures and frighteningly little sleep. And I'm busy with my own kind of boot camp that comes with the sale of both a building and business. There are inspections and paperwork and so many conference calls as Kelleher prepares to take over.

In those six weeks, we manage to close the deal. Kelleher will temporarily shut down Marino's before Thanksgiving so they can complete a much-needed kitchen renovation and some updates to the dining room. The plan is for them to reopen the new Marino's in the new year.

I have my first interview with Ladl, Nate Hawkins's consulting company. And despite my total lack of experience with job interviews, my vast experience with running every aspect of a restaurant seems to shine through. We schedule a second in-person interview for the Monday before the wedding.

Polly submits and successfully defends her dissertation. She's officially Dr. Marino, and she's got interviews lined up at four schools, all of them in New England.

And through all of it, I keep being friends with Toby. Just friends. Because the thought of shaking up that relationship amid the frenzy of checklists and contracts and plans makes me want to walk directly into the ocean. That's not to say I don't think about his tongue or his hands or his lips at odd intervals throughout the day, because I do. But our mismatched schedules make it much easier to pretend that nothing had changed.

For now.

And then suddenly it's October thirteenth.

The night before the wedding.

After a rehearsal dinner in the Marino's dining room that doubles as a family farewell of sorts, Polly and I are upstairs, washing off turmeric face masks before we crawl into bed, both exhausted and high on the giddy anticipation of the following day.

"Tomorrow is going to be incredible," I say, stacking my pillows so I won't wake up with a crick in my neck. I have to cruise direct an entire wedding, so it is imperative that I don't sleep cramped like I'm in a deep-water submarine berth. "Everything is good to go, it's going to be beautiful, and I think we might even have some fun!"

"I can't believe what a complete one-eighty you've done," Polly says, settling into her bed. Her face is shiny with layers of oil and moisturizer and something called a sleeping mask that I skipped because I'm too scared to try a new product and wake up with a zit the size of a pepperoni. "When I told you about the engagement, you looked like you wanted to snatch the ring off my finger and pitch it into the Charles River."

I wing a pillow over at her, aiming for her chest so as not to muss her mask. "I was just...surprised, is all."

"Because it was so fast?"

"That, and it didn't seem like you, getting married so young," I explain, thinking back to that shocking moment four months ago when this whole wild journey began. "You've always been so independent. Charting your course. You picked your path, and you followed it. All the way across the ocean."

Polly laughs, climbing into bed. Then she clicks off the lamp so our room is illuminated only by the streetlights outside. I feel a hitch in my throat as I realize this is probably the very last time we'll lie in bed next to each other in the dark.

"I never told you how Mackenzie proposed," Polly says out of the darkness.

I sigh. "That's because I'm a rotten sister who never asked."

A pillow wings back through the dark and slaps me in the face. In the four months she's been back in the attic, her aim has returned.

"I forgive you," she says. "So we went to Paris for a weekend trip Mackenzie had planned. She'd been several times before, but it was my first time, so we did all the touristy things —cafés and pastries and champagne and the Eiffel Tower. It was perfect. And on the last day, we went to the Musée Rodin, and right there in front of *The Kiss*, she pulled out a diamond ring and asked me to marry her."

"Wow," I say. It's a perfect proposal, especially for Polly, who's always been a sculpture fan. I know *The Kiss* is one of her favorites.

"And I said no."

I gasp, sitting straight up in bed. "What? Why?"

"Because it seemed fast! And it didn't seem like me or like part of the course I'd charted for myself." I let my own words wash back over me as I imagine it—Mackenzie standing there with a ring in *public* while my sister said no. "It was awful. We went to dinner after, and the restaurant was expecting a newly engaged couple. There was a bottle of Veuve Clicquot in one of those silver ice buckets by the table."

"Oh my god, you still went to dinner?"

"Yes! I didn't want to break up, I just didn't think I wanted to get married. So I was trying to keep the whole thing together," Polly says, groaning. "We got back to London and were sort of walking on eggshells, trying to find a way back to normal, when Mackenzie came down with this awful cold. Just coughing and hacking and so much snot—it was disgusting. So of course I went over to take care of her. I brought the good drugs and plenty of Kleenex, and I even emailed Mom to get her chicken noodle soup recipe."

"Excuse me, you *made* soup?"

"I know. I too was shocked."

Yeah, both the cooking and the caretaking are wildly out of Polly's wheelhouse. She has never liked being around illness, and that got worse after Dad died.

"Mackenzie was beside herself because god forbid there was a single task she couldn't do for herself. The woman is as bad a patient as I am a nurse. But in that moment I knew. I needed to take care of her, and she needed to let me. Forever, if we could. So after she took a twelve-hour Nyquil nap, I asked *her* to marry *me*."

"Holy shit, that's so romantic!"

"I mean, not totally, because she was still *really* full of snot," Polly says, laughing. "But those are the times when love matters most. When the plans have evaporated and everything is shit, if you can still look at the other person and say, 'At least I'm going through this shit with *you*,' then you know it's real."

I lie in bed, staring at the two remaining glow-in-the-dark stars that are still stuck over my bed with ancient gobs of sticky tack. And even though I want to run through checklists and contingency plans and check the weather for the eleventy billionth time, all I can think about is Toby. Because hasn't he always been that for me? The one I can go through shit with? The one whose hand I can hold when things go down? In twenty years, I haven't managed to fuck that up, so why am I so sure that changing the nature of our relationship would automatically nuke things? He already knows my secrets, my fears. He knows how to cheer me up and how to calm me down. He's always held a piece of my heart in his hands.

Why can't I just let myself give the rest to him?

Chapter 29

TOBY

Why was the shoe late for class?

It was tied up!

Sorry, you're probably asleep

The shoes.

I sit straight up in bed, my heart racing, because I forgot about the shoes.

Polly is due to walk down the aisle in—I fumble for my phone, which is shoved underneath my pillow—seventeen hours, and if I don't get out of bed and deal with her shoes, it'll be more like a hobble.

I climb out of bed, avoiding the squeaky floorboard so I don't wake Polly. I reach into my closet and pull out the first thing I touch, which turns out to be a pink fuzzy knee-length robe with a unicorn hood. I start to search for something a little less *insane* when Polly groans and rolls over in bed. I can't risk waking her up and ruining her pre-wedding sleep, so I shrug the robe on over my T-shirt, grab Polly's shoes from the box, and fly down the stairs as quickly and quietly as I can.

As soon as I emerge onto the street, I register that it's a little too cold to be wearing pajama shorts, but my adrenaline takes over, and I plant my butt on the stone stoop and begin to strap my feet into Polly's heels. They're navy silk, her something blue, with glass Art Deco brooches on the toes. Very twenties—very Gatsby, if Daisy Buchanan wore three-inch stilettos. They're beautiful.

Then I stand.

They're torture.

I start pacing. It's midnight, but since it's Friday, there are still a lot of people out on Charles Street, and they're looking at me like I might be in need of an ambulance. I am, after all, marching up and down the cobblestone sidewalk in black silk sleep shorts of the teeny tiny variety, a hot pink robe with a silver unicorn horn on the hood, and a pair of navy bejeweled high heels.

It's a *lot* of look.

So I head for a side street, which will be quieter and less likely to draw stares.

And as I walk, I do what I do best: I make lists in my head. I start with wedding tasks, running through my to-do list for tomorrow like I used to recite the prayers in CCD. Then I move on to the checklist for the rest of my life, which usually makes me despair. My first interview went remarkably well, but the second will be higher stakes. I could absolutely still fuck it up. If I do, I'll have to start a real job search. And regardless of what happens, I need to start apartment hunting. Which means I'll need all new furniture. I can take some things from the attic, but I think it's finally time to upgrade from the twin bed. I'll need dishes and cookware and a couch. Where you even get a couch?

Oh god, I'm going to have to drive down to Stoughton and go to IKEA.

And that's the thing that snaps my tether to rational thought. Because you can't go to IKEA alone, not if you want to buy furniture. Storage bins? Sure. An ottoman? Okay. A coffee table? Well, that depends on how many storage drawers it has. But when things like couches and dressers are involved, those boxes require a buddy. And Polly is getting married and Mom's moving to the Cape and I'm too scared to tell Toby that I probably love him so I can't ask him to go IKEA with me, because who knows what I might say in those aisles?

I feel my thoughts spiraling out of control. It's like when I was little and would twist the swings until the chains buckled. Once I picked up my little feet, the swing would start to spin, picking up speed, and there was no stopping it, not without scraping your knees something awful. You just rode it, spinning faster and faster and hoping you wouldn't wind up dizzy enough to throw up.

"Pippin?"

I spin around so fast that my (Polly's) heel catches on a cobblestone and I go down in a heap.

And that's when I realize that I'm in front of Toby's house. And that Toby's standing there in front of me, panting in running clothes.

"Are you okay?" he cries, reaching for my hands and helping me to my feet. Unfortunately, between the heels and the breakdown, I'm a bit like Bambi on ice, so Toby doesn't let go of me.

I don't hate that.

"Why are you out running?" I ask. I step back, because the warmth of him through this absurd pink robe is doing things to my insides. I make sure I'm steady on my borrowed shoes before I meet his eyes. "It's midnight!"

He cocks an eyebrow at me. "Why are you stomping around at midnight in pajamas and high heels?"

I level him with a totally undeserved glare. "You first."

"I had to take two weeks of nights in order to get off for the wedding, so I'm trying to get my body on schedule, get used to being up until seven a.m.," he says like it's obvious, then gestures to me. "Now you."

Unfortunately, my explanation makes much less sense. "I forgot to break in Polly's shoes," I say with a sniffle. "And I sort of had a freak-out, and I think I've destroyed my feet."

Because it's at that moment that I realize my toes feel like they're in a vise grip made of cheese graters and are maybe in danger of detaching from the rest of my body.

"Oh god, I'm going to get blood on Polly's wedding shoes!" I wail like a person having a breakdown. Because that's what I *am*.

"Well, it can be her something borrowed," Toby says with one of those eternal-optimist shrugs he's so good at. "Let me help you."

But I'm not ready to be helped. I'm *wallowing* and *spiraling* and I am not capable of getting off this swing yet. "You can't help me!" I cry. "These shoes won't fit you!"

Toby laughs. "That's not what I mean, crazy lady," he says, and then, without another word, he scoops me up into his arms. "I have actual medical expertise, if you'll recall, so let me help you."

I sniffle into his shoulder. He's warm and sweaty and smells like the ocean, and I can already feel my heart starting to slow.

"I can walk," I say as he starts toward his apartment door.

"All evidence indicates you cannot," he says. "So just hush and *let me help you*."

He manages to unlock the door to his apartment while barely jostling me in his arms, and the next thing I know I'm being welcomed into the cozy den of his home. It's still full of clutter and half-empty water glasses and open medical text-books and journals. But it's warm and it smells like him, and suddenly the spinning stops. Everything falls away except the fact that I'm in Toby's strong arms and he smells like sweat and cedar and—

I am in love with him.

Toby bypasses the couch and brings me into his room, setting me down on his bed before going into his bathroom. He emerges with an honest-to-god first aid kit, a white box with a red plus sign on it, and he cracks it open to reveal of full pharmacy of Band-Aids, gauze, scissors, and everything else you need to fix blisters or sew a foot back on.

"So...pre-wedding freak-out?" he says as his strong fingers begin to gently unbuckle the straps of the shoes from around my ankles.

"Sort of," I say. "More like...a *life* freak-out?"

"Well, you do have an awful lot going on," he says, cocking an eyebrow at me. My eyes cut toward the door—I can see directly into the kitchen, the scene of our dueling orgasms.

I'm about to get lost in the pleasure of those memories, but then Toby douses a gauze pad in what must be alcohol, because when he touches it to a spot on top of my big toe, I hiss in a breath.

"Sorry," he says, then leans down and blows on the spot, providing almost instant relief. Why does that work? Are there actual medical studies about the effects of blowing on a wound? Should I ask Toby that? Right now?

Jesus Christ, Pippin.

As usual, my brain is coming up with anything other than what I *want* to say. What I *need* to say.

And while I sit here and ponder ways to tell Toby that I am *definitely* in love with him, he cleans my poor burgeoning blisters and bandages my toes with special cushy Band-Aids.

"What would I do without you?" I say, still not ready to give voice to my real feelings.

Toby sits back on his heels and starts to pack away the supplies. He shrugs. "This is just basic first aid. Get yourself a Girl Scout and you'll be good to go."

"True, you aren't a great Samoa connection."

"Well, Siobhan's youngest is joining Daisies, so give me some time," he says with a wink. He digs some adhesive moleskin out of his first aid box and hands it to me. "You can put this inside Polly's shoes, and you'll probably need it inside yours too with all these blisters."

I let out a breath that's half sigh, half laugh. "Honestly, Toby, what would I do without you?"

"Google could have told you about this," he says. He snaps the lid closed and meets my eyes. "You're not helpless, Pippin. You're just overwhelmed." Then he reaches for my leg, his warm hand cradling my calf as he examines his work. "How's that feel?"

His long fingers are brushing softly against my bare skin, and when he looks up at me, his chocolate-brown eyes are like warm pools I want to sink into and never come out. My entire foot could be hanging off my body and I don't think I'd notice because the flood of warmth low in my belly would drown out the pain.

"Toby," I whisper, reaching down to brush his cheek. "I know I'm not helpless. But that doesn't mean I need you any less."

And then I cup his cheeks and lean down until my lips brush his, softly at first, then with more intention. Because while I still haven't figured out how to say what I need to say, I know I can show him.

He kisses me back immediately, his hands sliding up the backs of my arms and gripping me tightly, pulling me toward him, a groan rumbling up from somewhere low inside him. But then he pulls back, putting just enough distance between us that he can look me in the eyes.

"Are you sure?" he asks.

"*Yes*," I reply so quickly he barely has time to finish his question.

"No, I mean it, Pippin. Are you *sure*?" he says, his voice filled with vulnerability. And I can't tell if he's asking more for me or for *him*. "Because last time—"

"I'm sure," I say, my lips pulling up into a grin. "I've caught up, Toby."

A grin starts at the corner of his mouth, then quickly spreads across his face, into his dimple and up into the little crinkles at the corners of his eyes. If last time was a whirlwind of confusion and questions and concerns, this time feels like an absolute explosion—a full Fourth of July fireworks show —of *yes*.

We crash back into each other, and even though I've kissed Toby before, this feels new. This feels like the start of something, like a door has opened, one I can't wait to bolt through. He scoops me up and lays me back gently against his pillows, coming to rest beside me, his lips never leaving mine. And I immediately want to be closer. I want more. I throw my leg over his waist and pull him toward me, reveling in the way he rolls his hips against me. Toby, it seems, is also *very* sure about this, and the feeling of him hard against me sends a flood of warmth between my thighs.

But we're in no rush. It's like we have a decade of making out to catch up on. By the time his fingers reach beneath the hem of my T-shirt, leaving a trail of heat along my bare skin, I feel like we've been kissing for hours. His thumb traces a warm line beneath the swell of my bare breast, and just that, that barely-almost-not-quite-there touch makes me gasp. I am *made* of desire, but Toby stops again. He pulls back just enough to meet my eyes, his curls flopping over his forehead as he hovers above me.

"Are you *sure?*" he asks again, his eyes searching mine for any sign that I'm going to regret this. But there are none.

"*Yes,*" I reply, reaching up and tugging on one of his rogue curls. "We can stop and talk about it if you want. I'm ready. Or we can just…" I walk my fingers down his back and slip them beneath his running shorts to grab his muscular ass.

He grins and huffs out something between a laugh and a sigh of relief. "Thank *god,*" he says. Then he strokes his thumb across my nipple, and I'm gone for him. For this. I want him so badly I can taste it, and when I kiss him, our lips parting so I can brush my tongue against his, I do.

"I just have one last question," he whispers against my lips.

"I'm *sure,* Toby. I won't run this time," I say.

"I know, Pip," he says, running his tongue along my jawline and settling a warm kiss just below my ear that makes me moan into his. "I just wondered if maybe we could lose the unicorn robe?"

I bark out a laugh—I'd completely forgotten there was a glittery silver unicorn horn splayed across the pillow over my head. This man, my best friend, wanted me even when I was wrapped in hot pink fur like some deranged Muppet. My god, how did I get so lucky?

Instead of answering him, I sit up, shrug off the robe, and lose the T-shirt while I'm at it. I shove the waistband of my black silk sleep shorts and underwear down my thighs and shimmy and kick until they fly off my toes and into the corner of his room. Fully naked, I flop back onto the pillows, stare him directly into his eyes, and wink.

I swear the man stops breathing for a full minute. He sits up and lets his eyes roam over my bare skin and swallows. *Hard.*

"No more questions?" I ask.

He shakes his head, speechless.

"Good," I reply. And then I reach for the waistband of his running shorts and pull him back down to me. "I think we've waited long enough."

He's out of his clothes and laid out over me in seconds, and even though he just got back from a run, he smells salty and delicious. I lick a trail along his collarbone and pull him closer to me, his cock pressing into my belly. His hand skates down my chest, pausing to roll my pebbled nipple between his thumb and forefinger before dancing lightly along the curve of my waist and over my hip before finally dipping between my warm folds. As he brushes my clit, I let out a deep moan, my back bowing off the bed.

"You're so wet for me, Pippin," Toby says as he slides two of his fingers deep inside me, curling to find a spot that makes me see stars. "I will never get over how wet your pussy gets. For *me*."

I can't believe I've spent all these years being friends with this delicious man and I never knew he had a dirty mouth. I know immediately that the sound of those words coming out of Toby will never not turn me on. And I want more.

"Nobody has ever touched me like you," I say.

"And nobody ever will." His teeth sink into my ear before swiping at the sting with his tongue. I pant as his fingers continue to explore my pussy, my hunger rising like a fever. I roll my hips against him, chasing release, but he pulls his hand away. I nearly whine as he brings his hand to his mouth. "You are delicious, Pippin Marino," he says, his voice rasping as he sucks the taste of me off his fingers. "But I want to feel you come when I'm inside you."

Toby props himself up on one arm and reaches into his bedside table drawer, pulling out a condom and placing it on the tabletop. It's a dance I've done dozens of times, but I'm suddenly overcome with the desire for something new. Something I've never done before, since this is a night of absolutely delightful firsts.

"We've never actually talked about this, but I have an IUD," I tell him, my eyes cutting over to the condom. "And I haven't been with anyone since my last test. Which was clear."

Toby nods, trying to suppress a jubilant grin. "Same. Clear. And there hasn't been anybody else," he says.

I smile at him. "Good. Okay, well, if you're comfortable, then I'm, well…"

"Just you and me," Toby says, his eyes locking on mine. He takes my hands in his and strokes his thumbs across the backs of them. Then he slowly raises them until he's got my arms pinned over my head, lowering his nose until it brushes mine, his lips whispering against my mouth. "Nothing between us?"

"I want to feel you, Toby," I shudder as the head of his cock brushes against my swollen clit. "Just you."

"Thank fuck," he utters like the dirtiest prayer as he notches against me. I bend a knee to open for him, hooking my leg around his hip to pull him close.

"Now, Toby," I say. Now that I can have him, I can't wait another minute. I can't believe we ever wasted a moment not doing this. Not feeling *this*. I angle my hips to welcome him inside. "Please."

He grinds out a deep groan that starts in the center of his chest and rumbles in my ear as he slowly begins to slide inside me, stretching me, filling me. My eyes start to drift closed at the sensation, but I force myself to open them, to watch his face as he disappears inside me. His cheeks are flushed, his teeth sinking into his lower lip, his throat working as he swallows another moan.

God, he's so beautiful, my best friend.

As soon as he's fully sheathed inside me, Toby lowers his forehead to mine and lets out a long, shuddering breath.

"Is this real?" he says against my lips, his eyes heavy-lidded. I can feel the pounding of his heart against my chest. I can feel the hitch of his breath. I can feel the tautness of every muscle in his body as he tries to hold himself back. And all I can think about is the time I was nine and I found an old skeleton key in a cookie tin in Nonna's closet. I spent days wandering around the building, through the apartments, in and out of all the closets and around the restaurant kitchen, sliding it into various locks and attempting to turn it, until finally finally *finally* I ventured down to the basement and discovered an old wooden door I'd never noticed before. There was a great hulking iron lock on it, and when I fished that key out of my pocket and slid it in, the delicious click as it turned made me hiccup with delight.

That's how I feel right now. Like I've found where my key goes. Like everything fits, moves together, *belongs*.

"It's not a dream," I whisper, partially for Toby and partially for myself. Because nothing has ever felt this good, this right. Not in my waking life. Not ever.

Until he begins to move.

I feel the most delicious drag as Toby shifts his hips and slides out, then back in, bottoming out with a decadent groan.

"It's too good," he says, burying his lips in my neck, his fingers flexing into my hair and against my neck and shoulders, settling into a slow, mind-melting rhythm. "Goddammit, Pippin, you're perfect."

All I can do is whimper as his thrusts become more urgent, his hips canting so he catches my clit on each slide. I reach up and brush his curls back, feeling the sweat that is beginning to dampen his temples, heat pooling between us as his pace becomes punishing. I sink my fingers into his hair and tug as he pushes me closer and closer to release.

"What do you need?" he says, his hand cupping my breast, his thumb tripping back and forth over my nipple. "Tell me what you need to make you come."

My words have all left me—the tight coil of impending release sits low in my belly. All I can do is take his hand and guide it between us to the place where we're joined, and luckily I don't need to explain further. Toby gathers my slickness with two fingers and begins to circle my clit, mirroring the pace of his cock as he drags it in and out of me.

"Oh god, don't stop, please don't stop," I mutter, the words running together in a garbled plea for more and deeper and harder. I urge him on with my hips, beg by sinking my fingers into the corded muscles on his back, plead with him as his forehead presses against mine, our eyes locked together. "I'm so close, Toby. Please don't stop."

"Never," he says, then captures my mouth with his, his tongue tangling with mine. And when he pinches my clit between two fingers, my vision tunnels and I let out a scream people can probably hear down in Fenway. My molten orgasm ripples through my body like a stone in water, the reverberations growing bigger and wider until my ears are ringing with my release.

"Fuck, Pippin, I'm coming," Toby grinds out, following me over the edge, pulsing inside of me, the sensation of him filling me new and decadent and perfect.

He collapses, his warm body covering mine, rolling us onto our sides so he can gather me to his chest without crushing me. He plants soft kisses along my jaw as we work to slow our breathing.

He's still inside of me when I realize that I want to spend the rest of my life hearing Toby Sullivan call out my name as he comes.

Chapter 30

My phone beeps inside the pocket of my unicorn robe, which is lying in a heap next to the bed. I groan, rubbing far too little sleep out of my eyes as I lean over the edge of the bed. I am achy in all the best places from being worked over and soothed by Toby late into the night. It takes me a minute to dig through the folds of hot-pink fabric to find the phone and open the text message.

TOBY

> What did the patient with the broken leg say to their doctor?

I fall back onto Toby's pillows and roll over to see him naked and smiling, his phone in his hand.

"Well, aren't you going to answer?" he asks with giddy excitement. The man can barely contain himself.

I want to roll my eyes or groan, but something about how his wild curls are falling over his forehead but still not concealing that boyish spark in his eye makes me smile. So I tap back.

PIPPIN

What did the patient with the broken leg say to their doctor?

TOBY

Hey doc, I have a crutch on you.

And goddammit, I laugh.

"I knew it! I knew you thought they were funny!" he says, and I reach behind me to grab a pillow and whack him in the face with it.

"I think it's more that you're texting me from right next to me in bed and you're *naked*," I explain, lifting the sheet to glance down at his muscled frame, and his cock grows harder under my watchful gaze. "That's the only way I find those jokes funny."

"Well, that'll just have to be the procedure going forward," he says. He drops his phone onto the bed and rolls over to plant a kiss on my lips.

"You're awfully awake for someone trying to get onto a nocturnal schedule," I say as his hand skates up the outside of my thigh and comes to rest on my ass.

"Yeah, well, it's hard to sleep when reality is better than my dreams," he says. His lips trail along my collarbone, his tongue dipping low into the valley of my cleavage. I'm just about to pull him on top of me when my phone beeps again. Only this time it isn't a text message; it's the alarm I set last night, long before I went tromping out in pajamas and high heels and wound up in Toby's bed.

Because today is Polly's wedding day.

"Shit, I have to get moving," I say through a groan, because it is not the kind of moving I want to be doing. But there's lots to be done still before Polly walks down the aisle. There's makeup and hair, flower delivery and cake delivery and checking in with the caterers and the photographer. I-To-

Do even has a special checklist *just* for the wedding day, and that only adds to the giddy feeling I have from waking up next to Toby.

"Sorry, you can go back to sleep," I say, then lift his arm so I can snuggle up into the little nook of his shoulder. He reaches around with his other arm and envelops me in the warmest, most delicious hug of my entire life.

"How about this—you jump in the shower, and I'll run down to Starbucks and get us coffee and breakfast," he says. "What do you want, egg bites? Bacon gouda?"

My stomach growls, and I know it's going to be hard to find a moment to eat in the craziness of this day, so I tell him I want a bacon gouda and the biggest coffee they'll sell him. He climbs out of bed and puts on a pair of sweatpants and a Mass General fleece, and before he heads for the door, he pulls me in for another knee-melting kiss.

"You're not freaking out?" he asks.

"Not a bit," I tell him.

"Good," he says. "I feel like there are things to say, but maybe we can do that after the wedding craziness is done? I'd love to take you out for an honest-to-god date, Pippin Marino."

"I'm in, Toby Sullivan," I reply, my smile so wide I feel like my cheeks are going to crack.

Toby goes to fetch breakfast, and I climb out of bed, ready to jump in a hot shower, but then my phone beeps again. I reach for it, expecting another cheesy dad joke from Toby— maybe even hoping for one—but instead it's a text from Polly.

PIZZA

> Where are you??? The DJ called. He has
> the flu!

Shit. Well, it's not a wedding unless at least one thing goes wrong, and I'll take this over pouring rain. But this means my shower is going to have to wait, because I need to get back home and get this show on the road. There are brides to dress and fires to put out. So I fire off a text letting Polly know I'm on my way, then pull my sleep shorts and T-shirt back on, stealing one of Toby's sweatshirts instead of donning my ridiculous robe. I also rummage in his closet and find an old pair of flip-flops, and though they're about six sizes too big, they're a marked improvement over those torturous heels. I tap out a quick text to Toby as I head for the door.

PIPPIN

> Wedding emergency, rain check on breakfast! Maybe tomorrow morning after you bring me home from the wedding tonight?

I'm nearly outside before I remember that I left Polly's shoes at the end of Toby's bed, where he put them after taking them off me last night. I turn and hurry back, dropping down to fasten the straps and then looping them over my fingers so I can carry them without dinging them up. Then I head out, letting Toby's front door swing shut behind me.

I walk as fast I can in Toby's giant shoes, tripping occasionally over the cobblestones but managing to stay on my feet. As I head for home, I formulate a plan for the missing DJ. We can easily put together a patchwork of Spotify playlists and make Frantz our substitute DJ; he'll want nothing more than to spin his favorite records at his daughter's wedding. He'll also make a stellar emcee, announcing the dances and the cake cutting. Hell, I wouldn't be shocked if Frantz got the DJ sick himself so he could take over the job.

"Pippin! Hi!"

I blink myself back to the present to see Jen, Toby's ex-girl-friend, smiling at me from the sidewalk outside the dry cleaner. I must stare at her for a beat too long, trying to figure out if I'm hallucinating her in my underslept oversexed state, because she smiles wider and points at herself. "It's Jen McKinley? Toby's…uh, well…I was—"

"Of course," I say, partly because I recognize her and partly because *of course* I would run into Toby's ex-girlfriend the morning after I slept with him. Of course I'm the embodiment of the walk of shame while she looks like a #bossbabe in a navy pantsuit. Of fucking *course*.

"How are you?" I ask, because *what the fuck are you doing here* seems impolite.

"I actually just had an interview at MIT," she says with a mile-wide grin. "Yeah, the scientist running the lab where I worked in California turned out to be a total misogynist prick, so I have to get out of there. But they offered me a spot here, so it looks like I'm moving!"

"To Boston?" I'm sure I'm blinking *way* too fast, but I can't seem to control anything I do at the moment.

"Yeah! Isn't that wild?"

"The wildest," I say. Is that even a word? Or is it *most* wild? Could this matter any less right now? Because I'm standing in front of Toby's beautiful genius ex-girlfriend, and the *ex* part was entirely because there was a whole ass country between them, and now it looks like there won't be. "Does Toby know?"

"Yeah, I'm actually on my way to his place. We're supposed to meet for brunch. I mean, he doesn't know I got the job. I'm going to tell him over brunch. But he knew I was interviewing," she says. She's babbling, her cheeks reddening, and I can tell she's excited—about the job, and about telling Toby she's moving here. Jen glances at my borrowed sweats, at Polly's heels in my hand. "Is that where you're coming from?"

Jen interviewed for a job *here*. She wants to move here. She has plans to meet Toby for brunch *today*. And Toby never mentioned it. Not yesterday. Not before we kissed. Not the morning after he was *inside me*.

Oh god. I feel like I'm going to be sick.

"Oh, no, um, I was actually—" Oh god, why did I lie? I'm a terrible liar and I should have just come clean, but all I can think about is Jen being back here and all the times Toby acted weird when I asked about the breakup. "I was picking up my sister's shoes. For her wedding. From the, uh…cobbler."

The cobbler? Jesus, could I have told a more obvious lie?

"Oh, that's so exciting! Tell her I said congrats!" Jen says. Because she's the nicest person on the planet, and I'm a messy brat.

"It is. So I really should be going," I say, waving the shoes around like a crazy person. "Lots to do!"

And then I turn and trot off.

As I walk, I wait for the spiral. The panic. The freak-out. Because Toby's perfect, gorgeous, ex-girlfriend is back in Boston. And she's on her way to meet him for brunch, which he didn't mention. That should freak me the fuck out.

But it doesn't.

Because there's got to be an explanation for it, a way the return of Toby's ex-girlfriend won't get in the way of Toby and me. I mean, I *know* Toby. And after last night, I *really* know Toby. And I remember the look on his face when he asked me if I was sure, when he mentioned what happened last time. He looked terrified that I was going to run again. He wanted me as much as I wanted him, and this morning he was bursting with the kind of joy I've only ever seen on his face when he's been truly happy.

He was truly happy.

With me.

So even though Jen is moving back here, I'm not freaking out.

Much.

Chapter 31

TOBY

knock knock

You're supposed to say 'who's there?'

Pippin?

I burst into the apartment, shoes and fuzzy robe in hand, to find Polly, Mom, and Nonna strategizing at the breakfast table over pastry Mom picked up yesterday from our favorite bakery in the South End. The plan was for us all to have a nice leisurely breakfast with mimosas before the frenzy of the wedding overtook us. One last breakfast with the four Marino women under one roof.

Of course, I screwed all that up when I spent the night with Toby, and now I'm going to have to explain myself.

"Oh my god, you slept with Toby, didn't you?" Polly says, then gapes at me, her mouth open in a wide O of excitement.

Okay, maybe I don't have to explain myself.

"How did you know?" I ask, dropping into a chair and grabbing a chocolate croissant off the plate in the center of the table. Nonna pours me a mimosa, and I down the thing a little faster than I mean to.

"Um, you have a dopey look and you have sex hair and you're wearing giant men's flip-flops. Which, from the size of them, congrats," Polly says with a wink.

I shoot a look at Nonna, who holds up her hands.

"I didn't say a word," she says.

"As much as I want to hear every last detail—"

"Please, no," Mom groans, her Midwestern prudishness making her cheeks blush rosy red.

"As much as *I* want to hear it," Polly says, rolling her eyes, "we have to handle the DJ thing."

"Yeah, I don't actually think that's a problem," I say. "I'll call Frantz. You know he'll be excited to take over, and we can put together a couple of playlists to fill in the gaps. I just need to find my phone."

Because it's not in my hand. Polly's shoes are. I reach for my pocket, but my shorts don't have pockets. And the robe that's draped over my arm is empty too.

Which means I left my phone at Toby's.

"*Fuuuuuuuuck,*" I groan, picturing it sitting at the end of Toby's bed, where I dropped it while I was buckling Polly's shoes. "I left my phone at Toby's! I have to go get it!"

"Pippin, the woman who's doing our facials is going to be here in ten minutes," Polly says; she wants to make sure we all have perfectly prepped, pampered, glowing skin for her wedding day. "Then hair and makeup, then we have to meet Mackenzie and her family in Chestnut Hill for photos before the ceremony. Just call him and tell him to bring it over." She slides her phone across the table to me.

"I don't know his number!" I cry, because of course I don't. I've had it saved in my phone since the first time he gave it to me when we were twelve. That's probably the last time I knew what it was.

"Well, then, call Frantz with my phone," she says.

"But…I-To-Do! I don't have my checklists!" *Now* I'm spiraling—all my careful planning is going to fall apart at the finish line because I had sex brain and left my phone somewhere.

"Pippin Marino, I see you freaking out. Stop it, and look at me," Polly says, and I do, because I don't know what else to do right now. "This wedding is going to be fine, thanks to you. Even without your checklist. You are a boss bitch who can conquer anything. You have worked your ass off to give Mackenzie and me the best wedding day we could have imagined on an impossible timeline, and I will never be able to thank you enough for all your hard work. I love you, I love you, *I love you* for all you've done. And you do not need some app to get you through today. In fact, I'm glad you don't have it, because it means that instead of obsessively checking off tasks, you can let Jesus take the wheel or whatever and actually *enjoy* yourself. Which is the only thing I want from you today, you hear me?"

I suck in a deep breath through my nose and let it out, long and slow, through my mouth. I've been awake barely an hour and have already nearly had, like, three existential crises, to say nothing of my utter meltdown last night.

But I *am* a boss bitch.

And I *did* plan the fuck out this wedding.

And it's going to be *fine*.

Man, this newfound skill of talking myself down from spirals is coming in hella handy.

I take Polly's phone and pull up Frantz's number. "You know what, you're right," I say as the phone rings. "Let's get you fucking *married*."

Five hours and ten thousand photos later, I'm standing in the Bryans' sunroom, waiting to be cued to open the French doors and start my trek down the aisle. My dress is gorgeous and impeccably fitted, thanks to Birgit. My normally frizzy hair has been tamed into soft waves and swept up on one side, clipped behind my ear with a fresh ranunculus. I look and feel all kinds of amazing.

Polly was right. I didn't need my app, partly because I had today's checklist memorized and partly because everything went off without a hitch even without my intervention. And I was so swept up in enjoying it that I didn't spend a minute missing the weight of my phone in my hand.

I did miss hearing from Toby, though, and I've spent the entire day imagining this moment, getting to see him in the Bryans' garden while I stand at the front near the makeshift altar. I feel a tug low in my belly at the thought of him seeing me in this dress again; the next time we're alone, none of our touches need to be tentative.

This time he can *un*zip this dress.

But before we open the doors so I can finally see Toby, I turn to Polly, who is standing behind me with Mackenzie on her arm. With Dad gone and no desire to cling to any kind of tradition, Mackenzie and Polly decided to walk down the aisle together. So Frantz escorted Nora, and Mom and Nonna walked arm in arm. Mackenize's college roommate, Natasha, who is acting as her maid of honor, will go ahead of me.

I catch Polly's eye as she's taking a deep, centering breath.

"You look gorgeous," I tell her, and she does. Even more lovely than I imagined when she first walked out in that dress. Her curls are loose, and a crown of eucalyptus rests atop her head. Mackenzie's dress is more structured, less detailed, with thin straps and square neckline, the A-line skirt falling in crisp folds down to the floor. Her hair is pulled back in a low, sleek bun, and she has a thin bronze ribbon tied like a headband. They couldn't look more different, and yet they are undeniably a pair.

"Thank you," she says. "For everything. You did this. All of it, Pepperoni."

"Only for you, Pizza," I say. Then I reach into my pocket and pull out my gift for her. Even though her dress is something new, I feel like that's cheating. I pull the back off the little metal pin and fasten it to her bouquet. When she sees the tiny pizza attached to the ribbon, her eyes well.

"I love you," she whispers, fanning her eyes to keep the tears from falling.

"I love you too," I say, then turn to Mackenzie, pulling another pin out of my pocket. "And you too, Manicotti."

Mackenzie's eyes light up as she looks down at the metal pin I custom ordered from Etsy of a little pasta sleeve stuffed with ricotta and covered with marinara. I fasten it to her bouquet, and from the way her eyes are shining, I can tell the nickname is gonna stick.

I open the French doors and nudge Natasha down the aisle, turning one last time before I head out.

"Love you both," I say, gripping my bouquet tight to keep from tearing up. "See you out there!"

One of Polly's friends from undergrad is playing "Here, There, and Everywhere" on a classical guitar as I make my way down the aisle. The ceremony is taking place on the main patio, where chairs have been set up for the guests, and the end of the aisle features a wooden arch of warm autumnal blooms and eucalyptus over a vintage navy Persian rug Nora had in her office. It's beautiful, but I can barely take in any of it, because I'm searching the sea of faces for Toby. I spot him almost immediately, sitting taller than everyone around him.

He's wearing a navy suit, and his hair is styled the same way it was the night I kissed him on the bridge in the Public Garden. The sight of him fills me with warmth, and I flash a grin at him.

But his smile back is tentative. Something about it doesn't quite reach his eyes. And as much as I want to stop right there in the aisle, climb over the four people sitting next to him and ask him why he looks *nervous*, this is Polly's wedding.

So I make my way to the front and take my place.

Polly and Mackenzie come next, and Toby turns to watch them, so I can't search his face for clues. My mind immediately goes to the most catastrophic option, which is, of course, Jen, but I try shake that off. It takes actual effort this time, but I won't ruin what's between us. I promised him I was sure, that I wouldn't run. And I trust Toby. With my heart. With everything.

Polly and Mackenzie approach the end of the aisle, where Judge Terrell Coleman, Frantz's best friend from law school, waits to officiate the ceremony.

I glance back at Toby and see that he's looking right at me again. And with a searching expression, he mouths, "Are you okay?"

Oh, so he's worried about *me*. I don't know why, but that's an easy enough fix. I give him a smile and little nod, because there's really no way for me to communicate *I had to run off to take care of a situation with a sick DJ and left my phone in your bed, sorry* without attracting an awful lot of attention.

Still, Toby looks nervous for the rest of the ceremony, and while I try to pay attention to the vows and the joy on my sister's face, I can't help but steal glances at the man *I* love. I hope that the minute the ceremony ends I can find him, kiss him, and clear up whatever has him concerned.

Because I still haven't told him I love him, and I'm going to do that as soon as humanly possible.

Chapter 32

As soon as I make it back up the aisle and into the sunroom, I'm strategizing how I can get to Toby. But when I turn to look back, everyone has flooded the aisle, heading toward us for the cocktail hour that'll be held on the first floor of the Bryan family home. Trying to get to Toby through this door would be like trying to swim upstream salmon-style.

I turn and start to make my way toward the library, where cocktails are set up. Hopefully I'll be able to rendezvous with Toby there. But then Polly appears at my side.

"Pip, Frantz got waylaid by some guys from the firm—can you run ahead and make sure the playlist is going?" she asks.

"Of course," I reply, then turn and double-time it through the house. Frantz's elaborate stereo system is set up in the corner with Mackenzie's laptop plugged into it. I wake it up, type in the password she gave me, and fire up the playlist called "Cocktail Hour." Then I turn to stake out the door so I'll spot Toby as soon as he passes through, but a sea of humanity has appeared behind me, everyone pushing toward the bar at once. I rise up on my tiptoes, looking for his tall frame and his curls, but I'm boxed in. I decide to duck out the nearby patio door and circle around from the outside, and when I make my way through the garden and back into the house, I see Toby in the library immediately.

He's standing near the laptop where I just was, and now *he's* boxed in by the crowd at the bar.

"Go out that door," I call, mouthing the words dramatically because I'm sure he can't hear me over the Marvin Gaye that's coming out of the speaker directly beside him. I point at the patio behind him, and he turns and spots it. I gesture for him to go out and around and mouth that I'll meet him out back, hoping to god he can read lips.

But when I get back to the entryway, I run directly into a cater waiter desperately dabbing at the white shirt of a man I recognize as a US senator. His white shirt bears a rapidly growing red wine stain, and there's an empty glass on the floor at his feet.

"I'm so sorry," the waiter says, and I can hear from the tremble in his voice that he's near tears.

"Oh, it's okay, son—just need a little club soda, I think," the senator replies, and I quickly jump to the rescue.

"Senator, why don't you come with me, I can get you that club soda," I say, smiling at the waiter so he knows it's fine and accidents happen and he's not fired.

I lead the senator into the kitchen, where I know the backup bar supplies are waiting, and pass him off to the head caterer, who helps him with his shirt.

I try to head toward the garden to *finally* meet Toby, only this time I'm intercepted by the guy from the rental company where we got the extra exterior lighting.

"Fuse blew and the patio lights are out, do you know where the fuse box is?" he asks.

I don't, but I help him find Frantz or Nora.

Each time I try to find Toby, another small fire crops up. There's supposed to be one gluten-free, dairy-free, nut-free, keto meal for Polly's high school friend Ronaldo the marathoner, but it's missing—I find it in the back of the fridge, looking as bland and sad under its plastic wrap as you'd imagine. The valet runs over a nail and gives one of the guests a flat tire, so I make a quick call to roadside assistance to make sure it's taken care of before they leave. The photographer can't find the bathroom. The playlist ends, and Spotify decides Papa Roach is a good choice for cocktail hour—I've never run so fast toward a laptop in my life. Polly loses her bouquet, which she'll need to toss later; I find it next to the toilet in the first-floor bathroom. The flower girl accidentally drinks a glass of champagne punch and looks like she's going to hurl, and we narrowly avoided another red stain by whisking her off to a potted plant at the edge of the patio. And I have to help Polly pee by hoisting all that delicate lace on her dress. Twice.

Dinner is over and dancing has begun when I finally spot him. He's sitting at a table near the back of the tent, picking at a filet, looking dejected. And in a flash of inspiration, I know what to do. Because Dr. Nora was right. It's finally time to be *really* honest with Toby.

I hustle toward the front of the tent, where Frantz is happily playing DJ. Earlier I managed to convince him that swapping vinyl would be a real chore, so he's making Spotify playlists on the fly. And doing a pretty great job, I might add. Everyone on the dance floor is bopping boisterously to "The Power of Love" by Huey Lewis and the News.

"Hey, Frantz, can I throw a request at you?"

"Anything for you, Pippin!" Frantz says over the noise from the speakers. I've never seen a man look so happy at a wedding before.

"I need a little Billy Joel action," I say.

The opening notes of "We Didn't Start the Fire" explode across the dance floor, and despite the fact that it's an odd choice for a wedding reception and not an easy song to dance to, the crowd goes wild. Turns out an awful lot of people know an awful lot of lyrics to that song.

I make my way back to Toby, who has obviously noticed the odd song choice, and as soon as he spots me, he puts it all together. The night in the Public Garden. The violinist playing Billy Joel. He breaks into a wide grin.

"Wanna dance?" I ask, holding out a hand.

Toby rises from his chair, takes my hand, and immediately pulls me into a holding-on-for-dear-life kind of hug. "I haven't heard from you all day. I was so worried," he says into my hair. "You disappeared, and I thought maybe you were freaking out."

"First of all, I didn't disappear! I texted you," I say. "But then I left my phone at your house, and it turns out I don't have your number memorized, so I couldn't call to ask you to bring it over. I need to memorize it, by the way, because I should really know my best friend's phone number, to say nothing of my boyfriend. But I figured it wasn't a big deal because I'd see you here."

Toby looks confused. "I never got a text from you."

Now *I'm* confused. "You didn't?"

Toby pulls out his phone and shows me that the last thing I texted him was my response to his cheesy dad joke this morning when we were in bed. What I wouldn't give to be back there right now.

"Oh my god, I'm so sorry," I say. I'm *sure* I wrote a text, but now I'm not entirely sure that I actually *sent* it. "You didn't see my phone on your bed?"

"No, all I saw was that you were gone. I thought maybe you'd run again," he says. And now he looks sheepish, nervously scratching at the curls at the nape of his neck. "Especially after I ran into Jen at my place and remembered our brunch."

"I mean, that was a surprise. Especially the part about how

she's planning to move here," I say. "I worried that maybe you only broke up with her because she lived across the country and that you'd get back together now that she doesn't, but—"

Toby pulls back and looks at me, laughing. "I didn't break up with Jen because I moved," he says. "I broke up with Jen because she wanted to get married and I didn't."

I couldn't be more shocked if Billy Joel himself walked into this reception to give a private concert. Jen wanted a proposal? That was a conversation they had? "You didn't? Want to get married?"

"Not to her," Toby says, and I swear my heart bottoms out in my shoes. "Pippin, I've been in love with you for so long I don't think I remember *not* being in love with you."

"Oh my god," I whisper. *Is* Billy Joel here? Is this all a dream? Am I dreaming *right fucking now*?

"I know. And I didn't think you felt that way about me, so I put it away. I moved on. And that was fine until Jen said she wanted me to propose and I couldn't because I didn't feel about her the way I felt about you. And I knew I never would. It was you or nobody. So I moved back here to give it one last shot."

"I thought you moved here for Mass General?" I whisper.

"Let's just say that I got very lucky that the best Emergency Medicine program in the country happened to be down the street from you," he says. He reaches up and grasps my cheeks, leveling me with a look. "I moved here for you, Pippin. It was always you."

"But…when I kissed you on the bridge, you said it was a mistake," I tell him, my brain whirring. And here I thought telling him that *I* was in love with *him* was going to be a big deal.

"No, *you* said the kiss was a mistake. And I didn't want to pressure you and screw up our friendship, so I agreed with you.

But let me assure you, from my perspective, no mistakes were made."

I vaguely hear Billy Joel singing about British politician sex and the roar of the crowd singing along, but mostly that disappears into a dull buzz as I gaze at Toby. Who loves me.

"You lied?" I ask.

He nods. "Yes. I lied."

"But you planned to have brunch with Jen today, and you didn't say anything."

Toby throws up his hands like he's done with all these hurdles to our relationship. Like he's ready to kick them to the ground and step right over them. "Because I forgot! I was so out-of-my-head ecstatic that I finally got to have you last night that I forgot about Jen and her interview and having brunch. Fuck, Pippin, I think I forgot my own *name*. It just sort of flew out of my brain—all I could think about was how happy I was that maybe you felt about me the way I felt about you."

"Feel," I say. I reach up and brush back the curl that's sprung free from his hair gel and fallen into his eye. "Present tense."

"What?" He cocks his head.

"You said 'felt.' Past tense. But I have feelings for you in the present tense. Right fucking now, in fact."

A slow grin spreads across his face. "You do?"

"I love you, Toby. I took me a little longer to figure out I had feelings for you, but maybe I've had them for a long time. Maybe I was just too overwhelmed and distracted to realize that I was—*am*—actually in love with my best friend."

He breaks into a grin bright enough to light the entire city of Boston *and* its outer suburbs, then tosses back his head in a hearty laugh before sweeping me up into his arms. "Fuck. I love you, Pippin. So much."

"I love you too," I tell him, wrapping my arms around his

neck and never, ever wanting to let go. "Even when you're texting me the world's worst dad jokes."

He laughs again. "Or maybe *because* of them?"

I step back and shake my head. "What did that judge say? In good times and bad? Well, the dad jokes are definitely bad. But that's okay, because I love you anyway." I rise up on my toes and plant a kiss on his lips that quickly deepens, his tongue swiping against mine, my teeth nipping at his full lower lip. Now that I know how good it feels to be with him, I'm finding it hard to stop, but soon I start worrying that we're going to draw attention. We finally break apart, chests heaving, cheeks flushed.

Then Toby leans down and whispers in my ear, "I am never going to get tired of hearing you say that."

Epilogue
EIGHT MONTHS LATER

What did one boat say to the other?

PIPPIN

Are you up for a little row-mance?

TOBY

You've heard that one before?

PIPPIN

Yes, from you, you adorable nerd!

TOBY

See you at 6pm? At our spot?

PIPPIN

Wouldn't miss it

Happy Anniversary from I-To-Do!

The email makes my inbox ding, interrupting my latest expense report. Without thinking, I click the little icon to open it.

Happy one-year anniversary of beginning your wedding planning journey with I-To-Do! We love that you trusted us with the happiest day of your life. We wanted to let you know that there are even more happy days ahead with I-To-Do; we can help you plan your baby shower, an anniversary party, or even a vow renewal (it's never too early to think ahead!).

I groan and click unsubscribe before sending the email whooshing straight to the digital trash can. I am *out* of the wedding planning business.

I navigate back to my expense report, the only part of working at Ladl, Nate Hawkins's consulting group, that I don't absolutely love. But it's a necessary companion to all the travel I get to do. My suitcase lies open next to my desk, half unpacked from my last trip to Nashville and ready to be repacked for next week's job in San Francisco.

Nate offered me the job the week after the wedding, and I was happy to start as soon as we passed the keys over to Kelleher. I shadowed another consultant for a month before I was given my first client, a small French bistro in Indianapolis that was bleeding money because of a bloated wine list and a menu that left little room for error. I worked with them to streamline and refine the menu and hired a kick-ass new chef from Montreal. The five-star review from the *Indy Star* is now framed and hanging over my desk.

My phone dings with a reminder to get ready, so I close out of my expense report and head to my closet, pulling out the dress I found in a vintage shop on a recent Chicago trip. It's a pale robin's-egg-blue minidress with an A-line skirt, a nipped-in waist, and peasant sleeves. Very mod Marianne Faithfull vibes, and slipping into it brings me so much joy. Toby and I have been to a few more hospital galas together, and it's been fun expanding my closet beyond kitchen clothes. Sure, it's not a fire-engine-red sex dress, but I don't find myself needing a vacation from being Pippin very often these days.

I fluff my curls and push them back with a black satin headband, then slip into a pair of black flip-flops for the walk to meet Toby, my shoes dangling from my fingers.

The walk from our new apartment in Back Bay is short. Toby and I lucked out with finding the rental—one of the attendings at the hospital was vacating it for a house with a yard in Belmont. It's part of a chopped-up brownstone, and our living room and kitchen were once the ballroom of the old Brahmin mansion. It's grand and kooky, with windows looking out over the Charles River and the Esplanade, and the only thing that's better than the apartment is that I get to live in it with Toby.

It's almost six p.m. on a gorgeous June evening; the sun is still high in the sky, but the heat of the day has long burned off, the breeze from the river gentle and cooling. The Public Garden is crowded with tourists, commuters leaving work, people enjoying picnic dinners in the grass, and couples on dates. But I glide through the crowd effortlessly until I find him.

He's leaning his elbows on the railing of the bridge, gazing down at the still water below. He's wearing that dangerously tailored black suit that turns me into a puddle of want.

As if he can sense me, he rises and turns, beaming at me with a wide grin that sends joy bursting out of his very being.

"You ready?" I ask him.

"Oh, I've *been* ready," he says, bouncing on the balls of his feet like a kid on Christmas.

"Sorry, sorry, sorry," Polly says, squeezing around a family taking a photo on the bridge. "I'm falling down on the job, but this freshman showed up to office hours in tears begging for an extension, and— Oh, hell, it doesn't matter. Here you go!" She passes me a small bouquet of white peonies and pale pink roses. She canceled her evening class at Tufts, where she's an associate professor of art history, just to be here. "You know, when I promised to return the favor, I didn't think it would be this easy. I feel like I still owe you."

"Don't worry, we're square," I tell her, pulling her in for a hug. "This is exactly what I wanted."

"Should we get this show on the road?" Nonna asks.

"I think time is of the essence since this isn't exactly, you know, legal," Mom adds.

"Can we at least ask those tourists to move?" Toby's mother asks, eyeing a middle-aged couple in fanny packs, brand-new Red Sox caps, and Wicked Pissah T-shirts.

"Mom, relax, just let them do this their way," Toby's oldest sister, Siobhan, says.

There's some more chatter as everyone moves into place. Mom and Nonna pull Polly and Mackenzie toward them to my right, while Toby's parents, sisters, and their families form a very well-dressed mob to his left. And between us stands Fernando, now head chef of the all-new Marino's, who got ordained online just for us. I decide to stay in my flip-flops and drop my heels onto the ground. Might as well be comfortable.

"Yeah, let's start, because I love you guys, but I'm not getting arrested for you," Fernando says, pulling up the script on his phone. "Dearly beloved—"

"Skip to the good part," Toby says, cutting him off, never taking his eyes off me.

Everyone laughs, and the crowd around us begins to catch wind of what we're doing.

"Do you, Toby, take Pippin to be your lawfully wedded wife, to have—"

"I do. All of it," Toby says, practically vibrating.

"Okay, then," Fernando says, turning to me. "And do you, Pippin, take Toby to be—"

"You bet. Me too," I say, through giggles. "I mean, *I do*."

"Man, you guys are making this easy," Fernando says, quickly scrolling to the end of his script.

"That was the whole idea," I say, rising up on my toes. Toby meets me halfway, our lips connecting as the crowd around us whoops, cheers, and (in the case of Toby's parents) politely golf claps.

"Well, keep on kissing the bride, I guess?" Fernando says, looking quizzically at his phone.

"Oh, the rings!" Mackenzie says.

"Right! The rings," Fernando says, giving up and tucking his phone in his pocket. "You guys have the rings?"

I pull Toby's simple gold band off my thumb, where I placed it for safekeeping, as he reaches into his pocket and pulls out a matching thinner gold band, and with little fanfare but all the love in the world, we place them on each other's fingers.

"Okay, then, by the power vested in me by the Common-wealth of Massachusetts, the internet, and, uh, a perfectly legal park permit—I swear we're almost done, Officers!" I look up to see a pair of Boston's finest approaching what has become quite a crowd of onlookers. Toby and I look back at each other, wide-eyed and giddy, hands clasped; we're both practically vibrating. "I hereby declare you husband and wife. You may kiss again and then disperse before we all wind up in a paddy wagon!"

It feels like the entire garden explodes in cheers as Toby pulls me in for a kiss to end all kisses.

Or maybe the first of a lifetime.

"I love you, Pippin Marino," he says.

"I love you, Toby Sullivan," I reply.

And then we stroll off the bridge, hand in hand.

Acknowledgments

First, an enormous thank you to Stephen Barbara, my agent at Inkwell, who worked tirelessly for this book. I'm glad we found it a home with readers who love it. Thank you also to Amy Spalding, who did an absolutely incredible developmental edit. Your beat sheet changed the way I write forever. Thanks also to Allison Cherry for her eagle-eyed copyedits.

Simini Blocker illustrated this cover based solely on a vibes email I sent her, and man did she knock it out of the park. I have never loved a cover as much as I love this warm and lovely illustration of Pippin and Toby and Marino's.

Tiffany Schmidt was my wingwoman throughout this book. Thank you for the cheerleading and the inspiration and that one incredible text message that nailed the moment. You were always available for a brainstorming session or a quick read. Writing with you is awesome, but having you as a friend is even better. Thanks also to Jackson Pearce, who read an early draft and provided killer craft notes.

Rachael Allen, Gilly Segal, and Maryann Dabkowski were my first friends I ventured out with after COVID hit. Our writing retreat helped me get a lot of this story out, so thank you for inviting me!

This is the first book I wrote to music (I usually write to the ambient sounds of cafes, but thanks to COVID I had to find another way). So thank you to Hayward Williams for *Every Color Blue*, The Chicks for *Gaslighter*, Taylor Swift for *Folklore* and *Evermore*, and Jason Isbell for your entire catalog. And Bob

Seger's "Night Moves," oddly enough. If you want to see the playlist that carried me through this book, find me on Spotify.

Thank you to all the indie authors who've come before me, who left breadcrumbs behind for me to follow. I learned everything from you. Indie publishing is no joke, and I'm in awe of the indie romance community.

The biggest thanks of all goes to my husband Adam Ragusea, who never let me give up on myself. As I was wrestling with all the ins and outs of indie publishing, he knew just when to drop an "I'm so proud of you for doing this."

I wrote this book in the early days of the pandemic with both my children at home. I would escape to a local park, sit on a bench near a fountain, and hand write chapters in a spiral notebook. It was a time when I really needed joy, so I wrote some of my own. I hope it brings you as much joy now as it's brought me these last three years.

About the Author

Lauren Morrill is the author of spicy adult and sweet YA romance, including Sister of the Bride, Meant to Be (Delacorte) and It's Kind of a Cheesy Love Story (Farrar, Straus and Giroux). She loves all things romantic comedy and specializes in kissing books. Lauren lives in Knoxville, TN with her husband, Adam Ragusea, their two children, and Poptart the pup. You can find her online at www.laurenmorrill.com and you should definitely follow her on Instagram at @laurenmorrill so you call tell her to get back to writing when she's posting way too many stories.

Lauren also runs Procrastination Nation, a newsletter that is perpetually forthcoming. You can subscribe at https://laurenmorrill.substack.com/

Printed in Great Britain
by Amazon